Dishonorable Scoundrel

"Is there another reason more pressing—and perhaps more romantic—that would prevent your leaving Philadelphia?" Colonel Valentine inquired with a provocative lift to his eyebrow.

"I do not understand to what you refer," Sarah demurred in her most haughty manner. "My only other objection is that I have no affection for the English."

Colonel Valentine was not one whit abashed. "Come now, Sarah. I thought perhaps young Willing had a prior claim upon you."

"Brian is a dear friend and would endorse any decision I made," she said with dignity.

"How considerate of him," the colonel observed sardonically. "If you were my fiancée I could not contemplate a long absence with such magnanimity."

Sarah's cheeks flushed with anger. "Sir, you go too far. I am not some docile English, milk-and-water miss who will give in to your bullying. I might have expected as much from a British officer. The lot of you are nothing but dishonorable scoundrels."

Damn the chit! She needed a good spanking.

With that he grasped her slender wrists and hauled her against his chest, pinioning her arms behind her with one hand. She struggled, outraged, sputtering with fury, turning her head this way and that to escape the disturbing proximity of his lips. He raised her chin with his free hand and then his mouth was crushing hers—savagely, punishingly . . .

THE BEST OF REGENCY ROMANCES

AN IMPROPER COMPANION   (2691, $3.95)
by Karla Hocker
At the closing of Miss Venable's Seminary for Young
Ladies school, mistress Kate Elliott welcomed the invitation to be Liza Ashcroft's chaperone for the Season at
Bath. Little did she know that Miss Ashcroft's father, the
handsome widower Damien Ashcroft would also enter her
life. And not as a passive bystander or dutiful dad.

WAGER ON LOVE   (2693, $2.95)
by Prudence Martin
Only a rogue like Nicholas Ruxart would choose a bride on
the basis of a careless wager. And only a rakehell like Nicholas would then fall in love with his betrothed's grey-eyed
sister! The cynical viscount had always thought one blushing miss would suit as well as another, but the unattainable
Jane Sommers soon proved him wrong.

LOVE AND FOLLY   (2715, $3.95)
by Sheila Simonson
To the dismay of her more sensible twin Margaret, Lady
Jean proceeded to fall hopelessly in love with the silver-
tongued, seditious poet, Owen Davies—and catapult her
entire family into social ruin . . . Margaret was used to
gentlemen falling in love with vivacious Jean rather than
with her—even the handsome Johnny Dyott whom she secretly adored. And when Jean's foolishness led her into the
arms of the notorious Owen Davies, Margaret knew she
could count on Dyott to avert scandal. What she didn't
know, however was that her sweet sensibility was exerting a
charm all its own.

1-30 91

Sweet Pretender

BY VIOLET HAMILTON

ZEBRA BOOKS
KENSINGTON PUBLISHING CORP.

ZEBRA BOOKS

are published by

Kensington Publishing Corp.
475 Park Avenue South
New York, NY 10016

Second printing: December, 1990

Printed in the United States of America

Chapter One

The imposing red-brick houses on Fourth Street south of the High stood square and tall, resisting the damp March wind that swirled up from the Delaware River. Not a pleasant day in Philadelphia, but Sarah Ravensham, bidding a laughing farewell to her escort, seemed impervious to the weather as she ran up the marble steps of her grandfather's house. Absorbed in thoughts of her recent outing, she paid little heed to the gentleman coming out of the entrance and cannoned into him. His arms went out automatically to catch her lest she fall ignominiously at his feet.

"Such impetuosity, my dear young woman, will lead you into trouble one of these days," he chided.

Sarah looked up, her anger rising at the cool clipped tones that delivered the bland rebuke. She met a pair of dark hard eyes, which for a moment gleamed with a most disturbing light as her unknown rescuer imperceptibly tightened his hold upon her. He towered over her, a commanding, intimidating figure in a black, many-caped greatcoat that set off his well-muscled figure. Dark-haired, with a stern, tanned face, he had an air of mocking self-confidence Sarah found detestable. Not so did most men look at Sarah Ravensham, as if she were a willful child. He continued to hold her with an easy strength, watching her fruitless efforts to free herself with considerable amusement. Sarah, flustered and more than a little irritated by the encounter, realized good manners insisted she make some kind of apology for her reckless action, although her every instinct was to treat him with scorn.

"Excuse me, sir. I was heedless in my impatience," she said reluctantly, her stormy gaze belying her soft words. He released her immediately.

"Of course, Miss Ravensham. Glad to be of service." He smiled then, taking her breath away, for the change in his ruthless, rather cynical expression was quite alarming. "But do take care in the future. I am not so easily *bouleversé*, but you might not be so fortunate in your next victim," he drawled.

Before Sarah could summon the scathing reply he deserved, he took off his beaver hat, bowed, and walked briskly down the steps, turning left toward the High Street. Sarah watched him for a moment bemusedly, noting the upright carriage and decisive stride. Then tossing her head, she turned away. Really what an impossible man, treating her like a madcap schoolmiss. She would like the opportunity to give him his comeuppance. What a top-lofty man, and undoubtedly from his tone, one of the hateful British. What was he doing here? She hoped her grandfather had given him a cool reception. Well, she was not concerned with him. She sailed blithely through the front door, held open for her by the family butler, giving him a cheery greeting.

"Is Grandfather in his study, James? I want to see him." She handed her bonnet and pelisse to the butler, a tall black man of majestic mien and a head of tightly curled grey hair. His dignity was often sorely tried by Miss Ravensham's lack of decorum, but, long accustomed to her ways, he made allowances.

"Yes, Miss Sarah, and he has been asking for you."

Sarah hurried across the shining parquet floor to the large mahogany portal that guarded her grandfather's sanctum and knocked briefly before opening the door and poking her head inside. The elderly gentleman seated behind the Chippendale desk smiled and rose at her entrance.

"Come in, my dear. I was wondering where you were. Out gallivanting with young Willing, I suppose." Joshua Allen, in his late sixties, looked far from his age, a well-set-up man with a ramrod-straight back, a shock of white hair, and piercing blue eyes beneath bristling eyebrows. His gaze softened as he looked at his granddaughter.

"Not gallivanting, Grandpa, but improving my mind. We have been at the State House to hear the debate on Mr. Adams's Alien and Sedition Laws," she rebuked him cheekily.

"And what do you think of these latest efforts of our Federalists to keep Jefferson's rabble and the French fops in their place?" he asked, knowing his remarks would provoke a spate of argument from his aggressively democratic granddaughter.

"Iniquitous, that's what they are. I know that Mr. Jefferson's ambitions to have us declare war against the British, to aid our French allies, do not meet with

7

your approval, but Mr. Adams is too conservative to suit my taste, full of fustian. He had best beware, for his popularity has fallen greatly. But enough of that for now. Who was that haughty gentleman I met on the doorstep just now? An Englishman, no doubt." She perched on the arm of a chair to interrogate her grandfather.

Joshua Allen, although a power to be reckoned with in the merchant circles of Philadelphia of which he was a reigning figure, and an influential voice in the ruling Federalist Party, rarely exerted his authority over his wayward granddaughter, charmed as he was by her piquant personality and youthful spirits. Not a beauty in the classical mould, Sarah's attraction lay in the mobility of her expression, the infectious tilt of her generous mouth, and the gaiety that flashed from her deep brown eyes. Her nose was a trifle too retroussé to be fashionable and her small chin had a determined set that hinted at a character stronger than that of most young girls who frequented Philadelphia society. There was no faulting her elegant slim figure, gowned this afternoon in a trim wine-colored merino walking dress, nor the chic style of her chestnut curls cut in a carefully modish disarray. Sarah Ravensham could look the very epitome of a proper Philadelphia miss, but appearances were deceiving as her grandfather had cause to know. She was as strong-minded as her dear mother with a quixotic quality that his daughter, long departed and still mourned, had never possessed.

He sighed. He would miss her, but she must answer this invitation of her paternal relations, no matter how repugnant she would find the idea.

"Come, come, Grandfather, I have a feeling you are

8

hiding a budget of worrying news from me. That won't do. It will upset your liver. And I wager it has something to do with that toffee-nosed type who has just left."

"That is no way to address Colonel Valentine, my dear, a very distinguished and brave soldier in His Majesty's Service."

"Pooh, just as I expected, a stuck-up Britisher. What was your business with such a man?"

"Since it has to do with you, my dear, I will overlook your impropriety this time. Sit down, Sarah. I have something very serious to discuss with you concerning your father's people." Joshua Allen sighed, his normal benign countenance darkening as he recalled the past.

"Oh, Grandpa, I don't want to hear, if it promises to be as tiresome as all that. I know it depresses you to speak of those times, of Mother, and all that happened. I refuse to acknowledge my English relations who were so cruel to Father." Sarah concluded bitterly.

"It's not quite that easy to dismiss them, my child. There were faults on both sides, and now the Ravenshams want to redress old wrongs. We cannot be so churlish as to refuse Lady Ravensham's pleas. She has written a most civil letter to me, and also enclosed a missive for you. Colonel Valentine assures me her health is failing and not improved by this long estrangement. We must discuss this whole affair calmly and without rancour."

"I am listening, Grandpa." Sarah responded with a subdued air. She knew how upsetting it was for Joshua Allen to recall the past, those days when his

9

beloved only daughter had married a British officer stationed with Gen. Sir William Howe's forces occupying Philadelphia during the late War for Independence. Sara was a committed citizen of the United States of America and had little use for the British who had handled their former colonies so cavalierly. Unfortunately she was half-British herself, the product of that tragic romance, much as she might wish to ignore the fact.

"Colonel Valentine has just delivered a message from your grandmother, Lady Ravensham, who begs my indulgence and hopes that I will allow you to pay a long overdue visit to England so that she can meet her granddaughter before it is too late. Colonel Valentine will escort you on the voyage if you consent to go. And I really think you must, my dear. You owe it to your father's memory. And perhaps, in London, you can discover some evidence that will remove the unjust stain from his reputation." Joshua Allen sighed, brooding over the tragedy that had scarred his daughter's brief life and had brought her young husband to an early grave.

"But, Grandpa, it's been almost twenty years since Father's disgrace. What could I discover now? And I will hate being patronized and humiliated by those Ravenshams and all their uppity friends, like that Colonel Valentine. Imagine being forced into his company for weeks aboard ship, ugh!" Sarah did not voice her most urgent objection, her anxiety at leaving her grandfather for so long a period. He was her refuge and a loving security, the only family she had ever known. She knew he would not appreciate being reminded that his own age made any long absence worrying.

"I am sure you will find Colonel Valentine an unexceptional escort, once you have come to know him better. I was quite impressed with the fellow. But before you make up your mind to refuse, here is your grandmother's letter. I am reluctant to persuade you to any course of action that will make you unhappy, Sarah, and I will of course miss you intolerably, but my conscience and my instincts tell me you must accept this invitation. Unless there is a more pressing reason for you to stay here?" Joshua Allen raised his eyebrows in inquiry. Sarah assumed he was referring to her expected engagement to Brian Willing, an event she knew her grandfather favoured, but she was unwilling to think about that now, or discuss it. This news from England needed much consideration. With a soothing and affectionate kiss on her grandfather's cheek Sarah departed, taking with her the controversial letter.

Chapter Two

Sarah could not explain why she sought the refuge of her bedroom to read Lady Ravensham's letter. She had no secrets from her grandfather, but she did not want to expose him to further pain, to the remembrance of those long-ago years that he tried to banish from his mind. Although he shared much with his beloved granddaughter, he did not want her scarred by his unhappiness. Despite the untimely death of her mother, Sarah had never felt deprived of love. She looked around the room that had sheltered her for most of her nineteen years, the pink-and-white-sprigged dimity tester and draperies adorning the canopied bed, the graceful Chippendale furniture, especially built to her grandfather's order for her sixteenth birthday, the mementos of her childhood and adolescence, a dog-eared teddy bear, a much-loved doll, and the samplers that she had worked so rebelliously. Orphaned young, she had never suffered deprivation of care and protection. She repaid her grandfather's love in kind. She would never do anything to cause him disappointment or grief, but she did not fully understand why he wanted her to travel to England. She opened Lady Ravensham's letter:

My dear Granddaughter,

It is with some apprehension that I break the silence of years to write and invite you to visit me in London. You may find you are unable to accept my apologies for this regrettable estrangement, which was not of my doing. Your grandfather, a proud man, could not accept that his son was termed a traitor. For generations Ravenshams have served in the army with never a slur upon their name. On the contrary many of your ancestors have covered themselves with glory on the battlefield, a credit to their family, their regiments, and their country. Despite the overwhelming evidence against your father I never believed the allegations against him or your mother. He would never have committed treason. But your grandfather refused to mention his name, and moreover refused to allow me to write to either your mother or you. I do not excuse this attitude, but I felt I must honour his wishes. Now that he has gone, I yearn to redress old wrongs, to welcome you into your proper place in the family.

Please my dear, if you have any charity, do accept my invitation and travel to England so that I may see you before it is too late. Colonel Valentine, who is kindly delivering this letter, will see to all the arrangements for your voyage, which I realize might be a perilous one for a young girl. I await your coming with impatience and be assured you have all my love,

Your grandmother,
Amelia Ravensham

Though determined not to be moved by her grandmother's words, Sarah could not help feeling compassion for the lonely old lady, restrained by her overbearing husband, forced to withhold the natural sympathy and interest she felt for her son's widow and child. Sarah knew some of her parents' story, but she sensed that much had been hidden from her. She knew that her father, second son of the Earl of Ravensham, had been a major in the Second Brigade of Guards that had occupied Philadelphia under Gen. Sir William Howe during the winter of 1777–78. Howe's officers had enjoyed the occupation—dancing, theatricals, banquets, cards—all the pleasures of a sophisticated society lavishly offered by citizens of a city not at all committed to the cause of independence from their rightful king.

Out at Valley Forge the rebel general, George Washington and his pitiful remnant of troops had starved and shivered in the bitter winter while within the city the well-to-do merchants and pacific Quakers had refused aid and comfort to their countrymen while entertaining His Majesty's forces. Sarah knew that her grandfather had not favoured the rebellion, his loyalty to the king strengthened by the economic ties that his merchant firm, Allen and Smithson, had formed with London. Joshua Allen was not an overt Tory. He had managed to straddle the issue of independence with much adroitness, and his position was such that neither the British nor the rebels had wanted to offend him. His chief allegiance was to his daughter, the lovely Elizabeth Allen, who had early attracted the attention of the most aristocratic officers in Howe's train. Even the charming and ebullient Maj. John André had joined the bevy of her admirers, but she had fallen deeply in love with Maj. Richard Ravensham, and within a few months of their meeting they had married. Joshua Allen, although disturbed by the rashness of the courtship and marriage, had been unable to deny his daughter her heart's desire.

Within weeks of the marriage Howe had evacuated his forces and Major Ravensham had been detached to serve with Gen. Johnny Burgoyne in New York, leaving behind a pregnant and apprehensive bride. That was when the trouble began. Major Ravensham was accused by the War Office in London of treasonable activity, of aiding and abetting the rebels, seduced from his duty by his American wife, so the accusation read. Before his court-martial and trial could be scheduled, he was killed on a routine patrol in the wilds of the upper New York colony. Witnesses believed he deliberately rode into enemy fire, preferring to die rather than face disgrace, for the evidence against him seemed insurmountable. He was dishonorably discharged from the Guards posthumously.

Elizabeth Allen, so loyal and devoted to her young lover, had denied to the end that she had been implicated in the accusations leveled against him. Indeed, although she was not an avowed Tory, she cared little for politics, unlike her daughter who had grown up in the capital of the new republic and followed its fortunes with a passionate dedication. But the rumours, the disgrace, her husband's own family's belief in his guilt had completely destroyed her. She died giving birth to Sarah. If the small orphan had not been blessed with a caring if grieving grandfather, her own fate might have been equally tragic. Joshua Allen never believed his son-in-law was a traitor, and those who challenged him received short shift. He wrote once, in anger, to the Earl of Ravensham, refuting the charges against his son-in-law and telling the Ravenshams of his daughter's death and the birth of a grandchild but never received the courtesy of an answer. He did not try again. All communication between the two families was severed. Lady Ravensham's letter was the first breach in that twenty-year silence.

Sarah, growing up in the beginning years of the struggling new republic, knew little of her parents' story. Her grandfather's coterie never referred to it, respecting Joshua Allen's obvious desire to draw a cloak over the whole affair. Many of his colleagues were, like himself, reluctant rebels, accepting the separation from England with regret, but pragmatic enough to recognize a *fait accompli*. They were businessmen, not politicians.

It was laughable to think that Major Ravensham had been tempted from his duty by Joshua Allen's daughter or by any Philadelphia rebel for that matter. The whole regrettable affair was brushed over and forgotten until Sarah learned of it from a jealous spinster, a one-time rival of her mother.

Joshua Allen had subdued his own anger and told her honestly and kindly of the absurdity of the

16

charges, minimizing the spiteful tales, and assuring her that her father was a man of honour and dedication, but he could not deny that his view was not shared by Major Ravensham's superiors or his own family. Of his own grief, that the denunciations had contributed to his daughter's death, he said little, preferring to minimize the tragedy that might darken his granddaughter's life.

She had not been deceived, but she blamed his accusers, not her father, and she still did. That censure, combined with lessons of the perfidy of the British in dealing with their late colonies, had transformed her into an ardent patriot. She thoroughly disliked all things English and had vowed never to set foot in the cursed country or have anything to do with its citizens. Now she was being asked to renege on that vow.

Perhaps, because she had grown up under her grandfather's aegis, Sarah, at a very young age, had taken an interest in matters not usually engaging a young girl. Joshua Allen was on excellent terms with all the great men of the new republic—John Jay, Charles Pinckney, Alexander Hamilton, even the redoubtable Gen. George Washington. All these men were stalwart Federalists, as was Joshua Allen himself. Currently the ruling party was at odds with Thomas Jefferson's Democrats over the French war. Jefferson, as passionate a Francophile as his rival Hamilton was pro-English, determined to aid France in her struggle against England. Joshua Allen, although annoyed by the English efforts to restrict its former colonies' trade, still preferred to do business with British merchant houses rather than those of the

17

revolutionary junta in France. He had a great deal of respect for the economic acumen of Alexander Hamilton, who had resigned as Secretary of the Treasury to become a general of the army, but still managed to keep a firm hand on the new country's finances.

Sarah, accustomed to discussions of trade deficits, balance sheets, cargo insurance, and their political implications, understood the financial problems inherent in founding a new republic but did not endorse her grandfather's more conservative views. She found President John Adams prosy and dull, his starchy manner and weighty orations annoying. Mr. Jefferson's enthusiastic endorsement of the French Revolution found favour in her eyes, and she was not reluctant to discuss the opposing stands with whomever would listen, much to her several beaux' dismay.

Today she had prevailed upon Brian Willing, the chief contender for her hand, to take her to the State House to listen to the debate on the restrictive Alien and Sedition Laws, Adams's effort at repressing dissent, much to that young gentleman's discomfort. And she had not been reticent about her own opposition to legislation aimed at thwarting immigration and free speech, democratic principles to which she was firmly wedded.

The thought of visiting England, where George III's ministers were conniving against her government, raised her hackles. She had no doubt that Englishmen were arrogant fribbles who would patronize her and her country, which she would find infuriating. Just look at that Colonel Valentine, for example. Her grandfather might find him acceptable, but she did not—and the thought of spending long weeks on a sea voyage enduring his condescension was unbearable. She hoped her refusal to answer her grandmother's pleas for a reunion would shake his equanimity. She had never before encountered a high-born Englishman, that specimen being in short supply in her country. If Colonel Valentine represented his countrymen and class, she hoped she never met any again. Her cheeks reddened and her eyes flashed as she thought of his high-handed approach at their meeting. No doubt he was accustomed to simpering misses falling at his feet or batting their eyes in grateful appreciation of his notice. Well, he would not receive that kind of reaction from her. She was annoyed with herself for allowing that brief encounter to disturb her usually cheerful spirits, but Englishmen, and particularly Englishmen of his type, infuriated her with their lords-of-the-earth manner. No doubt he believed she should be grateful for the Ravenshams' attempt to heal the breach in the family—eager, even, to be entertained by them. She tossed her head, remembering again his strange appraisal of her.

For once she did not agree with her grandfather. She pitied Lady Ravensham, victim of a harsh unbending husband, but she despised her timidity in not defending her son and contacting her daughter-in-law. Sarah was not of a vengeful disposition but she could not banish from her mind the cruelty of her English relations. She was American through and through and she wanted nothing to do with the Ravenshams, nor their ally, the detestable colonel. She would tell her grandfather that a journey to London was out of the question.

Setting her chin, Sarah decided she would waste no more time on the vexatious English. She would concentrate on preparing for the dance that evening at Mrs. Powel's elegant house on Third Street, to which Brian Willing was escorting her.

Chapter Three

Prepared to enjoy herself, Sarah entered Elizabeth Powel's magnificent ballroom that evening on Brian Willing's arm. She knew she was looking exceptionally well, in her marigold-yellow silk gown with its new empire waistline stitched in tiny seed pearls, and with more of the pearls highlighting her chestnut curls that were arranged in a fetching, simple style. Her wide topaz eyes glowed with excitement. But some of her irrepressible spirits were dimmed at the sight of the tall figure in red regimentals standing nearby, who watched her entrance with an enigmatic smile. Ignoring his mocking gaze, she greeted her hostess charmingly, thanking her prettily for the invitation. As she and Brian prepared to move on, Mrs. Powel stopped her with a hand on her arm.

"My dear, Col. Lucien Valentine wishes to be presented to you," her hostess said.

"I am delighted to have this opportunity to meet you formally, Miss Ravensham. Our encounter this afternoon lacked propriety, I think you will agree," he greeted her, his eyes glinting with amusement as he observed her sudden confusion.

Despite herself Sarah felt a blush of mortification rise to her cheeks, remembering the strong clasp of his arms when he rescued her from her tumble. But he need not think that contretemps had put her in good charity with him. Now, as imposing a figure as he cut in the hated red uniform, she did not forget he was one of the despised British, and an army officer at that. She acknowledged the introduction with a cool nod, gazing at him with what she hoped was icy indifference which, to her annoyance, had little effect.

"You were most gallant, Colonel. I do not think you have met Brian Willing," she introduced the pair, aware of Brian smouldering at her side as he eyed the tall officer.

"Now that we have been properly introduced I hope I may beg the honour of a dance. I am sure your card will be rapidly filled and I must make my bid early." The officer's cool address set Sarah's back up but she was in no position to give him the set-down he deserved, with Mrs. Powel standing by smiling graciously and Brian glowering at the intruder. Before she could reply, Brian intervened.

"You have promised the first dance to me, Sarah, and I believe all your others are claimed," he reminded her.

Brian, a cousin to Mrs. Powel, and a member of the well-established Willing family, rarely felt at a loss in Philadelphia society, but the British colonel had put him out of countenance, and he felt a vague resentment at the fellow's interest in Sarah. Brian was an attractive young man of average height with a shock of blond hair and warm blue eyes, which had caused

22

many a young woman to envy Sarah his obvious devotion. Since their days in leading strings Brian had trailed behind the madcap Sarah with a determination that never faltered. He wanted her for his wife and had proposed several times, a match that both Joshua Allen and his own parents encouraged. He reminded her that now she was nineteen, well beyond the marriageable age, and she must decide soon or she was in danger of being left on the shelf.

But Sarah continued to refuse and laughingly told him not to be a goose, she was not yet quite antiquated, nor was she prepared to settle down to domesticity. She enjoyed her status as a reigning belle. Though fond of Brian, she did not return his ardour and felt much was lacking in their relationship. He did not make her heart stop, nor her blood race. She was enough of a romantic to hope that the man who claimed her as his wife would provoke just such emotions. Still, she felt a deep affection for Brian, even if she could not return his devotion, and she did not want him to come to cuffs with the annoying colonel, who had already caused her enough discomfort.

"Of course, Brian, I have not forgotten. I am afraid the colonel must be disappointed. My dances are all promised," she said coolly, delighted to give the Englishman the affront she thought he deserved. Although he took his refusal with a smooth courtesy, she was surprised to see in those dark cold eyes a flash of annoyance. The aquiline face, so stern and controlled, betrayed little emotion, but Sarah sensed that beneath the polite facade lurked a ruthless will and a self-assurance that was not often bested. She suspected that Lucien Valentine was not a man accustomed to rejection, nor would he countenance it. Still he had no recourse but to accept her rebuff with grace in Mrs. Powel's ballroom. As he murmured his disappointment, she took Brian's arm and prepared to turn away.

"You cannot postpone the inevitable forever, Miss Ravensham," he added, in a voice only she could hear. "We will have another opportunity when your watchdog is not around to protect you, and the demands of civility won't prevent me from taming your temper." He bowed and crossed the room to solicit the hand of a sparkling brunette who welcomed him eagerly.

"Really, what an encroaching fellow. I did not like his tone," Brian protested crossly. Always quick to spring to Sarah's defence, and jealous of any man who paid her attention, he had not liked the officer's possessive manner.

"Yes, he is most irritating, but let's not bother about him. He's not worth discussing, and the set is about to begin," Sarah replied. In truth, she was feeling very annoyed with herself for allowing the colonel to shake her composure once again. Despite herself she could not help watching the colonel as he escorted his partner toward the set just forming, chatting easily and obviously charming her with ease. His dark hair shone under the light cast by the huge chandelier, and his tall distinctive figure caught the attention of other feminine eyes beside her own. Unlike most of the gentlemen present he did not powder his hair, wearing it instead in a short military crop that highlighted his firm features. No doubt he wanted to set his own fashion, Sarah concluded uncharitably. What was it about him that goaded her temper? She should have responded in a light careless fashion and not become unsettled by his rather intimidating manner. Her dislike of the British was deeply engrained, but her feelings toward the self-assured colonel could not be explained entirely by her prejudice. Determined not to allow the recent clash of wills to upset her normal equanimity, she smiled enchantingly at Brian in an effort to banish his sulks. She would not allow the arrogant officer to spoil her evening.

"Stuck-up popinjay," Brian muttered as they took their places on the dance floor.

"Now, Brian, he's quite an impressive figure of a man," Sarah teased.

"It's that uniform. All you girls go down like ninepins before those regimentals. Remember he's an Englishman and you have never cared for those fellows," Brian warned, unwilling to be soothed.

"Quite right. And Colonel Valentine is the epitome of all I dislike, but let us forget him. He's not worth arguing about," Sarah said a trifle sharply. Accustomed to surrendering to her stronger will, Brian yielded to her wishes.

Sarah, her spirits restored, chatted happily away with him and all the while kept her eyes from the tall figure some distance away from them. Fortunately her adversary and his partner were not included in their set so that the movements of the dance did not bring them in contact. It really was unfair to plague Brian, she decided, but he did get on his high horse if he suspected she had any interest in another man. Not naturally flirtatious, Sarah was sometimes driven by

Brian's possessiveness into imprudent behaviour. But she did not intend to follow that course with Colonel Valentine. She could not fathom why his sardonic manner threw her into such a pother, but, as she would not be seeing any more of him, it hardly mattered. He had evidently come to Philadelphia on some military mission but soon would be returning to England. What he felt about her did not matter. Banishing all speculation about his presence in their midst, she entered gaily into the figures of the dance.

Elizabeth Powel's soirées always attracted the elite of both government personages and Philadelphia society. Her husband, Samuel, had been mayor of the city as well as the possessor of considerable wealth and taste. Despite his death from yellow fever some five years before, Mrs. Powel continued to entertain in the grand manner as befitted the daughter of one of the most prominent merchant families in the city. John Adams, not a particularly social man, believed she set the best table in the capital and enjoyed her "sinful feasts" of jellies, sweetmeats, sillabubs, and twenty kinds of tarts. Sarah, usually of good appetite, tucked into the lavish spread of delicacies with less than her usual enthusiasm. She refused to speculate on what was causing such a lack of interest in Mrs. Powel's superb supper.

She and Brian had joined several longtime friends for the repast, and Sarah shook off her black mood, unwilling to let her unease spoil the others' pleasure. The badinage across the table was the usual rollicking repartee, but Sarah was not to be allowed to dismiss the colonel so easily from her thoughts. Martha Delaney, one of her bosom bows, a cheerful blond minx, overly plump but with a winning smile and faultless complexion, leaned across her escort and asked Sarah, "I see you have met the fascinating colonel. What a fine figure of a man. I vow he has us all in a taking. What do you suppose he is doing here? Did he say?"

"What does any Englishman do here but connive to prevent us forming an alliance with the Frenchies," Brian intervened bitterly.

"I don't know what he is doing in America. He called on my grandfather today, but Grandpa is such a clam about his affairs. Probably some complicated trade issue. What does Napoleon call the British, 'a nation of shopkeepers'?" Sarah jeered, unwilling to reveal the real object of her grandfather's meeting with Colonel Valentine.

"Soldiers are not shopkeepers, my dear, and furthermore, I understand he is the younger son of an earl," Martha sighed longingly.

"As a patriotic American you should disdain titles, Martha. I am ashamed of you," Sarah riposted.

"Well, I do think titles are affected, and undemocratic, but he certainly has a distinguished, aristocratic air, which is quite irresistible. I wish he would ask me to dance." Martha, not one whit abashed by Sarah's rebuke, continued to rhapsodize.

"That's no way to talk, my girl," reprimanded Martha's fiancé, a well-set-up if somewhat pompous young man. "You are an engaged woman. Let's have no more of it."

"John's absolutely green that he can't strut around in a dashing uniform before your admiring eyes, Martha," Sarah teased, eager to distract her friend's attention from the disturbing British officer.

"Nonsense, Sarah." John responded, not amused to be the butt of Sarah's gentle humor. "I have little use for the military. I may have been just a child, but I remember all too well all those Hessians, and the English weren't much better."

"I cry pax, John. And I must get back to the ballroom. My next partner is waiting." Sarah rose with Brian and bid a laughing farewell to the merry group around the table. Sarah stood for a moment looking about the dance floor. Brian was reluctant to leave her side, but he was promised to another partner for the upcoming gavotte and perforce had to claim the lady. Sarah fanned herself impatiently, looking for Andrew Carter, whose initials scrawled on her card signified he was her next partner. She saw him at last crossing the entrance from the supper room, a worried frown on his bovine face. But before he reached her she was swept up closely against a red jacket and marched around the edge of the ballroom.

"How dare you commandeer me in this fashion, Colonel Valentine. I am promised for this dance," Sarah sputtered, struggling against the iron-hard arm that prevented her escape. But mortified to see that they were the cynosure of all eyes as they circled the edge of the ballroom where the next set was now under way, she realized that, short of causing a scene, she must accompany her abductor.

"I am sure your partner is devastated at being deprived of your company, but I had no recourse since you refused my civil request for a dance," the colonel replied suavely, as he propelled her ahead of him into a deserted anteroom. "Mrs. Powel assures me we will be undisturbed here and I have quite a bit to say to you." He released her and, pushing her gently down onto a silk-covered settee, loomed over her in what Sarah considered a menacing fashion. One look at his impassive face convinced her he would not allow her to leave. She had no idea what had provoked such treatment, but she had every intention of letting him know she resented his domineering ways. Her first reactions to this high-handed redcoat had been correct. English misses might find such arrogant behaviour acceptable but she did not, and she would not be tardy in signifying her displeasure.

Chapter Four

Now that he had achieved his purpose in removing Sarah from the dance floor, Colonel Valentine abandoned his brusque manner and seemed intent in charming Sarah out of her bad temper.

"Your escort this evening did not approve of my requesting a dance, I notice. Does his proprietary air mean you have consented to marry him?" he asked, ignoring the speaking look she gave him.

"I fail to see that is any of your business, Colonel Valentine," Sarah answered angrily, surprised by the turn of the conversation, but not willing to be distracted by his ploy. "How dare you drag me off for this interview in such a scandalous manner. Like Brian I have little use for the British, especially the military, a prejudice that is most understandable, I am sure you will agree. And your behaviour has done nothing to change my views."

"We are no longer enemies, Miss Ravensham, and I hope you do not completely share that young man's bias, although I greatly fear you are still a rebel," he replied with amusement, obviously not impressed with her anger.

"Well, I do. I may be half British myself, but my sympathies are wholly American. And I must say you represent all that I find most despicable in that nation of arrogant, patronizing, affected popinjays," she sputtered.

Raising one eyebrow mockingly at her strong words, Colonel Valentine continued, "And how many of us have you had occasion to meet to make such a judgment? You really are impetuous, Miss Ravensham, and prone to jump to conclusions, I fear. I am perfectly harmless. I regret that I was forced to remove you from the dance floor so ruthlessly, but I doubt if you would have accompanied me willingly. I rarely find myself reduced to such straits in order to converse with a young woman."

"English girls may approve of such ill manners, but let me tell you I do not," she retorted.

"You might profit from studying British manners, my girl, but let us not get involved in further arguments. My time here is limited and I have other responsibilities than those imposed by Lady Ravensham's request. I take it you have read your grandmother's letter and talked it over with Mr. Allen." He eyed her blandly.

"I see no reason why I should confide in you, Colonel. But I will tell you I have no intention of leaving my home and my grandfather to journey to England, where I would find a very chilly reception, I am sure," she said waspishly.

He sat down beside Sarah on the small settee, ignoring her efforts to move away from him. His masculine presence so close to her made her heart

31

pound nervously.

His lips tightening at her shrinking from him, Lucien Valentine spoke reassuringly, "Listen to me, Miss Ravensham. You do not understand your grandmother's need for a reconciliation. She had no recourse but to obey her husband when he forbade any contact with his American relations, but she never agreed with him. Now she is clutching at this last opportunity to make amends. Surely you do not include an ailing old woman in your animosity toward all things British. I cannot believe you are vindictive."

"Indeed I am vindictive toward the British. And you do nothing to allay my feelings, parading around in that uniform. Here, in Philadelphia, we have not forgotten what that implies."

"But not all of your countrymen were such passionate rebels. Your own mother found a British officer quite to her taste," he answered gently.

"Yes, and look where that relationship led her," Sarah answered, wondering that he should so tactlessly refer to her parents' tragic fate.

"I do not share the War Office's belief that your father was a traitor, and I championed his innocence with your grandfather. The Ravenshams are old friends of my family and, whatever you may believe, they are people of honour. I know your father would never have betrayed his country, no matter how deep his love for your mother," he said quietly, and with a sincerity that impressed Sarah despite herself.

"But his father did not share your views," Sarah protested, unwilling to be cajoled.

"Your grandmother never believed the accusations, and this estrangement was not of her making. She was

32

of a generation that did not defy her husband and she had to obey his orders. Now she wants to make what reparation she can before it is too late. Surely you will not deny her," he urged Sarah. She distrusted and disliked him, that was apparent, but he was not about to concede defeat. He rarely encountered a young woman who did not bow to his charm, his charismatic masculinity, and his well-born status, and he had to admit that Sarah Ravensham's antagonism was a refreshing challenge.

Sarah could feel her resolve weakening under the stare of those dark eyes, which caused tumult to her senses, but she was not yet ready to surrender.

"My grandfather would miss me if I went on such a long journey, and I love him. He is the only family I have ever had or needed," she still protested.

"I do not doubt your devotion to him, but he is willing to loan you to your grandmother for a visit, and, indeed, thinks you might profit from such a meeting," Colonel Valentine answered her objection smoothly. "Of course, there may be another reason, more pressing—and perhaps, more romantic—which would prevent your leaving Philadelphia?" he inquired with a provocative lift to his eyebrow.

"I do not understand to what you refer, Colonel," Sarah demurred in her most haughty manner. "My only other objection is that I have no affection for the English."

"Come now, Sarah, do not get on your high ropes. I was alluding to young Willing. I thought perhaps he had a prior claim upon you." Colonel Valentine was not one whit abashed by Sarah's effort to turn aside his impudent question.

"Brian is a dear friend and would endorse any decision I made," she said with dignity.

"How considerate of him," the colonel observed sardonically. "If you were my fiancée I could not contemplate a long absence with such magnaminity."

Sarah's cheeks flushed with anger. "I am not engaged to Brian Willing, sir, and I am not amused by your raillery. You presume too much, and your professions of belief in my father's innocence do not deceive me. I have no doubt you would say whatever was expedient to gain your way. I am not some docile milk-and-water miss who will give in to your bullying. You are a British officer and therefore a dishonorable scoundrel."

Damn the chit! She needed a good spanking. "Indeed," he said coolly. "Quite dishonorable."

With that he grasped her slender wrists and hauled her against his chest, pinioning her arms behind her with one hand. She struggled, outraged, sputtering with fury, turning her head this way and that to escape the disturbing proximity of his lips. He raised her chin with his free hand and then his mouth was crushing hers—savagely, punishingly.

No one had ever treated her like this, no one had ever taken such liberties. Sarah was shocked to find an unfamiliar passion welling up in her, a most unlady-like desire to respond to his kiss. This infuriated her more than anything so far, and the second he released her she struck him with all her strength across the face.

"How dare you treat me so. I am not some doxy to be handled in such a fashion. I will not listen to you another moment, and I will not forget how you have

34

treated me." She rushed from the room as if from the devil himself.

"Damn it. That was foolish of me, but she put my back up." Lucien grinned ruefully to himself. She was a maddening little handful but a loyal and spirited one. He was both intrigued and angry that she had provoked his temper. And he had probably sealed Lady Ravensham's fate. Sarah Ravensham would never travel to England now.

her thoughts. She flushed hot... she could not deny his
attraction. In the same way... she could not seem to
dismiss... in either coldness or... proper disinterest so
perhaps... reorganizing her ride... the most inconve...

Chapter Five

Later that evening in the privacy of her bedroom Sarah read her grandmother's letter again. Despicable as she found Colonel Valentine, she had to admit she was moved by his description of a repentant old lady regretting the long estrangement from her granddaughter, and the cruel judgment of her husband that had forced her to reject any belief in her son's innocence of treason. Normally of a sunny and forgiving nature, Sarah did not hold grudges nor was she prey to vindictive actions. She realized that much of her reluctance to answer her grandmother's invitation came from her furious reaction to the colonel. He had mocked her, attacked her patriotism, and, finally, with that brutal kiss, had aroused all of her hatred of the British to a fever pitch. She would be exceedingly loath to accept either his protection or his presence on a long sea voyage to London. She was accustomed to being admired, even deferred to by her beaux, and the colonel's treatment had confused as well as angered her. Much as she disliked him, she could not deny his attraction. At the same time, she could not bear to think that he might believe his arrogant tactics had persuaded her to change her mind. She was, however, honest enough to accept the fact that her reaction to him was scarcely a basis on which to refuse Lady Ravensham. Finally, her dilemma still unresolved, she blew out her candle and settled into a restless sleep.

The morning found her still muddled but determined to lay her problem before her grandfather, since he had never failed her. She met him for breakfast, masking her disquiet with a gay smile and a kiss atop his white head. He was not deceived and commented disapprovingly on her languorous air and pale cheeks.

"Too much dissipation, my girl, that's what's wrong. I will speak to young Willing if he cannot bring you home at a decent hour. Much too much of this revelry. It is affecting your health," Joshua Allen growled, not liking to see his beloved granddaughter in low spirits.

Sarah roused herself to bite determinedly into her toast and gulp her chocolate. "Nonsense, Grandpa, I was not very late, and it is not my riotous social life that has set me brooding. I could not sleep after reading Lady Ravensham's letter and discussing it with that maddening Colonel Valentine. Whatever can Mrs. Powel be thinking of to invite a British officer to her dance?"

"He is considered quite an eligible young man, my dear, even in our fervently democratic society, and certainly Elizabeth Powel is no republican. He is much sought after by all Philadelphia hostesses, and their daughters, too, I believe," Joshua Allen reproved

Sarah with a twinkle in his eye.

"Brian called him a stuck-up popinjay," Sarah said.

"Yes, well I can see that young Willing would think him a threat. But Valentine's no popinjay, my dear. He's a brave soldier, with many battles behind him for all his sophisticated manner."

"Oh, Grandpa, you're just being contrary, like Martha. She thinks he is most captivating and finds his drawing room air—or is it arrogance—positively charming. She quite put John's nose out of joint with her admiration." Sarah chuckled, remembering John's pompous disapproval.

"John will have his work cut out for him with that little baggage," her grandfather conceded. "But seriously, Sarah, you must not judge Lucien Valentine as an enemy just because he is a British soldier. Those old hatreds must be forgotten. It is to our country's advantage to make an ally of England, especially now that France is behaving so recklessly."

"I'm sure you know best, Grandpa," Sarah agreed demurely.

"You're not sure at all, missy, so don't come over me with those false smiles. Soothing the old gentleman, are you? Well, I'm not taken in for a moment. You will think and do exactly what you wish." He smiled indulgently, thinking what a delightful picture Sarah made gracing the breakfast table on this bleak March morning in her turquoise-blue morning dress, accented with a fresh white fichu, her curls tied with a matching ribbon.

"Grandpa, that's not fair. I always listen carefully to your strictures."

"Yes you listen very prettily, my dear, but as to

heeding my advice, that's quite another matter, eh?"

"And what is your advice about this journey?"

"You know I think you should go. Whatever your feelings, you owe it to your parents' memory."

Joshua Allen was quite solemn now, and Sarah had to be impressed with her grandfather's obvious desire that she accept her grandmother's invitation. She knew he did not want her to leave him, but Joshua Allen was a man to whom duty and honour meant a great deal. She did not know what to say.

"Well, I will leave you to think about it, my dear. General Hamilton is calling upon me this morning and I must ready myself for the appointment." Dropping a light kiss on her curls, Joshua Allen left the room. Sarah, watching his upright figure walk briskly to the door, sighed. How could she think of leaving the dear man who meant so much to her as companion, advisor, and beloved parent? All she had ever known at his hands was love and protection. How could either of them bear the long parting?

Joshua Allen's thoughts echoed his granddaughter's as he sat in his library awaiting the visit of Alexander Hamilton, late of the president's Cabinet and now Inspector-General of the new republic's small army. When Hamilton was Secretary of the Treasury he had often called upon Allen for advice on a particularly stubborn piece of economic legislation, but Allen had no experience in military matters and could not but wonder what the new commander wanted of him.

At ten o'clock precisely James ushered the dapper and worldly general into Allen's sanctum. The two friends greeted each other warmly. Hamilton had always been a favorite of Allen's, although at times he deplored the younger man's vanity and hotheadedness. Hamilton, at forty-one, had already accomplished more than most men in a lifetime. Under average height, his erect stature and quickness of step gave him a commanding presence. Quick to take offense, he was equally quick to forgive and his adherents were many.

The illegitimate son of a cadet branch of the Scottish nobility, Hamilton had been born on the Caribbean island of Nevis, had emigrated to the colonies at an early age, and had rapidly acquired an education and access to important men and affairs. With an astute legal mind allied to an impulsive temperament, he was not everyone's choice for high government office, but General Washington had soon discovered that his young adjutant was a man of rare administrative talents as well as martial bravery. Hamilton had married well to Elizabeth Schuyler, daughter of a wealthy New York landowner, and had risen under Washington's aegis to a position of prominence in his adopted country. His masterly essays had persuaded many doubters to endorse the new constitution, but his recent espousal of the British in their struggle with the French had made him many enemies. Allen respected him and, for the most part, shared his sympathies.

After an exchange of civilities, Hamilton lost no time in stating the object of his visit. His thin features were drawn into firmly disciplined lines, his blue eyes stern as he looked across the desk at his host.

"You may know, Allen, that the French, with Jefferson's misguided cooperation, are doing all in their power to pull us into a war against His Majesty's government. And the combination is a powerful one. One reckless act and we could be fighting before the year is out. If we must be drawn into the struggle, I would much prefer to put our limited resources at the disposal of the British, who are standing stalwart against these cursed revolutionaries." Hamilton stated his case succinctly.

"You were once a fervent revolutionary, yourself, Alex, if I remember," Allen chided.

"Those were different times and far different circumstances," Hamilton retorted angrily. "Our quarrel with the British was primarily a parliamentary one, as you know. The French are radical, willing to throw out all restraints to aid their new order. I have no patience with them, nor with Jefferson's mealy-mouthed acquiescence to all things Jacobin."

"I think you would secretly prefer we were still ruled by King George, my dear fellow," Allen answered, not surprised by Hamilton's distinct Anglophile leanings.

"Not at all, although I do think our quarrel with the mother country might have been settled in a more amicable way than complete severance of the connection. But that is hindsight. What I am worried about now is that fellow Genêt and the Frenchies dabbling in our affairs. They are into every department, their spies are everywhere. I have recently routed a few in the army, I can tell you," he stated with satisfaction.

"Yes," Allen agreed. "I am sure the army is getting a thorough overhauling, and about time too, with poor old Henry Knox not up to the demands."

"But my plans for the army and the continuing

peace of this country are constantly endangered by French spies and their sympathizers. I can trust very few," Hamilton said.

Allen, suspecting that Hamilton suffered from paranoia about the French, wondered what the young general would call upon him to do.

Hamilton sighed, then shook off his somber thoughts and offered his shocking suggestion.

"I understand your granddaughter is traveling to England shortly to visit her paternal grandmother, Lady Ravensham." Hamilton spoke with assurance, lifting an eyebrow wryly when he noticed Allen's expression.

"I suppose it is impossible to keep a secret in this town. It's a hotbed of gossip, and, I assume, you have your own spy network." Allen, remembering bitterly the talk at the time of his daughter's tragedy, was not at all pleased that his private business was the subject of tittle-tattle.

Hamilton hurried to placate Joshua Allen. "Do not be angry, old friend. My source was Col. Lucien Valentine, who is far from indiscreet. Valentine is here to confer with me privately about arrangements to thwart the French from forcing our country into an unwanted and, I may say, unaffordable war."

"That's all very well, Hamilton, but I fail to see why my granddaughter's plans concern you," he responded stiffly.

"I am hoping she will consent to carry some secret documents to Pitt for me. I dare not trust the diplomatic channels or even a special courier. I am afraid there are Jefferson sympathizers on my staff, and a leakage could prove disastrous. Colonel Valentine will be traveling with her and can keep an eye on her, but no one will suspect such a charming and well-brought-up young woman of intrigue." Hamilton knew his suggestion would meet with repugnance and braced himself to receive his friend's objections.

Allen was appalled. "It's unthinkable to expose her to danger. She is not a devious girl, and it would be impossible for her to dissemble."

"She is a patriot, I know, and a lovely one, who would disarm the devil himself," countered Hamilton, who, although happily married, had never lost his taste for the ladies, an admiration reciprocated enthusiastically by a legion of women. "Why not put it to her? I promise to tell her honestly of the pitfalls and to abide by her decision."

"After you have cozened her into accepting. I know your methods, Hamilton, and my granddaughter is as susceptible as any to your particular brand of charm."

"My friend, this is no light matter, but a most serious situation. I would not put your granddaughter at risk if there were any other way. And besides, there will be little danger. Valentine is a sharp fellow, well capable of guarding your ewe lamb. Let us hear from her and see if she wants to serve her country." Hamilton appealed brazenly to Allen's own patriotism, knowing how disturbed the merchant was at the conditions now prevailing, and shrewd enough to warrant that business mattered a good deal to Joshua Allen. With trade in its present chaotic condition, even the solid firm of Allen & Smithson must be feeling the pinch.

Joshua Allen brooded, knowing the truth of Hamilton's assessment. Both the French and English navies endangered American trade, boarding vessels unauthorized, impressing seamen, lifting cargoes, and acting in a reprehensible manner that the nascent American navy was powerless to prevent. Washington's neutrality proclamation angered the French, and John Jay's treaty with the British denied American access to the traffic in the West Indies in the lucrative cargoes of molasses, coffee, sugar, cotton, cocoa, and coffee.

"I would think the British had enough on their plate what with the Irish rebellion, Napoleon's efforts against their ally Austria, and their attempts to dominate the sea lanes," Allen argued. "Why should they bother with us?"

"Because they do not really believe in our independence, and we are too lucrative a market for them to surrender gracefully. No matter how invidious the British treatment, it is still in our interests to keep relations with our former masters sweet, rather than connive with the French against them. The English will prevail against Napoleon in the end, you know." Hamilton spoke determinedly.

"Perhaps. In any case, European squabbles do not interest me, but my granddaughter's welfare does."

"She is half English herself, need I remind you," Hamilton spoke gently, not wanting to upset Allen any further.

But Joshua Allen, always a fair man, sighed, and admitted the justice of Hamilton's claim. "Yes, you are right. Well, we will ask her, or rather you will. I refuse to offer any advice either for or against the project. It must be her decision alone."

"I will be satisfied to rest my case in Sarah's

44

hands." Hamilton barely suppressed a sigh of relief. He had every confidence in Sarah Ravensham's eagerness for adventure, and, if the project were put to her adroitly, he believed he could persuade her.

Chapter Six

General Hamilton's confidence in his ability to convince Sarah was not misplaced. When she entered the library a few moments later, he stood and received her greetings with a warm smile. What a lovely young woman she was. And how fortunate Valentine was to make the long sea voyage in her company, the lucky dog. Hamilton sighed, his reputation for gallantry and dalliance coming to the fore as he thought of the myriad romantic opportunities ahead. Still, he must not be distracted from his mission.

"Good day, General Hamilton. How nice to see you. And how is Mrs. Hamilton? Is she with you on this trip?" Sarah beamed on the urbane general, whom she had known from childhood and always admired for his astute mind and chivalrous manner.

"Alas, I had to leave her with the children in New York. As always, you are looking ravishing, my dear Sarah." He smiled graciously on her.

"Thank you, General." She turned to her grandfather. "Did you want me for something special, Grandpa? I am about to go shopping."

"I think you must postpone your expedition, my dear. General Hamilton has a particular favour to ask of you." Allen looked at his granddaughter affectionately but his tone was serious.

"Anything I can do, of course, General Hamilton," Sarah replied and seated herself.

"I wonder if you will be so amenable when you hear what I require," Hamilton said. "I understand from your grandfather that you are planning a trip to England to see your paternal relations. Is this correct?"

Sarah raised her eyes enquiringly. What could her invitation to London have to do with General Hamilton?

"I haven't precisely decided yet. Grandfather thinks I should go, but I am reluctant to leave him and, unlike you, General, I find the English not exactly to my taste," Sarah replied boldly. She well knew, as did all of Philadelphia, of the general's conflict with Jefferson over the French alliance.

"Well, I hope I can persuade you to make the trip." Hamilton was not annoyed by her obvious aversion toward a visit to England. Her anti-British feelings were well-known and made her all the more suited for his purposes. He continued speaking.

"I know you are a sincere patriot, Sarah, and would not want to see the country we both love plunged into an ill-advised war that can only lead to suffering for our people. If Mr. Jefferson has his way we might eventually find ourselves in just such a position. He is a man of profound ambition and violent passions and must be stopped from embroiling us in quarrels that do not concern us."

Sarah suppressed a smile with difficulty. Hamilton's description of his rival could be applied equally well to his own temperament, but she had enough wisdom not to suggest such a parallel. "I certainly do not want to see America at war with either England or France," she assured the general.

"If Jefferson has his way, we will be at war and within months. Elbridge Gerry is on a mission to France, which I regard as very suspect. If we are dragged into this European struggle, I want to be sure we are on the right side. A country led by that monomaniac Napoleon does not deserve our support." He spoke unequivocally.

Sarah wondered if his opposition to the French alliance was sparked as much by his animosity to Jefferson as it was by a real belief that such a course would be disastrous to his country. Rumours were rife that Hamilton had been intriguing with George Hammond, the British special emissary. His own motives were not simon-pure. Still she said nothing.

"What I want you to do is to take an important document to London, to William Pitt. It is advisable—in fact, for your own peace of mind, essential—that you know nothing of the document's purport. But believe me when I say that it is vital to peace." Hamilton's sincerity convinced his listeners that he had no doubts about the necessity of this mission.

Sarah turned to her grandfather. "Grandpa, what do you think? Should I undertake General Hamilton's errand?"

"It must be your decision, my dear. Only let me say that I tend to agree with General Hamilton as to the seriousness of the situation, and I share his views about Mr. Jefferson's influence and political hopes." Joshua Allen spoke slowly, not liking the position into which Hamilton had forced him, but unwilling to repudiate his longtime friend.

"You will be well protected on the voyage," Hamilton assured her. "Colonel Valentine will be aboard ship and he will keep an eye on you. Perhaps that is an inducement, eh?"

"Not at all General Hamilton." Sarah answered tartly, annoyed at the blush that rose to her cheeks at the general's unwarranted suggestion. "I am sure Colonel Valentine is a brave soldier, but I cannot view the prospect of weeks in his company as anything but a tedious duty—if, indeed, I undertake this affair."

"Sarah, unlike many of the Philadelphia misses, does not find Lucien Valentine a romantic figure," Joshua Allen explained.

"Oh, no?" said Hamilton. "But he is considered quite a beau and a nonpareil as well as a brave soldier, Sarah. At any rate I know I can trust him to keep an eye on you. I will not deny that what I am asking you to do poses some dangers."

"Well, it sounds like a great storm in a teacup to me but, since you are certain of the necessity, General Hamilton, I will go to London and deliver your message to Mr. Pitt." Sarah was aware that she had made a momentous decision. She was rather excited to be involved in a matter of such importance and also quite relieved to have made the decision once and for all to go to England.

"You will make an attractive secret agent, my dear. I quite envy Valentine his duties," Hamilton teased. Then his demeanour and voice changed. "I cannot thank you enough, Sarah, and be assured you are doing your country a great service. Your grandfather will let me know of your sailing date, and I will contact you soon. It is important that as little time is lost as possible, so I hope you will expedite your plans and be on the high seas without delay."

Hamilton bowed in a courtly manner over Sarah's hand and bid Joshua Allen a warm farewell. He walked from the room briskly, as if a great load had been lifted from his shoulders. Joshua Allen watched him go with mingled emotions. He admired the bantam cock and shared to some extent his assessment of the political perils ahead, but he was perturbed that Hamilton had embroiled his granddaughter in his machinations. If anything happened to her, Hamilton would answer to him.

Chapter Seven

Sarah, although not naturally timorous, experienced several qualms of apprehension in the absence of the dynamic and persuasive Alexander Hamilton. Neither her grandfather nor Brian Willing helped calm her emotions about the coming voyage. Brian, irate that she was leaving on a long visit to England, renewed his proposal of marriage, insisting that an engagement would protect her from London's licentious society. She had great trouble dissuading him without damaging his feelings. And then her grandfather had his own worries about the danger she might encounter. She reminded him somewhat caustically that both he and General Hamilton had felt she would be ably served by her protector, Lucien Valentine. What she did not tell her grandfather was that most of her uneasiness sprang not from her fears about carrying General Hamilton's message to Pitt but from her looming meeting with the English Ravenshams. She had additional doubts about spending those weeks aboard ship in the disturbing colonel's company, too, and could not tell her grandfather about their last tempestuous confrontation. Fortunately she had not been forced into the colonel's company since Mrs. Powel's dance, so she had not experienced the embarrassment that might have occurred after that interview.

Meanwhile her erstwhile adversary was entertaining disquiet of his own. Lucien Valentine had strongly opposed Hamilton's choice of messenger for the Pitt document. He would have preferred to carry the letter himself and chance a confrontation with a French agent on what was, at bottom, a military mission. He had been brought round to accepting Sarah as the safer alternative but still felt at heart that it was no job for a woman, especially a gently bred female scarcely out of the schoolroom.

Lucien had a soldier's taste in women, confining his romantic excursions to those matrons of easy virtue who understood the rules of dalliance or the demi-reps whose business was pleasing men. He avoided chaste young women, debutantes, and country belles whose chief concern were the marriage stakes. The second son of the august Earl of Lenminster, he did not need to worry about marrying and producing the obligatory heir. That was his brother Alistair's responsibility. As a serving soldier he considered marriage a trap, which he had successfully evaded—although at times it had been a near thing for he was considered a very eligible *parti*. His father had bought him a cavalry commission at an early age, and his natural aptitude and reckless courage had won him rapid promotion not entirely due to the earl's connections and well-filled purse. At twenty-eight he was young to be a colonel but he had earned that rank on battlefields throughout Europe. Since France had declared war on England six years ago, he had been involved in every action to defeat the French republic and recently served on the Austrian Archduke Charles's staff during the Italian campaign that had culminated in the Treaty of Campo Formio.

His notable talents on the battlefield were equaled by his exploits in the bedroom, which had earned him quite a reputation. Still, he considered women a diversion, not to be taken seriously, necessary at times but not vital to the real business of life. He had never met a girl like Sarah, of good family but independent, antagonistic to him, and not susceptible to the flattery and flirtatious ploys that had stood him in good stead in the past. Perhaps it was because she was an American and had absorbed some of the brash former colony's spirit.

But he found her infuriatingly attractive, an unlooked-for complication. His interest had been piqued by her prejudice against Englishmen, her mercurial moods, and her undeniable appeal to the senses. While not in the mode of accepted English beauty which was blond-haired and blue-eyed, she had her own sparkling allure. He feared Sarah could provide more trouble than he wanted at this stage in his life and cursed the day he had come to Philadelphia. She had dealt quite a blow to his *amour-propre* and, though he was tempted to make her pay for it, good sense came to his rescue. There was only one relationship possible with a girl like Sarah and he was not prepared to offer her marriage.

He had no illusions about what matrimony entailed. He had seen too many of his comrades succumb to the lure of an enticing face and figure with never a care for the mind or character of the beloved. Very few women were fitted to follow the drum and certainly an American would spurn such a life. He did not intend to play the tame lap dog to a wife's demands and he would never leave the army. Seeing the danger, he planned measures, like a good campaigner, to avoid it.

This sea voyage held more perils than those a French agent might provide. Lucien suspected that General Hamilton found his position rather amusing. Lucien smiled grimly. Well, his best defense was to keep his distance from Sarah, which would disarm the enemy as well as ensure that his own emotions would remain under control. No doubt he was flattering himself to think she held him in anything but aversion. She had certainly gone to some lengths to assure him she found him unacceptable in every way. He had been a fool to kiss her, although that had happened as much from anger as desire. Still he was having difficulty in forgetting how seductive that brief caress had been. Maddening minx! This nursemaid chore promised to be challenging in more ways than one.

Not one for prolonged introspection, Lucien, when faced with an obstacle, usually met it straight on and this was what he intended to do with Miss Ravensham. He set off for Joshua Allen's house prepared to come to terms with Sarah Ravensham without delay.

Unaware of what faced her, Sarah was enjoying her morning chocolate, her thoughts not entirely concerned with the perils of her upcoming voyage. She admitted to herself that General Hamilton had beguiled her into an errand that might cause more complications than she had originally believed. Not the least of these was a close association with Colonel Valentine. From her first meeting with that lordly gentleman he had possessed a talent for upsetting the even tenor of her days. She could not deny his attraction, remembering that impressive figure, the stern features that could lighten into a whimsical, alluring smile, and, beneath all his careless banter, the real sensuality she sensed without actually understanding it. But she could not forget he was an arrogant Englishman.

He may have been astute enough to treat her grandfather with respect, and apparently General Hamilton, well known for his British proclivities, considered him both intelligent and courageous, but then neither of them had been treated to his condescension and cynical approach to women. No doubt he was accustomed to the easy conquest of the ladies, witness Martha Delaney's reaction to his physical assets. But Martha was a flibbertigibbet, not known for her common sense, and a notorious flirt despite her engagement.

Sarah herself found him annoying, patronizing, and at their last meeting, more than that, insulting. He did not like being thwarted, and his brutal kiss proved she had caused him to lose that much-vaunted English self-control, although she was not proud of her own conduct at that interview. She bit her lip in frustration, remembering that kiss. She should have responded with icy dignity but instead had reacted like an innocent schoolgirl, frightened of being ravished.

Well, she did not welcome the idea of him as a

watchdog on the coming voyage, but she would see to it that she did not repeat her previous mistake with Colonel Valentine. At their inevitable next meeting she would behave with cool circumspection, and let him know she was not available for flirtation or romantic shipboard dalliance. They would have to establish some kind of relationship but it would be formal. She could not forget that his close friendship with the Ravenshams meant he would be most apt to agree with them about her father's imputed treachery despite his denials. She could never entertain warm feelings about a man who felt thus. No, she would make it quite clear to the haughty colonel that, though she might be forced to accept his protection, that did not imply any other bond between them.

Sarah's firm resolutions concerning her future attitude toward Lucien Valentine were put to the test much sooner than she had expected. While she was conferring with the cook, James's wife, Liberty—an apt name, Sarah had often thought, for the fierce little woman who managed her husband and indeed the whole household with quiet determination—James brought her the news that Colonel Valentine had called and was awaiting her in the drawing room. James must be impressed with their visitor, if Sarah was not, otherwise he would have insisted he wait in the hall.

She looked ruefully at her plain blue cambric morning dress, not the costume she would have chosen to receive the colonel. She needed the armour of her best apricot morning dress for the confrontation, but she had no time to change. Then reproving herself for such vanity she marched across the hall. After all, what did it matter how she looked to the colonel? What mattered was that she remain distant and imperturbable in the face of his mockery, not her usual open style, and that she offer a firm rebuke over their last encounter, if not pointedly ignore it altogether.

Lucien watched the militant figure approach him with some amusement. He was determined that this interview would go according to his wishes and Lucien Valentine was not a man accustomed to being denied, certainly not by a chit of a girl.

Meeting his bland gaze, Sarah called on all her reserves and greeted him.

"Good morning, Colonel Valentine. This visit is most unexpected," she said frigidly.

"I suppose you are alluding to our last meeting. I must apologize for that. I fear you must hold me in contempt, for my loss of control. I can only plead extenuating circumstances. You are very enticing, Sarah, and you made me angry," Lucien spoke cajolingly. She was looking damned attractive now, temper adding an appealing glow to those creamy cheeks and a sparkle to the topaz eyes, which continued to regard him with scorn.

"Hardly the behaviour of an officer and a gentleman, Colonel. Do you kiss every female who angers you?" she asked.

"Not unless they are as attractive as you," he responded audaciously. "It will not happen again— unless, of course, you show unmistakable signs of welcoming my advances," he smiled, softening the stern features, and exerting the charm that had so often served him in good stead with recalcitrant

57

females.

Sarah, to her dismay, found her resolution to treat him coldly melting away under the seductiveness of that smile and the warm gaze he turned upon her, however hard she tried not to be beguiled by his practiced address.

"I accept your apology, Colonel Valentine, and now I must excuse myself. I have several pressing chores awaiting me," she replied.

"Miss Ravensham, can we not sit down and talk about our common mission. It seems General Hamilton has powers of persuasion I do not possess. I understand you have consented not only to visit your grandmother but to carry his letter to Mr. Pitt. I commend your courage, but it will be my responsibility to see that you do not suffer from your patriotism. If we are to travel on this voyage, which may pose perils, do you not think it foolish to be at daggers drawn? I promise not to encroach on any limits you set to our friendship, but I hope you will not let our past passage at arms influence your future conduct. I will not believe you have accepted my apology otherwise," he coaxed.

Sarah, now thoroughly confused, had no choice but to seat herself gingerly on one of the brocade chairs and indicate that he might do likewise. She was not at all pleased that he had somehow managed to gain the upper hand with his patronizing talk of a future relationship. He might come over his various women friends with such tactics but she was not so easily deluded.

"Colonel Valentine," she began, with as much dignity as she could summon. "I have agreed to

General Hamilton's request. But you both exaggerate the dangers of this errand, I believe. Who would suspect me? In other words, I am hardly in need of a protector. We American girls are quite capable of fending for ourselves."

Lucien's lips tightened, annoyed both at her adroit set-down and at her refusal to take the dangers ahead seriously.

Sarah could barely hide her satisfaction that she had slipped beneath his guard. He was much too sure of himself, and he need not think a few specious words would eradicate that brutal kiss.

"My dear Miss Ravensham, the general is quite right to put you on your guard. I have some experience with these French agents, and they can, like their master, be ruthless. If you are not careful, you could place yourself in a dangerous position. I disapprove of your being involved, as I know your grandfather does, but I intend to see that nothing happens to you. For that I need your cooperation. So whether you like it or not, Sarah, we are bound together in this mission," he spoke earnestly, all attempts at flirtation absent.

Sarah, impressed despite herself by his serious manner, so different from his usual approach, realized that she had been taking her promise to General Hamilton too lightly. Influenced by Hamilton's engaging manner and assurances of her safety under Colonel Valentine's aegis as well as by her own patriotic conviction, she had heedlessly leaped into a situation that might be dangerous. Sarah was no coward but she was no fool either. Nor was she naive enough not to acknowledge the truth of Lucien Valentine's warnings, based as they were on his past experiences. Meeting his eyes, from which all trace of mockery had vanished, she accepted the fact that she must depend on him and somehow that decision calmed her fears. She must trust him and put her life in his hands, which, strangely, she was not reluctant to do. When it was a matter of duty, she knew he would spare no effort. Oh, he was a clever devil, disarming her on the one hand, and on the other, forcing her to accept his protection.

"I am sure we will brush through this mission with success, Colonel, and I promise to do all that you advise when it comes to the matter of my safety. I find you arrogant and annoying, but I am convinced you will do your utmost to see that I safely arrive in London with the document. I will go no further than that, but that should satisfy you," she answered gravely.

"It does not satisfy me, Sarah, but I expect it is the greatest conciliation you can offer. Perhaps by the journey's end I will have succeeded in changing your opinion of me. I intend to try, I warn you, but in the meantime I am grateful for your trust." He smiled at her again with that insinuating charm that threatened all her resolutions to keep him at a distance. "I will see you on board ship if not before. And I am glad that we have resolved some of your animosity." He bowed and left the room before she could form the caustic rejoinder she had planned to tender.

Chapter Eight

Sarah leaned over the railing of the packet, which was slipping from the Philadelphia harbour on the evening tide. She blinked the tears from her eyes, determined not to surrender to the emotions that this painful separation from her grandfather had provoked. He had put a brave face upon it, and so had she, in deference to his feelings, but she knew her absence would mean loneliness and worry over her safety for him. She was sailing toward an unknown future, having no information about her Ravensham relatives nor their London life beyond the sketchy words of her grandmother's invitation. The reunion Lady Ravensham wished for so ardently could prove to be a disaster, and how would the other members of the family receive her? Somehow that meeting loomed much larger in her mind than General Hamilton's mission. So much depended on their welcome. Perhaps Colonel Valentine could give her some idea of what to expect from the Ravenshams. She hated to ask him or to reveal her dread of the family, but she needed more information about them, to arm herself for acceptance or rejection.

As if he had been conjured up by her thoughts, Lucien Valentine appeared silently at her shoulder, well wrapped in a stylish greatcoat against the late March winds buffeting the sails now unfurling above them. Standing in her leeward, he sheltered her with his imposing bulk from the gusts that stirred the chestnut curls beneath her securely tied bonnet.

"You must be prey to some melancholy at seeing the last of Philadelphia and bidding farewell to your grandfather, Sarah. You are a brave girl to undertake this voyage. I know few English misses who would face what's ahead with such courage." He spoke warmly, surprising her with his perception and sympathy. He alluded, she knew, not only to her parting from her home and grandfather, but also to the mission on which they were embarked. His words reminded Sarah of the precious papers she had sewn inside her petticoat, feeling that her reticule and her baggage were not secure hiding places. Sensing that he was awaiting some kind of rapproachement from her, an acknowledgment that their passage at arms in the past must now be put aside in the face of the common danger that confronted them, she answered his offer of understanding.

"I will certainly miss Grandpa, but I am not so faint-hearted that I don't relish the chance of some adventure." Sarah, although reluctantly admitting that Colonel Valentine's protection comforted her, was not about to confide in him her real fears about the voyage—that she felt apprehension about the coming meeting with the Ravenshams, and real doubt about being able to discover any proof of her father's innocence. Although an impelling reason to travel to England, she felt it would not receive much encouragement from Lucien Valentine, and she was not secure enough in their new relationship to confide in him.

"I am here to see that no adventure more exciting than a shipboard flirtation occurs," Valentine teased, hoping to distract her from any somber thoughts. He genuinely admired her courage in taking on the Hamilton mission. Certainly none of the well-bred ladies he knew in London would be either fitted or eager to accept such a challenge. Sarah was annoyingly hot-tempered and prickly about her country, but she had the virtue of her faults, loyalty and devotion to those she loved. There was nothing frivolous in her manner, only an engaging light-heartedness Lucien found distinctly appealing after a surfeit of bored and blasé society women.

Sarah, always quick to rise to the bait, replied, "Oh, surely, not with you, Colonel. You are quite above my touch." Sarah refused to be patronized, not recognizing Lucien's words were attempts to assuage her uncertainties about what lay ahead.

"I wonder why you should entertain such an idea. I find you most appealing," he continued to plague her, enjoying the fire in her bright eyes and the glowing colour either the fresh sea breeze or his provocative words had brought to her creamy cheeks. Although her charms were not in the accepted mode she was truly captivating, and Lucien chided himself for flirting with her. That way lay trouble, he knew.

But Sarah did not take him seriously. Despite her many beaux and popularity among her Philadelphia set, she did not think every man she met was bowled over by her charm. And she was convinced the colonel preferred more sophisticated companions.

"I think you had better concentrate on your objective, Colonel," Sarah reproached him, confused by his whimsical tone, "which is to keep an eye out for agents who might interfere with our plan. I am sure your talent for expert dalliance can await your arrival in London. I am not a suitable target for your gallantries."

"Now I wonder why you should doubt my sincerity," Valentine responded, unaccountably annoyed at her assessment of him. "You have been listening to tales unfit for your chaste ears. You should not believe all you hear, Sarah. You wound me deeply."

"Colonel Valentine, I think I should make one thing clear. I have accepted your escort on this voyage because Grandpa and General Hamilton advised me to do so. I am not undertaking this trip for amusement. And may I remind you that my chaperone, Mrs. Amberly, is prepared to see that I behave in a proper manner? See that you do so, also."

He raised his eyebrows sardonically. "I will accept your precepts, Sarah, if you will call me Lucien. I find it very daunting when we are co-conspirators to be addressed, in those quelling tones, as 'Colonel Valentine.' If I promise to behave, will you call me Lucien?"

"Oh, you are impossible," Sarah chided, laughing despite her intention to act with staid decorum. Lucien Valentine was not like her Philadelphia beaux who accepted a set-down and treated her with the utmost respect. Still, she supposed he was right. How foolish to be at daggers drawn with the man who had been selected to guard her against misfortune.

"I will make a bargain with you, Lucien. We will stop this silly sparring with words, and I will welcome your protection, but please treat me like an adult. If General Hamilton believed I was grown-up enough to undertake this task, you should treat me accordingly." Sarah spoke seriously, intent on impressing the colonel with her maturity.

"I stand reproved," Lucien responded, laughter in his eyes. "I would do nothing to shake your faith or prevent you from confiding in me if you sense something or someone suspicious aboard this ship. You must lock your cabin door securely at night. In the daytime I will be hovering nearby to see that no harm comes to you. If my presence prevents some of these young sprigs from paying you attention, I regret it, but you must be alert to danger. Trust me, Sarah, and remember we both desire a safe outcome to this mission. Let me escort you below now, and you can see to your unpacking. I hope your cabin is comfortable."

Sarah, taking one last look at the receding skyline, accepted the colonel's arm and turned from the rail. He might try to set her mind at ease as to his intentions, which he insisted were strictly protective, but she could not control her own feelings. Their relationship promised problems for her, she was convinced.

Below, he inspected her cabin, which could barely hold her wardrobe and the bunk much less an intruder. He seemed satisfied that her accommodations were as comfortable as possible under the conditions.

Joshua Allen had booked passage for Sarah on the first available packet sailing for Plymouth, and the safest, for the ship was sailing in a convoy of two armed merchantmen, but it was not a luxury vessel. The colonel would have preferred to sail on a British ship of the line, but this had proved impractical. There must be no suspicion that Sarah was aught but a traveler journeying to meet her English relations, so she sailed aboard an American packet. Perforce Valentine had to do the same.

After he left the cabin, Sarah did not immediately look to her unpacking. Normally she would have been accompanied by a maid, who would have assumed this task for her, but her own Cissy had not wanted to travel so far distant from home, and neither Sarah nor Valentine were willing to chance employing a new abigail. Sarah, often impatient at the restraints polite society insisted on imposing on a well-bred girl, was annoyed enough at the presence of Mrs. Amberly, the wife of a British diplomat, who was sailing home to her children and had agreed to chaperone Sarah. Mrs. Amberly allowed that American girls were far too free and easy in their ways, and said that, if Sarah hoped to make the best impression on her British relatives, she had best observe the prescribed customs of their society. Sarah had not taken to Mrs. Amberly, a rather languid matron, who had simpered at Colonel Valentine when they were introduced. Sarah accepted the fact that she must endure the lady's surveillance, but she did not welcome it.

In all the badinage above board in the welter of sailing, she had forgotten to ask Colonel Valentine about her grandmother and what she might expect in

London. Oh, dear, so many problems, and she felt again beneath her skirt to make sure the paper entrusted to her was safe. How happy she would be when both she and the paper reached their destination safely.

Thinking of the paper, Sarah frowned. If it was as important as General Hamilton believed, why had he not given the paper to Colonel Valentine, who certainly held his every confidence? She feared she was not cut out to be a conspirator. All this huggermugger. She could not think for a minute she was in any personal danger, although her grandfather had warned her to confide in no one. At the last minute he had almost forbidden her to go, alarmed at the pitfalls she might encounter and cursing Hamilton for cozening him into approving of her services as a messenger. Though apt to be an alarmist where Sarah's welfare was concerned, in this case Joshua Allen had every reason to worry.

Chapter Nine

Life aboard ship, which Sarah had expected to be
constricting, proved exhilarating. The Atlantic, which
could be turbulent in early spring, had decided to
offer its more benign aspect, and Sarah discovered she
was a good sailor, delighting in the brisk breezes and
the furl of the sails as the packet cut its way through
the grey-blue waters. This happy adaptation to the
roll of the ship had not been her chaperone's portion.
Soon after they had sailed out of Delaware Bay, Moira
Amberly had taken to her bunk, a victim of seasickness. Sarah dutifully visited her, willing to offer what
comfort she could, but the sufferer wanted only to be
left alone, soothed by cloths dipped in eau de cologne
and submitting to the ministrations of the brisk but
kindly stewardess, who was accustomed to passengers
suffering from *mal de mer*. So Sarah was able to roam
the decks, enjoy the bracing winds, and make the
acquaintance of her fellow passengers. Two or three
young men sailing to England on business or embark-
ing on leisurely travels were eager to attend her, and
Sarah, friendly and open by nature, saw no reason to

discourage them.

Lucien Valentine made no effort to join her train of admirers, but she was always conscious of him looming in the background, his sardonic eyes ever alert. Although she had protested that she did not want him to carry out the threatened shipboard flirtation, now that he had retreated from any attempt to alter the terms she had laid down, she was irked by his compliance to her strictures. She did not know what she had expected, but she had to admit that his attitude of casual friendship protected her. A study of the passenger list had assured her that no overtly suspicious types might have an interest in her mission, so she relaxed and prepared to enjoy the voyage.

Among her admirers she numbered Lt. Philip Fairlie, of His Majesty's Navy, who had been visiting his sister in Philadelphia on his recent leave and was now sailing to meet his ship in Plymouth. Sarah had been introduced to the young naval officer by Brian Willing, who had come to bid her bon voyage, and reluctantly made Lieutenant Fairlie known to her. Delighted to be free from Brian's proprietorial ways, Sarah had welcomed his acquaintance with enthusiasm and found his company on this long voyage pleasant and undemanding. For his part Lieutenant Fairlie hailed Sarah with flattering eagerness, which soothed her *amour-propre*, that had been damaged by Colonel Valentine's recent indifference to her charms. Unlike the aloof colonel, Lieutenant Fairlie had none of the arrogance and stiff-necked attitude that infuriated Sarah. A blond, open-faced young man, a bit above middling height, his engaging air of candour and obvious delight in Sarah's company was just the tonic she needed, and he early staked a claim as her most persistent cavalier. Philip's attentions and the absence of her chaperone enabled Sarah to enjoy her days at sea and relegate her errand for General Hamilton and the coming reunion with her grandmother to the back of her mind. However, she was not allowed to forget entirely.

After less than three days at sea Lucien reminded her that her situation was not as halcyon as the waters upon which they sailed. He approached her after the convivial dinner she had shared with Lieutenant Fairlie and the ship's company, requesting a word alone. Puzzled at Colonel Valentine's grim expression, Sarah put off Philip's importunities and retired with the colonel to a secluded corner of the saloon.

"Is something troubling you, Lucien?" she asked.

He answered her question with one of his own, "Aren't you seeing a lot of Lieutenant Fairlie? I see that Mrs. Amberly is still racked by seasickness, although I can't quite see why since the sea is as calm as a millpond. She should be watching over you," he said, frowning.

"You worry too much, Lucien. Philip is an unexceptional young man and very pleasant company. Mrs. Amberly's presence is not necessary to make me behave, you know. I have some notion of how to go on." Sarah was piqued by his own attitude toward her, accustomed as she was to masculine attention, and annoyed that he thought her free and easy in her ways. But Lucien Valentine was not impressed with her efforts to dismiss his criticism.

"We know nothing of Lieutenant Fairlie. He may be all that you say, but I am not entirely convinced that he is merely a young naval sprig sailing to join his ship after a visit to his sister in Philadelphia. And I have reason to be suspicious of anyone so assiduously cultivating you." He spoke harshly.

"That's not very flattering, Lucien," Sarah said teasingly. "He may just be attracted by my *beaux yeux.*"

"No doubt he is, but we cannot be too careful. You may have forgotten that message you are carrying, but let me assure you I have not, and neither has some interested party. My cabin has been thoroughly searched. Have you noticed whether your possessions have been disturbed?" Lucien asked soberly.

A chill went through Sarah at this ominous news. She wrinkled her brows in an effort to remember whether there was any evidence of this. "No, no, I don't think so. If anyone was rummaging around, he was most careful." Sarah tried to retain her composure, but she flushed guiltily.

She was not prepared to tell Lucien where she had hidden the document. He might be all he said, and General Hamilton and her grandfather might be perfectly right in their assessment of him, but she was not so sure. She did not completely trust him. Perhaps it would be going too far to think he was a French agent. Certainly his war record and the judgment of men in high places must be taken into account, but, while good sense insisted that she agree, her emotions told her otherwise. Was it because he did not take her seriously and, when not flirting with her, treated her like one of the nursery set? Did she really want him to make love to her? A *frisson* partly of anticipation, partly of fear, shook her. Lucien Valentine was not one

71

of her usual beaux, content with a few surreptious meetings or light roguish glances. Why did he put her so out of countenance, she wondered. After all, he was abiding by her rules of conduct.

"You must trust me in this," he said. "I have had some experience in thwarting French machinations. There is little doubt that somebody on this ship believes I am carrying dispatches or other material home. I have been watched since my arrival in the colonies," he assured her abstractedly.

"We are not the colonies. We are the United States of America, and unless you British abate your arrogance, we will join the French against you," Sarah responded angrily. Really he was too aggravating, chivying her about spies and treating her like a mindless miss. She would not put up with it.

"Sorry, my dear, a regrettable slip of the tongue. I would not offend your sensibilities for a moment. I know what a loyal little rebel you are," Lucien teased, throwing off his gloomy mien and seeming determined to soothe her alarm. He should not have raised needless worries in her head. He was more than capable of protecting her from harm.

"Don't be so patronizing. If General Hamilton had not been so pressing, I would not have considered cooperating with you on this ridiculous mission. I have troubles enough of my own." Sarah, unaccountably annoyed that the enigmatic colonel did not take her seriously, decided she had had enough of his badgering.

"I seem to have gotten off on the wrong foot with you, Sarah, and I regret that. I cannot help being British, you know, and I am as concerned as you are for the mutual safety and cooperation of our countries. General Hamilton is an astute man, not given to idle fancies, and he is quite right to scorn a French alliance. America is not in a position to hazard her new independence by assisting her former allies. That way lies madness."

"The French are only attempting to throw off the yoke of royal authority." Sarah responded heatedly. "As a republican I endorse their efforts. The people have suffered terribly."

"Oh, I quite agree that the Bourbons behaved badly, but the French revolutionaries are not Virginia gentlemen, my dear. They are equally intemperate, even vicious in their treatment of the supporters of their king's follies. You cannot condone the guillotine or the murder of the royal family."

"No, of course not. But you are probably exaggerating the excesses," she said stubbornly, unwilling to agree to the justice of his statements. "In any revolution the innocent suffer. King Louis and Queen Marie Antoinette ignored all the peaceful attempts of their subjects to redress their wrongs and now they have paid the penalty. They should have seen the storm gathering."

"Well, we must agree to differ on the French methods of achieving their ends. We are no longer enemies, you know, and in this enterprise we are allies at least. And a more attractive co-conspirator, I have never had." Lucien smiled in that devastating manner that Sarah found so disturbing. She really was no match for him when he tried his wiles upon her.

"I promise, Lucien, I will be most vigilant, and, if any untoward action makes me suspicious, I will inform my watchdog at once," she assured him, hoping to calm his fears as to her safety. She believed he had alarmed her to some purpose because, after all, he was an experienced military man, well versed in the intrigues of European courts while, as a sheltered Philadelphia miss, she knew nothing of tortuous Continental politics. How fortunate her country was to be protected by the vast expanse of the Atlantic, although even that imposing bulwark suddenly seemed less of a safeguard.

"I only intended to warn you, not upset you unduly. I am sure our enemies do not suspect such a charming young woman of intrigue. But take care. And now I must bid you good evening. Your cavalier is becoming impatient, I see." Lucien smiled, knowing his teasing would restore her equilibrium and unwilling to pursue the real fears he had for her safety. He would see to it that no harm came to her, from Lieutenant Fairlie or any other source. On that he was determined. With a bow he left her to her musings and went out on deck. Sarah, more annoyed at his abandonment than disturbed by his warnings, looked after him in puzzlement. He was such a difficult man, one minute charmingly skilled at light repartee, the next completely serious about his duty, yet never accepting her as an adult, a woman capable of attracting him. To Lucien Valentine she was just a troublesome child with whom he was burdened for this voyage. Once in England, her mission accomplished, he would probably never give her another thought.

Although he was one of the hated British and they had crossed swords more than once, the prospect that their relationship might end when she had served her purpose lowered her spirits. Surely she could not be harbouring romantic notions about the colonel. That would be foolish indeed. She would abandon such ideas forthwith. They could only be mirages induced by this voyage that brought them together. Once she had arrived in London, he could be relegated to his proper sphere, that of an enemy, or at least a sometime acquaintance.

Chapter Ten

Colonel Valentine's warning concerning Napoleon's agent did not trouble Sarah so much as her continuing doubts about the colonel himself. She was convinced he was an experienced philanderer and, if he could play false with women, why not with other matters? She had only his word that his cabin had been searched. On the one hand she wanted to trust him, to know that he would protect her from any danger. On the other, his expert handling had thrown her into confusion. Was she being beguiled by her emotions, when she should be using her good sense? Her grandfather and General Hamilton spoke glowingly of the colonel's character, courage, and military exploits. It seemed very unlikely he would be in the pay of the French, enemies of his country, which he had sworn to defend. But other traitors had cunningly played the patriot, and appearances could be deceiving. Look at the falsified evidence that had convicted her father. And men like General Hamilton and Joshua Allen did not know of Lucien's advances toward her. They did not look at him in that light. Still, if they had such faith in his courage and capability, why hadn't they allowed him to carry the document? She was not completely convinced by the excuses they had offered to persuade her to accept the mission.

She might be forced to look elsewhere if there were indeed a French agent aboard, but she would keep a wary eye on Lucien. He would not soothe her suspicions by his practised lovemaking either. General Hamilton might be convinced it was in their country's interest to become allied with the British, but she did not so easily abandon her longtime hatred of their late enemy. All the colonel knew about the document's whereabouts was that she had secreted it safely, and in justice to him, she had to admit, he had not asked her. Surely, if he had wanted possession of it, he would have made some effort to wring that information from her, but he had not. He had seemed all that was honest and trustworthy, even explaining that he thought the indifferent attitude between the two of them was necessary for her safety. Oh, she was confused and angry at herself for her doubts, and at Lucien for being English and for arousing in her this welter of emotion. Not for the first time she wished she had not consented to make this voyage.

While Lucien's motives continued to puzzle Sarah and his public indifference piqued her vanity, apprehension dragged her. And the worry was not entirely due to that enigmatic gentleman and her mission. Nagging at her constantly was her concern about the future meeting with the Ravenshams. Shielded during the years of her childhood by her devoted grandfather, she had rarely brooded over the accusations of treachery that had darkened her parents' lives and caused their early death, once she had learned the tragic story. In a less loving and protected environment she might have suffered from the stigma, but Philadelphia society held a healthy fear of Joshua Allen's anger and he would allow no gossip to shadow his granddaughter's life. Although she had a strong republican contempt for the British as a whole, Sarah's real scorn was reserved for the Ravenshams, who had turned so cruelly against her father. Pompous regard for family honour was not a quality that appealed to Sarah. Even if her grandmother had craved her forgiveness, tried to make amends, Sarah, normally not of a vengeful nature, could not entirely banish her long-held resentment and instinctive dislike of what she believed the Ravenshams represented. Certainly the little contact she had heretofore experienced with well-born Englishmen and women had done nothing to make her alter those opinions. And Lucien Valentine and Moira Amberly were not helping matters, she sighed in frustration.

Recovered from her seasickness after a few days, Mrs. Amberly belatedly undertook her chaperone duties, in a manner bound to raise Sarah's hackles, and in far too desultory a way to suit Lucien's ideas of propriety. Mrs. Amberly's worldly air and pretensions irritated her charge who could find few common interests with the lady who had disliked living in Philadelphia and was not reluctant to say so. She spent much of her day in the salon, rarely venturing on deck, regaling whatever of the company would listen about the trials of the city and the society she had found both boring and provincial. Listening to the languid yet caustic tones of the lady, Sarah felt bound to protest when Mrs. Amberly complained of the home Sarah loved. But her own good manners prevented her from arguing overmuch with her chaperone, although her thoughts were writ large on her expressive face, as Lucien noticed to his amusement. He, too, found Mrs. Amberly rather tedious, but he had reasons for cultivating that lady and, allowing none of his boredom to show, applied himself with some skill to entertaining her, which she allowed with every sign of enthusiasm.

Mrs. Amberly, in her late thirties, attractive in the traditional mode of cool blond English beauties, found her charge much too lively and independent for her taste. "Well-bred English girls would never be allowed such license. Too bold, by far, these colonials," she told Lieutenant Fairlie one evening.

Her criticism was not well received, founded as it was on jealousy and the knowledge that Sarah's youth and high spirits challenged her own reputation as a reigning beauty. The young lieutenant, who had early fallen victim to Sarah's natural ways, protested that Miss Ravensham was a welcome relief from the shy colourless misses he had encountered in Bath and Cheltenham. Mrs. Amberly was quick to point out that he had spent little time in London, perhaps did not have the proper entrée, and so did not comprehend how ton life in London was conducted.

Sarah's most important asset in Mrs. Amberly's mind was her relationship to Lady Ravensham, a doyenne of that closed circle whose approval was sought by many of London's most starched hostesses. Moira Amberly did not approve of her charge or even like her overly much, but she was careful not to offend

79

Sarah overtly. However, her condescension sent that forthright young woman into the boughs. Sarah also did not enjoy watching Colonel Valentine's attentions to her chaperone, who preened herself under his studied courtesies, implying that such a suave and well-born officer would prefer the company of a woman of her mature charms to a heedless chit.

Gradually Sarah, for the most part, hid her fears about the upcoming meeting with the Ravenshams, and managed to relegate her secret mission for General Hamilton to the back of her mind as the packet sailed relentlessly toward landfall.

A favorite with the young people aboard, she never lacked for companionship, and Lieutenant Fairlie continued his assiduous attentions, obviously fascinated by Sarah's open, honest conduct. Colonel Valentine, for his part, beyond the most cursory politeness, largely ignored her, only occasionally raising a wry eyebrow at the high spirits displayed by Sarah and her company of naval officers. His indifference and disapproval irritated Sarah, although his manner was exactly what she expected of an arrogant British aristocrat. His obvious preference for Mrs. Amberly's company only strengthened Sarah's original opinion that he regarded her as a tiresome colonial, available for casual gallantries, even a kiss or two, but not really worthy of his time. She preferred to forget he had said that the events in which they were embroiled demanded such an attitude, that it would not do for them to evidence any sign of more than the most casual acquaintanceship. Sarah, her reactions to the colonel fluctuating wildly from one extreme to the other, did not find this sensible and protective manner very satisfying and, in a spirit of defiance, decided to ignore his attempts to remain aloof.

She had persuaded herself that she must have more information about the Ravenshams and that Lucien Valentine was the only one who could supply it. She needed all the ammunition she could find to face what she had decided would be difficult adversaries. Despite her grandmother's kind letter, she was not convinced that the rest of the family would welcome her enthusiastically. She was not even sure of what the rest of the family consisted. Lucien must tell her, and without any more soul-searching she decided to approach him that very evening and discover what she could about her unknown family.

Uncertain as to which tactics would prove effective with Lucien, and unwilling to admit that she was really seeking a subterfuge to allow her some time with him, Sarah felt both embarrassed and exasperated—but not enough to abandon her quest. Unaccustomed to employing the ploys usual with young women who sought men's company, Sarah tackled the problem in her usual forthright manner. After dinner when the company gathered in the salon, she walked up to Lucien quite boldly and asked him if he would grant her some words in private, ignoring Moira Amberly's raised eyebrows and words of protest. The colonel seemed to find nothing untoward in her action. After politely securing the permission of her chaperone, who could not resist the request coming as it did from a man with whom she wished to remain on good terms, he coolly escorted Sarah from the salon.

Their passage did not go unremarked by Lieutenant Fairlie, who glowered fiercely at the back of the colonel, the idea of a tête-à-tête between Sarah and that officer being repugnant to him. He was not rash enough to interfere, to make his objections known, for he feared Colonel Valentine would ignore him and he saw no means that would not be damaging to his own self-esteem of preventing the interview. Lucien Valentine often inadvertently made Lieutenant Fairlie seem bumbling and callow, a humbling condition. He despised himself for admitting that he was no match for the imposing officer, but he could at least pretend otherwise to Mrs. Amberly. He would brook no criticism of Sarah from that lady who had a great deal to say about her charge's "fast" behaviour and brash colonial manners as evidenced by her forcing herself forward that way. Perforce, Lieutenant Fairlie had to listen to this spate of ill-natured invective without speaking, but he escaped as soon as possible.

Chapter Eleven

"Sarah, I am not sure it is wise of you to single me out in this fashion," Lucien reproved her as they paced the deck. His words were tempered with a smile, for how could he object to her presence when she looked so enchanting. Impervious to the brisk winds, her creamy cheeks aglow with colour and the light of mischief sparkling in her changeable eyes, Sarah provided a welcome contrast to the jaded London ladies who usually sought his escort. Unlike Moira Amberly he did not find Sarah's colonial manners crude or fast, but refreshing and provocative, too much so for his peace of mind. What Mrs. Amberly considered boldness, he believed was courage and determination in the face of danger.

As if she had read his thoughts, Sarah tucked her arm confidingly in his and said saucily, "My chaperone is in despair with me. She thinks I am much too forthcoming and was quite out of countenance that I sought this private talk with you. Encroaching American miss, that's her judgment, I know. She disapproves of me, I fear."

"Mrs. Amberly is quite up to snuff. Knows how young girls should go on. You must be guided by her, Sarah," he reproved, a twinkle in his eyes.

"Nonsense. I am quite tired of her criticisms and patronizing manner. You would think I was a member of the demimondaine the way she goes on," Sarah replied, aware that she could be shocking the colonel.

"You should not speak that way, or even know about such women," he answered almost automatically, watching her from beneath hooded eyes, impervious to her attempts to shock him.

"Fustian. You don't believe such nonsense. I am not such a ninny I don't know how you men go on. Anyway, if I were the staid and sheltered miss you all would have me, I doubt if General Hamilton would have trusted me, or Grandfather allowed me to undertake such an important role."

"You are right, but I am beginning to think we would have been better served to have thought of some other courier," the colonel teased.

"You do exaggerate the dangers—but enough of that. What I really want to ask you is what can I expect from my Ravensham kin. I know so little of them. My grandmother's letter was kind, but what of the rest of the family? Will they welcome me?" she spoke seriously now, her anxiety apparent.

"Of course, you may find a little wariness at first, but with your winsome ways, I am sure you can bring them around," he offered, knowing his words would arouse her.

"I'm not sure I want to bring them around," Sarah retorted in indignation. "You British are so condescending. They should want to bring me around, as you put it. They are the guilty parties, treating my father with such injustice."

"Your grandfather was the real culprit, and do not think his decision to ostracize your father caused him any joy," Lucien said soberly. "He truly mourned the loss of his second son, and, no matter how misguided his motives, he really believed the War Office charges. His family pride suffered terribly. As did your grandmother's."

"What kind of father was he that he could distrust his son, believe that slander?" Sarah argued. "I refuse to feel compassion for him. My grandfather never believed a word of it, and he is not that partial to your countrymen."

"Joshua Allen is a far different type of man, my dear, and was far closer to the situation. Still, I think Lord Ravensham regretted his actions, and I know your grandmother wants to heal the breach. She is a gentle old lady, fair-minded, and lonely, I suspect. She truly wants a reconciliation and the company of her vivacious granddaughter."

"But what of the rest of the family?" Sarah persisted. "Surely there are other Ravenshams, a new head of the family."

"Yes, the present Lord Ravensham, your Uncle Ronald, has a son and a daughter, your cousins, Alan and Angela. Your uncle has an important post at the Foreign Office. I know Pitt confides in him. Ronald was the third son and quite young, barely down from Oxford, I believe, when your father died. The elder brother, the heir, died from a fever. The Ravenshams have suffered much tragedy, but all seems set fair now. Alan is a likely lad, still at Eton, and his sister, older by three years, has just made her come-out. She's a beauty, and very popular. I am sure you will be fast friends, and she will introduce you about, and show you how to go on."

"Mm, perhaps." Sarah sniffed, irritated with his assumption that she would need guidance among the perils of London society. "Your Angela may think I am much too brash a colonial, just as you do. I gather you approve of her, and think I should accept her as a model."

Lucien's lips twitched with amusement. "What a little cat, and showing her claws, I see. Don't fly up in the boughs. Angela has no part in the family feud and will no doubt welcome a new attractive cousin happily. Don't borrow trouble where none exists, Sarah. The whole regrettable affair happened so long ago. I cannot believe your uncle holds to those old animosities. Don't decide to take the Ravenshams in repugnance before you have even met them. Your grandmother does not go out in society very often and will depend on the present Lady Ravensham and Angela to introduce you to the ton."

"I'm not sure I want to be introduced. That is not why I am going to London," Sarah replied, still annoyed that he felt Angela, unlike herself, was such a pattern card of beauty and grace. "And is the present Lady Ravensham as exceptional as her daughter?" she asked tartly, aware that her reaction was peevish.

"Lady Ravensham is a very pleasant lady and will behave properly toward you, I am sure," Lucien responded, his eyes alight with laughter.

"They sound a bit chilly, but then it hardly matters. I will not be staying long. Grandfather wants me to mend relations between our families and bring some comfort to my grandmother, but, since I intend to return to Philadelphia as soon as possible, what the other Ravenshams think of me, or society's approval is of little moment," Sarah said decisively.

She had no intention of joining that brigade of London misses, concerned with beaux and fashions, trying to impress a world in which she would never feel comfortable. Let Angela Ravensham bat her eyes at the colonel. She would not stoop to ingratiating herself with such tactics, although she admitted it would be fun to shake that annoying officer out of his self-control.

"I will tell you what I want someday, my inquisitive lady," Lucien answered, unwilling to be drawn, regretting his words as soon as they were out of his mouth. By God, she would tempt a saint, argumentative and provocative and all the while presenting an enticing picture as she gazed up at him and wet her lips nervously with her tongue.

They had stopped for their interview in the protection of a gunwale that hid them from the view of any passing crewman. Sarah's eyes widened in puzzlement at his words, unaware that her glance goaded him into abandoning the prudence he had clung to so precariously during the past few days. A muscle twitched beside that controlled mouth and, before she could speak again, he jerked her ruthlessly into his arms and she felt his lips warm and sensuous on hers. This kiss was far different from the punishing one she had suffered in Mrs. Powel's anteroom. Although it began as an effort to stop her questions, this time the passion and the skill of his caress evoked a far different

87

response.

Sarah could not disguise the shudders of delight that shook her as his lips roamed across her cheeks and eyes, to the tender place beneath her ears and traveled lower. No man had ever kissed her there, at the opening of her low décolletage, causing unimagined sensations rippling through her body. The deep hammering of his heart resounded against her, evidence that he was as shaken as she was by the unexpected gusts of passion that caught them in its grip. She felt his muscles harden as her arms moved across his shoulders and her hands grasped that dark windswept hair. This was not the reserved patronizing, arrogant Englishman she had known but a man lost in the pleasure of the moment, beyond all thought or reasoning. His skilled lovemaking forced from Sarah a response she had not dreamed herself capable of feeling, her mouth opening under the demand of those drugging lips.

Mindless beneath the onslaught of emotion, she knew not where this tempest was leading them but, before she could surrender completely, a sudden clang of metal against the winches disturbed the night. Nearby a sailor was wandering about, and his intrusion broke the spell. Lucien recovered before Sarah and released her abruptly, his expression a mixture of anger and frustration. Then his face was quickly masked by that imperturbable aloofness she found so annoying.

"Forgive me, Sarah. That was inexcusable. Sea voyages are apt to promote such moments, I fear, but I had no intention of using you thus. Please accept my apologies," Lucien said stiffly, the words forced from the stern lips that just a few moments before had asked a far different response.

Angry and disappointed at his reaction, Sarah was determined to show an equal indifference, although her pulses were still pounding. She would never let him know how his kisses had disturbed her. "Oh, come now, Colonel, let us not refine too much on a few kisses. I am just surprised that you lost, if only momentarily, that famous British reserve. It's very gratifying."

Lucien smiled a bit grimly but accepted her valiant attempt to return to normalcy. "You are a minx, Sarah. Your grandfather should have spanked you more often when you were in pigtails," he replied, composedly.

Soon after, they parted. Sarah was eager to cool her overwrought senses and to wonder at Lucien in the sanctuary of her cabin. As for Lucien, he walked the deck, cursing his impetuosity, and determined to relegate Sarah to that company of women whose only use was distraction and light dalliance. He knew he was deceiving himself, but he must guard himself from future encounters that offered such temptations. He would not, must not, get involved with Sarah Ravensham. There could be no future for him with her as long as she held him in such dislike. And would he want her to feel differently?

Sarah, trying to compose herself for sleep, wished shamefacedly that she had not responded so ardently to Lucien's kisses. How foolish of her to even dream that those kisses had meant more than he claimed, a momentary surrender to the isolation and romantic situation in which they found themselves. He would never have tried such tactics on the very proper misses of his own world, her cousin Angela for example. Had she led him to believe she was available for such an experience? Well, she would disabuse him of that notion and not allow him to treat her so cavalierly. She would keep her distance from him in the future. She would not be treated as some light-minded miss, a credulous colonial. Still, her pride had suffered when he had so quickly repudiated his lapse. What was he really like underneath that aloof facade? Would she ever come to know the real man, and, if she did, what would it mean to her? They were oceans apart in their beliefs, their loyalties, their backgrounds. Folly, that is what it was for her to think they could ever reach a real understanding. From now on she must guard her heart, and remember that the colonel was naught but her watchdog, and an arrogant Britisher at that.

Chapter Twelve

Dressing for dinner on her last night aboard ship, Sarah searched absent-mindedly for her mother's gold locket. She wore it rarely for she was afraid of losing this prized possession. She thought she had left it on the top tray of her trunk in the velvet pouch that held her small amount of jewelry. Finally she discovered it on the clothes folded neatly below the first layer. She wrinkled her forehead in perplexity. Now that she looked carefully, it seemed that her belongings were not quite in the same order in which she had left them. Her dresses, which the kindly stewardess had pressed and hung carefully behind the door of the cabin, hung askew, and the counterpane of her bunk looked to have been twitched hastily over the bed linen. Could someone have been rummaging through her things? Certainly there had been ample opportunity.

The weather had turned nasty the last few days and the passengers had been forced to seek amusements other than strolling the decks. Mrs. Amberly had found the renewed roughened seas more than she could bear and had retired to her cabin with another bout of seasickness. Sarah, not unhappy to be released from her chaperone's vigilant and critical eye, had spent the time playing hilarious games of loo in the main salon with Lieutenant Fairlie and his fellow officers. Neither Colonel Valentine nor other more sober members of the passenger list had intruded on the boisterous group, which meant that there had been ample time for some unknown person to search her cabin. Could it have been the colonel?

Sarah sat down suddenly on her bunk, feeling a bit sick. She had light-heartedly dismissed the idea that a French agent was on this ship, that such a person suspected her to the extent of violating her privacy, pawing among her most intimate belongings in the hope of discovering some sign of her mission. Fortunately she always wore the document pinned to her petticoat when she dressed for the day or evening. If she had favoured the flimsy muslin gowns which were all the rage with the more fashionable belles of the day, that shocking mode would have revealed her secret, but fortunately the weather insisted on warmer and more concealing dress. At night she always locked her cabin door and slept with the precious document under her pillow.

Who aboard could be the French agent? Certainly the young naval officers must be excused, and aside from them there were only a dozen or so other passengers, a few respectable couples journeying abroad to visit relatives in England, several merchants and factors bound for the big counting houses of

London, not one of them capable of spying—or so she had thought until now.

After a considerable debate with herself Sarah decided not to appraise Lucien Valentine of this latest development. If he were the culprit, she would only be warning him that she had discovered some reason to regard him with distrust. Much as she might want to banish these nagging doubts about his good faith, they kept reoccurring, no matter how hard she fought against them. Every instinct led her to believe in him, but she must not endanger the safety of the document by behaving recklessly. If he were indeed a traitor, then all was lost. If he were not, and Sarah knew how easily some actions could be misconstrued—her father's experience proved that—then she would be accusing him of a monstrous crime, for which he would never forgive her. And for which she would never forgive herself.

She realized suddenly that his good opinion of her mattered, a surprising conclusion she conceded ruefully. Despite their passages at arms, those caresses that had roused in her such turbulent emotions, she felt at heart that Lucien Valentine was a man of integrity. No doubt his lighter moments led him to philander with women only too eager to welcome his favour—light skirts and matrons with casual morals. But Sarah had learned early that a man might have the most dishonourable intentions when dealing with women and yet be an absolute pillar of probity in his political or business life. General Hamilton, himself, was an example. She would be wise to remember that, especially as she would soon be experiencing the licentious and loose life of English society, of which she had heard some horrifying tales. She must be mindful of Colonel Valentine's reputation with women. Even Betsy, engaged to a desirable *parti*, had found him captivating. He had certainly tried his obvious lures with herself, and, to her sorrow, she had not been indifferent.

Oh, what a coil this whole affair was—French agents, political intrigue, an unknown family to be faced, and the disturbing if arrogant English officer about whom all her troubles seemed to revolve. Never had she wished more eagerly for her grandfather's wise counsel and protective arm.

Catching up her Norwich shawl and giving no more than a cursory glance at her reflexion in the glass, Sarah hurried from the cabin. She ignored the delightful picture she made in her deep-blue moiré gown, her cheeks flushed with the colour her troubled thoughts had brought.

In the dining salon there were quite a few empty places, since the newly inclement weather had forced all but the most stalwart sailors to remain below decks. At the captain's table, Moira Amberly's place was vacant and two other passengers had failed to appear, leaving Sarah, Colonel Valentine, and two naval officers to entertain the captain. Normally, Mrs. Amberly sat on the captain's right, an arrangement that seemed to please that gentleman, a tall, portly man of middle years, with piercing blue eyes in a tanned face. Tonight his expression was unusually grave as he signified he wished Colonel Valentine to take the seat on his right, and there was then an informal post all around with Sarah seated on the colonel's right and next to one of the naval officers.

Lieutenant Fairlie and his young companions had not been invited to such august company, and sat across the salon at a table for six, where they seemed quite merry and undeterred by the storms. Sarah wished she could join them.

She had not seen Lucien alone since their encounter two evenings ago on the upper deck. She smiled reflectively, despite her worries, for she seemed always to be deciding on what face she should wear for that gentleman after one of their passionate embraces. Really no wonder he presumed. She behaved no better than the worst of light-skirts in his company and then turned upon him like a shrew, when she knew in her heart that the fault was as much hers as his. But this evening his attention was all for the captain, and after the briefest of greetings, he turned from her to continue talking with that gentleman. Sarah, after a desultory exchange of light conversation with her naval neighbor, was left to her own thoughts, a not unwelcome condition as she had much to resolve. But suddenly her musings were interrupted by the captain's answer to one of Lucien's questions.

"It was as we suspected," the captain was saying. "A French naval ship, which hove to just beyond the horizon. I was quite relieved to know that our escort vessels were nearby, and they closed up at the sight of the Frenchie."

"Is the ship still there?" Lucien asked curtly.

"Yes, but it does not seem anxious to announce its presence, or take any belligerent action. By tomorrow we will be entering the channel. It will hardly challenge us there." The captain appeared more puzzled than worried about the enemy ship.

"Let us hope not, but with the best part of our fleet with Nelson in the Mediterranean, it behooves us to be prudent. English ships have been attacked in the channel before," Lucien answered, not too reassured.

"You army chaps never lose a chance to cast a slight at the other service. 'Tis the same in our forces, not that our navy is much to speak about, or our army either, unfortunately. Perhaps General Hamilton will be able to change that." The captain continued to speak of the challenges facing Hamilton, and the disturbances on the frontier of the new republic, but Sarah suspected that Lucien, for all his appearance of polite attention, was still brooding over the French ship and the meaning of its strange behaviour. Could it have been sent to aid the mysterious French agent aboard their packet in the search for the Pitt message? She could not believe that, but then this whole situation was puzzling, including Lucien's involvement in it.

At the conclusion of the meal, when the company rose, Lucien, who had hardly noticed her through the whole of dinner, turned to assist her with her shawl and then suggested she have coffee with him in the salon. "It seems our usual company is thin this evening, and it is hardly an evening for a stroll about the decks," he teased, reminding her of their last meeting.

Sarah, who had every intention of refusing his civil invitation, found herself meekly accompanying him to the salon. He settled her in a chair, a bit apart from the main grouping. Lieutenant Fairlie, coming in shortly afterwards, made a movement toward her, but encountered the colonel's forbidding frown. He quickly changed his mind and joined his fellows at the card table far from their sequestered corner.

"Mrs. Amberly is indisposed again, I see," Lucien commented sardonically. "She seems rather a fragile woman. Let us hope she will recover in time to serve as a congenial escort for you in the coach from Plymouth to London."

"Are you worrying about the proprieties, Lucien? I believe you use them to suit your own convenience," Sarah replied a bit waspishly. Did Lucien also escort Mrs. Amberly above deck and dally with her in the moonlight? Sarah found this notion not to her taste.

"What a little shrew you are, Sarah. Could it be that you resent my attentions to that very respectable lady? Let me assure you, I have all I can do to cope with you." He was delighted to see her blush at his suggestive words.

"I am quite sure you could cope with a legion of women, Colonel. Why you wish to waste your time with an innocent naive miss like myself, I cannot imagine," she countered, determined not to be put out of countenance by his outrageous allusions.

"I intend to tell you why, when we have completed our current business," Lucien said lightly. "And if you expect another apology for what happened the other evening, you will be disappointed, my girl. You were as much at fault as I was, so don't toss your nose in the air and behave as if you had been ravaged by a practiced seducer."

Sarah implied by her disdainful silence that she found his remarks unworthy of an answer, and sipped her coffee daintily.

"It's unfair to put you up in the boughs, Sarah,

when I crave your good opinion. What I really want to discuss is our delivering of Hamilton's message, now that we are within sight of land, if not safety," Lucien said seriously. "We still have to fear interception, I believe."

Sarah, remembering the French ship and the search of her quarters, barely repressed a shiver of anxiety. For all her apparent sang-froid, she was not foolish. Danger still stalked them and, in the absence of any other protector, she would just have to tell Lucien of her fears.

"I was in two minds as to whether to tell you or not, and I may be imagining it all, but I believe my cabin was searched sometime this afternoon while I was in the main salon playing cards with Lieutenant Fairlie and his friends," Sarah confided in a rush, abandoning her suspicions. If the captain trusted Lucien, could she do less when so much was at stake?

"Tell me exactly what happened, Sarah," Lucien demanded, all humour vanished. She answered as best she could, trying to minimize her reactions.

"I have not asked you where you hid the message, Sarah, because I fear you do not entirely trust me, and perhaps I have not behaved as I should to deserve your confidence. But the next twenty-four hours, during the landing and disembarkation, could be fraught with danger. I am warning you again to be on your guard, and I will do my best to see that all goes smoothly. Until we reach your grandmother's London house, I will be on tenterhooks. Guarding one slip of a girl is far more arduous than facing Napoleon's cavalry, I am discovering." He spoke wryly, but with an undertone of gravity.

Despite herself, Sarah was impressed by his sincerity. She wanted badly to believe in Lucien, but the welter of emotions he aroused in her made reasoned thought concerning him difficult. She was convinced he was a loyal and courageous officer where his duty to his country was involved. But in his personal relationships she could not be sure of his reliability. Whatever deceptions he practiced on the women who aroused his interest, he could be trusted to do his soldier's duty, she decided. Nevertheless, she did not tell him where she had hidden the packet, keeping that vital information until she reached the security of her grandmother's drawing room. Evidently her doubts and decision was writ large on her face.

"I do wish you would trust me, Sarah," Lucien said, studying her face carefully. "In this we are not enemies, but you will persist in viewing me as some ogre, determined on betrayal, seduction, and who knows what other base crimes." Lucien sighed, his disappointment evident, and Sarah realized she had lost her chance to confide in him. Rather than being angry he seemed more sorrowful over her lack of confidence, but she refused to surrender. He escorted her back to her cabin eventually, but as she bade him good night in the hallway, he looked at her quizzically and said, "Since you have already damned me in intention, it might as well be in deed, my fiery colonial." And he pulled her into a hard embrace, kissing her warmly, before she could protest, had she been so inclined. But to her eternal shame, she responded, helpless before the insinuating passion that only Lucien could evoke.

"Perhaps that will keep you awake for a moment or

two. I know it will for me. Good night, Sarah." He bowed briefly and was off down the corridor before she could summon up a reply.

won, I know it will for me. Good night, Sarah." He found in the poor, muddled about the corridor for she could summon no reply.

Chapter Thirteen

Sarah's first glimpse of England inspired more awe than comfort as the ship swept around the rugged coast of Cornwall where the jagged brown cliffs rose determinedly above the angry waves battering ceaselessly against the rocks. From Land's End, past the Lizard sailed their vessel, entering at last into calmer waters off Devon and into the natural haven surrounded by gentler promontories that formed the port of Plymouth. As she stepped ashore, thankful to feel firm ground beneath her feet after so many weeks at sea, Sarah could not but be impressed by the mass of ships, the scurry and bustle of one of England's chief seaports, the very ground from whence the Puritans had sailed to the New World to escape persecution in the old.

Moira Amberly sniffed peevishly at the scene that Sarah found so exciting and romantic. She did not find Plymouth exciting, only tedious, one of her favorite words. Indeed, to Mrs. Amberly all but London society and the exercise of her own charms seemed tedious, Sarah decided. After weeks at sea, exposed daily to that lady's finicky notions Sarah's patience was exhausted, although her manner remained courteous. Moira Amberly had certainly not proved the happiest choice for a chaperone.

Lucien secured a carriage for them and their luggage, which he extricated quickly from the huge mound unloaded onto the pier. Whatever his faults, there was no denying his efficiency, and Sarah was grateful for his protection, although she was loath to admit it. For some reason she felt much more fearful now that they had actually arrived in Plymouth than at any time during the voyage. If French provocateurs were going to attempt any treachery, it would be now, perhaps their last opportunity to steal the document. Lucien, too, seemed apprehensive, keeping a careful eye on the surrounding citizenry, but obviously seeing nothing to cause him disquiet.

As they drove along a fine raised esplanade with smooth green lawns stretching, below on their left, to the sea, Lucien reminded Sarah that it was from the Hoe that Sir Francis Drake had spied the Spanish Armada approaching as he played at bowls. Nearing the center of town, he indicated the quay from which the *Mayflower* had sailed, and the Citadel whose century-old ramparts hid a welter of military barracks. Plymouth was not only a commercial seaport and naval base, but also an army depot, redolent of all the British power that Sarah found so offensive, but she was too fascinated by the sights and sounds of the town, by the relief of stepping onto dry land, to challenge Lucien's pride in the might of his country.

The large coaching inn, which he had chosen to receive them, obviously catered to only the very best quality. Its courtyard bustled with fine carriages, hostlers and servants scurrying to and fro and sleek horses being hitched and unhitched from the traces. Inside the inn a jovial landlord and his white-aproned wife hurried to make them welcome and to escort them to the bedrooms and private parlour Lucien had miraculously secured for their night in Plymouth. Sarah, relieved that she was not expected to share a chamber with her chaperone, thanked both landlord and Lucien prettily for the accommodation and whisked into the commodious bedroom to restore the ravages of travel. She needed some time alone to refresh not only her body but her spirits.

Now that they had landed in England all her qualms and misgivings about this journey returned fullfold. Leaving the ship broke her last link with America, Philadelphia, and her grandfather. Henceforth, she must rely on her own courage and wits, although she was now fairly convinced Lucien could be trusted to guard her person and her message until she reached London. His duty done, would she then see the last of him, bored with the colonial miss who returned his kisses but not his confidence? Sarah tossed her head angrily. She would not be beguiled by that gentleman; who was no better than he should be and doubtless panting to resume relationships with the many women who awaited him in London— women no doubt more skilled in flirtation and passionate love-making than the credulous girl who had responded so avidly to his caresses. Well, there would be no more of that, now that they were off the ship. She had been a victim of propinquity and his skilled love-making.

From now on, relations between Colonel Valentine and herself would be completely circumspect and, when he had delivered her to her grandmother and walked out of her life, she would be as relieved as he to have this troublesome acquaintance ended. Sarah spoke harshly to herself but no matter how she rationalized the sense of her argument, she could not repress a pang of unhappiness at the prospect of seeing the end of Lucien. Oh, well, she had not seen the last of that maddening man yet, and there was still the packet to convey safely to London. She must not forget enemies could be all around and not relax her guard.

After refreshing herself from the ewer and basin of hot water placed on the commode, Sarah gave a last pat to her hair, smoothed her skirt to make sure no betraying bulge showed through the lightweight blue merino stuff of her walking dress, and prepared to join her companions in the parlour. Now which door led to that room, she wondered, having not paid close attention when the innkeeper's wife had shown her to the chamber. Two doors opened on either side of the wide room, and one into the hall. Well, she must just make a stab at it. Walking to the left-hand door, Sarah tugged it open and walked into a room similar to her own. Before she could retreat, realizing her mistake, a tall figure in a rich wine-coloured, frogged dressing gown rose from a chair before a desk and regarded her with no little surprise.

"Well, what have he here? I had no idea the "Crown and Garter" provided such amenities," he drawled in a hateful sneering voice, his lip curling with disdain. He looked Sarah over rather as if he were considering the points of a thoroughbred mare up for auction.

Sarah, although considerably taken aback by both the unexpected encounter and the stare of the haughty stranger, replied coolly enough, "I beg your pardon, sir, a mistake on my part. I thought this was the private parlour bespoke for me and my companions." She made to back out the door but was arrested by the insolent voice of the man whose privacy she had interrupted.

"My mistake, also, I perceive. Obviously not one of the muslin set, but certainly not of the ton. An American possibly?" One dark eyebrow rose questioningly. He had now crossed the room to stand in front of Sarah and, although he made no move to prevent her from darting back into her chamber, she had the feeling he would stop her if she did move. He was altogether a formidable-looking creature—tall, lean, and with an air of distinction spoiled by the disdainful sneering expression that appeared to be habitual, for deep lines of cynicism and weariness scored his face. Sarah was not so innocent she did not recognize those worldly eyes and curled lip marked the libertine, a man who had experienced most of the vices of life.

"Yes, I have come from America and am on my way to London. Now, if you will excuse me, I must find my friends," Sarah met his stare unflinchingly. He had made no effort to introduce himself and she in turn refused to offer her own name. For a moment an ugly light gleamed in the dark eyes that watched her, then his lids came down and he shrugged lazily, as if bored with the encounter.

"Of course, my dear. Perhaps we will meet again."

And he turned away as she reentered her bedroom. She locked and bolted the door behind her, as if shutting out a wild tiger, for she felt she had indeed just emerged from a contest with a half-tamed beast, just barely leashed.

Going through the door to the right, she joined Mrs. Amberly and Lucien in the parlour separating the chambers of the two women. She found herself reluctant to discuss the strange meeting. Mrs. Amberly would have had some caustic comment to make, inferring that Sarah had once again acted in a compromising manner, and Lucien . . . well, she could not imagine what his reaction would be, but it was best to forget the whole episode.

The trio discussed the next day's journey to London, and Lucien informed Sarah he had sent a message ahead so that her grandmother would know at what hour to expect her. Moira Amberly showed an avid interest in Sarah's meeting with the Ravenshams, which did not deceive her charge. Sarah suspected that her chaperone wished to take advantage of her current position and ingratiate herself with Lady Ravensham and her circle. Sarah was no stranger to attempts at such encroachment—even in Philadelphia's more open society, social climbing was not unknown—and Sarah recognized in her chaperone some quality of the parvenu, despite that lady's claim to an exalted standing in the London ton. After weeks in her company, Sarah had to exercise all her charity to treat Mrs. Amberly with a modicum of politeness. Once she had reached London, she fervently hoped to see little of her—just as she would see little of Lucien, though that eventuality did not seem to cause her equal satisfaction.

Lucien, noticing Sarah's heightened colour when she joined them at the tea table, wondered what maggot she had in her head now. It was unlikely she would tell him, he thought. She had recently relegated him to the status of a mere troublesome acquaintance, an attitude he would challenge in his own good time.

Sarah had prided herself on successfully hiding her contretemps with the disdainful stranger from both Lucien and her chaperone, but she had congratulated herself too soon. The following morning, emerging from her chamber in bonnet and shawl en route to board the coach Lucien had hired, she chanced upon the man, caped and ready for the road, also taking his departure. Unfortunately, Lucien, whose room was across the corridor, witnessed the brief bow the man gave Sarah and the raking glance he bestowed on her as he passed. Lucien frowned. Here was a coil. Sarah must be warned.

"Have you met that man, Sarah, who gave you such an outrageous look just now?" he asked preemptorily, annoyed and quite ready to take her to task.

"Just in passing," Sarah answered shortly.

"Well, do not allow him to introduce himself further," Lucien said tersely. "That is Theron, Marquis De Lisle, one of the most notorious rakes and libertines in London. No decent young woman should acknowledge him in any way. Not that he often appears in respectable society for he is quite beyond the pale."

"Why, Lucien, you make him sound so intriguing. Is he also a well-known philanderer? I am discovering that London may hold all sorts of surprises—and not unattractive ones either," Sarah riposted, amused at Lucien's admonitory tone. So, he did not like the idea of her meeting the objectionable Lord De Lisle, eh? Though she privately had to agree with Lucien's assessment of the man, she certainly had no intention of meekly following his instructions, telling her who she should find acceptable or not. It was time that Lucien realized she had a mind of her own.

"You little witch," Lucien returned. "You are just trying to send me up. But be warned, Sarah. De Lisle is no companion for an innocent young girl, not that he would be interested, for respectable women of any sort do not attract him. He has a vile reputation, and all of it deserved. Do not let your inclination to score off me lead you into imprudent behavior." Lucien realized he was refining too much on the affair but he had not liked the look De Lisle had cast on Sarah. Lucien found the notion of Sarah attracted to such an unsavoury type maddening in the extreme and reminded himself that women often thought such a man could be saved by the love of a good woman. But surely Sarah was more sensible than that—so why was he worrying? She would find admirers enough in London without encouraging such an unsuitable follower. And Lady Ravensham would see to it that Sarah was protected from men of that sort and introduced to proper young sprigs, who would no doubt keep her thoroughly occupied, another prospect that Lucien found unaccountably depressing.

"Come along," he chided. "The sooner we reach London the better. You are a sore trial to me, Sarah."

"How relieved you will be to discharge your duties when we reach my grandmother's. I am sorry your escort of me has proved so tedious," said Sarah, now thoroughly annoyed by Lucien's lecture and brusque dismissal of her.

"That wasn't what I meant at all, Sarah, and you know it, now stop trying to engage me in a quarrel. It's too early in the morning for that." Lucien threw off his irritation and resumed the teasing manner that masked his feelings so effectively. Not until he had seen Sarah and Mrs. Amberly comfortably disposed in the carriage and had mounted his own horse to ride alongside of the vehicle did he begin to wonder at De Lisle's presence in the Plymouth inn, so far from his usual haunts. Why would a man of his stamp and proclivities be at the seaport? Lucien remembered that De Lisle had a French grandmother and had spent a great deal of his time in Paris before hostilities had broken out between the two countries. Could he possibly be involved in some kind of sinister intrigue? He would bear further watching.

Chapter Fourteen

After two days sequestered in a coach with Moira Amberly, Sarah's nerves were at the breaking point. Normally able to take the rough with the smooth, she found an unrelieved diet of that patronizing lady's company more than her normal cheerful temperament could accept with equanimity. Mrs. Amberly, obviously not any happier than Sarah at the enforced intimacy, spent the hours journeying to London warning Sarah of the perils she faced in launching herself on that strictly conducted world and expressing her doubts that Sarah would comport herself properly even in the unlikely event she received acceptance.

How aggravating, but wise of Lucien, who had hired the coach—and the most luxurious and comfortable one available—to ride beside it. Not for him wearying hours cooped up with the ladies who by the end of the journey had taken each other in severe dislike. As the coach neared the metropolis, Sarah was relieved to note that Mrs. Amberly had at last exhausted her warnings and lapsed into a sullen silence, for which Sarah was exceedingly grateful. She had enough on her mind without parrying her chaperone's barbed comments.

Although Lucien had been most solicitous of their comfort, when they halted en route, and had kept the hired coachmen up to the mark, he had spent very little time with them, much to both ladies' disappointment. But as the coach passed Richmond and crossed over the Thames, Sarah put all thoughts of her traveling companions behind her, concerned now with the coming meeting with her grandmother. After all, a rapprochement with Lady Ravensham was the reason for this trip. She would cling to that thought and dismiss all images of the disturbing encounter aboard ship with Lucien. Once in London she would see very little of him—just as well for her peace of mind. Never had she missed her grandfather's comforting companionship more. His love and support would have done a great deal to calm her fears and put her confusions to rest.

As they entered the outskirts of London, Sara forgot all her anxieties, entranced by the sights of a city she had never expected to see. Although Philadelphia was far from a country hamlet, indeed the hub of the new republic and a dignified, growing capital with its gracious red-brick Georgian state buildings and the lavish town houses of the country's most prominent citizens, nothing had prepared her for the immensity, the noise, and the variety of London. The place was teeming with life, itinerant vendors hawking their wares, carriages and drays crowding the cobbled streets, and in the distance imposing buildings with the patina of centuries reminding travelers that indeed London was the center of a nation of traders and adventurers, the focus of Englishmen's pride and ambition.

Lady Ravensham's residence on Park Street rose majestically beyond imposing marble steps, its facade at once intimidating and luxurious. Sarah stepped eagerly from the coach, barely acknowledging Lucien's proffered helping hand. She turned to bid a relieved farewell to Mrs. Amberly.

"Good-bye, Mrs. Amberly and thank you for your care of me on the voyage and journey here." Sarah was aware of the perfunctory acknowledgement, but her thoughts were concentrated on her meeting with her grandmother and she had little time to spare for the tiresome woman who had done her best to quell Sarah's natural good spirits.

"Not at all, my dear. It was a pleasure. Although I know you are eager to meet Lady Ravensham and I would not intrude on your reception, I hope to see you again and, perhaps, you will convey my respects to your grandmother and suggest a future meeting." Mrs. Amberly did not intend to lose the advantage this fortuitous chaperonage of Sarah had given her. Indeed, contact with the august Ravenshams had been her sole reason for accepting the boring duty. She did not dream that Sarah was astute enough to realize her intentions.

"I am sure my grandmother will want to tender her gratitude to you personally, Mrs. Amberly. Good-bye and again thank you." Sarah devoutly prayed she would not be present at that interview. Lucien, waiting patiently at her side, signaled the coachman and the carriage rolled away.

"Not apprehensive, are you, Sarah? Believe me,

your welcome will be all that you desire. Come, I know your grandmother is anticipating this meeting and we must not keep her on tenterhooks." He spoke gently, taking Sarah's arm and ushering her up the steps.

Obviously the household was alerted for her arrival, for the great mahogany doors parted and the butler and two footmen stood ready to greet her and accept her baggage.

"Good afternoon, Miss Ravensham, Colonel Valentine. Lady Ravensham is awaiting you in the drawing room," the butler announced, waving his minions to their duties.

Summoning up all her composure, raising her chin militantly, much to Lucien's amusement, Sarah marched across the lofty hall in the butler's wake, determined to show that very proper major-domo that even colonials knew how to behave. Her shaking hands clutched her reticule tightly. Not for anything would she betray her fears to the colonel.

"Miss Ravensham, and Colonel Valentine, milady." The butler flung open the drawing room doors and announced the visitors.

Sarah had not known what to expect, but the fragile old woman, white hair impeccably coiffed, in a deep-garnet gown of fashionable cut, did not appear fearsome. As Sarah curtsyed and moved to greet her, she was surprised to see tears in the faded-blue eyes.

"At last, my dear. How I have waited for this day. And how kind of you to accede to an old woman's request and leave your home and your grandfather." Lady Ravensham embraced Sarah, her fragile arms trembling. "And thank you, dear boy, for persuading her and escorting her on what must have been a long wearying voyage." Lady Ravensham smiled tremulously at Lucien.

"Not at all, ma'am, my pleasure. I will leave you two to get acquainted. I know you have a great deal to say to one another and I would not intrude."

"Can we not offer you some refreshment after your trip, at least, Lucien?" Lady Ravensham recalled her manners, smiling gratefully on the officer.

"I must report to headquarters, immediately, Lady Ravensham, but I will avail myself of your hospitality another time. I would not want to lose my advantage with Miss Ravensham, for once she meets all the London bucks she will have no time for a tired old soldier like myself." Lucien raised one eyebrow quizzically, and Sarah felt like hitting him. She knew very well he was putting on this act for her grandmother's benefit, and probably to ensure he would see her soon to discuss the delivery of the message to Mr. Pitt. She wished she could give it to him now and be rid of the whole affair. Sarah chided herself for her childish reaction due, no doubt, to travel fatigue and the emotions this meeting with her grandmother had induced.

"Of course, dear boy. We quite understand, and I hope to see you often now that I have such an attraction," Lady Ravensham answered.

"If you will permit, I will come tomorrow and take Sarah for a drive in Hyde Park, a fitting introduction to London." His glance at Sarah was full of meaning.

"You will like that, my dear." Her grandmother, eager to encourage Lucien's interest in Sarah, assured Sarah. "Lucien is quite a hand with his curricle, a regular nonpareil."

"I am sure I will, ma'am. And I will be delighted, Colonel, to have you show me the sights of the town," Sarah said, accepting prettily and well aware that Lucien wanted the message delivered as quickly as possible so that he could wash his hands of her. Obviously he regretted giving way to those momentary romantic impulses engendered by the long sea voyage, and his enigmatic statements about their future relationship meant little. He had to keep her in a sweet temper, since she carried the message to Pitt. She would be a fool to expect more. London gentlemen of the ton may have developed a nicety of manner, but their true characters left much to be desired by one accustomed to candid and sincere expressions in her companions. For all Lucien criticized the notorious Lord De Lisle, there was little to choose between them. Her pride would never allow her to show her disappointment at such cavalier treatment. Sarah bid Lucien a stiff good-bye, thanking him primly for his care of her on the voyage, and ignoring his amusement at her attempt to put him at a distance. Under her grandmother's indulgent eye she could not tell him how she really felt.

Chapter Fifteen

Sarah and her grandmother dined alone that evening, at the broad mahogany table in the vast dining room, served by Peverel, the butler, and two footmen, a rather overwhelming experience for Sarah used to much less formal mealtimes. Portraits of long-ago Ravenshams lined the walls of the spacious room and seemed to frown down on her, intimidating and severe, many of the gentlemen in uniforms and the ladies unsmiling and conscious of their position. Lady Ravensham showed no such aloofness and plied Sarah with questions about her grandfather and her life in America, and signified with touching gratitude how happy Sarah's arrival had made her. Although she spoke with affection of Sarah's cousins and with pride of her son Ronald, Sarah thought the old lady yearned for a closer relationship, a bond that only Sarah could offer. Sarah could see, too, that the excitement of her visit had tired her grandmother, and she pleaded the stress of travel to excuse an early retiring.

"Of course, my dear. We cannot make up for years

of absence in one evening. I look forward to many comfortable coses. I have so longed for the opportunity to try to explain the tragedy of my husband's rejection of Richard, and his refusal to even listen to a word about your mother. I know it hurt you and your grandfather very much. Perhaps I cannot make up for the estrangement of twenty years, but I dearly want to try. And Sarah, when you write your grandfather, please send him my gratitude for allowing you to make this long journey. I know he must miss you dreadfully, for you have always been everything to one another. I would not have him think I am uncaring of his sacrifice in surrendering you to me, even for a short time, but I hope you will stay many months. I will, of course, write him myself but he will welcome your assurances." Her grandmother paused and her tired blue eyes gleamed mistily at the thought of Sarah returning to America.

"Grandfather understands, and he was most anxious for me to visit you and end this long estrangement. I will miss him, of course, for until now he has been the only family I have known, and I love him dearly." Instantly Sarah regretted her reminder of the breach, as she saw it hurt her grandmother.

"As you will come to love me, too, although I don't deserve it. But come, I am an emotional, silly old woman. I want you to enjoy your time here, my dear. Tomorrow we will make some plans for your entertainment, a new wardrobe, and I believe I will come out of retirement and chaperone you to all sorts of parties where you can meet young people. You will not want to spend all your hours with an old lady. Angela and Margaret, Lady Ravensham, will take you about too.

I want you to be happy here, my dear." Lady Ravensham's sincerity could not be doubted, and Sarah determined to thrust all homesickness and longing for her grandfather from her conversation, if not from her mind, when she was with her grandmother.

"Thank you, Grandmother, and now we had both best retire, to gain strength for the delights ahead." Sarah spoke lightly, trying to calm the highly charged atmosphere that obviously was sapping her grandmother's strength. She gave her a warm good-night kiss on the cheek and retired to the bedroom so thoughtfully redecorated for her use. The soothing shades of apricot and ivory in the silk hangings on the four-poster bed, the graceful new Chippendale furniture, the comforting coal fire in the shining grate all eased Sarah's strangeness. She was touched by the efforts made for her comfort and, abandoning all worries about the coming meeting with the other Ravenshams and Mr. Pitt, dropped quickly into restoring sleep.

On awakening the next morning to a bright April day, Sarah sprang from her bed and rushed to the windows that overlooked Hyde Park, ignoring the tray of chocolate the maid had placed by her bedside. A few early riders cantered their horses beside the greensward bordered by beds of glowing daffodils. London had donned its gayest dress for her this lovely spring morning, which did much to raise her spirits. Normally an ebullient girl, she refused to allow the coming meeting with the other Ravenshams to lower her spirits, although she conceded it was hardly possible to expect the same warm welcome from the rest of the family she had received from her grandmother. Polly, the young woman selected to serve her since she had not brought her own abigail, a solecism noted by Mrs. Amberly with lifted eyebrows, helped her dress, choosing a light-yellow muslin with a sprigged redingote, well suited to the unexpectedly balmy day.

Sarah, never one to stand on formality, won Polly's heart with her friendly, open manner. She had always dealt easily with the servants in Joshua Allen's establishment, where she was a great favorite. She had seen no reason to explain to Mrs. Amberly that her own longtime abigail, their butler's daughter, Cissy, would have been miserable so far away from her family, in strange surroundings, so Sarah had assured her she could do without her for her brief stay in England. Polly took to her new mistress and eagerly explained Sarah's lack of side in the servants' hall, insisting that, for all her taking ways, Miss Ravensham was a real lady, and not a crude colonial as they might have expected.

Sarah, unconscious of the interest her arrival had generated below the stairs, finished her large breakfast in her bedroom, and then waited for a summons from her grandmother, who stayed abed in the mornings to husband her strength. Although she was impatient to explore London, she knew she must pay her grandmother the courtesy of a morning visit.

"My, what a cheerful sight you are, my dear," Lady Ravensham greeted her granddaughter when Sarah at last was admitted to her presence. "I am such an old slug-abed. I must bestir myself, but, until your arrival, I had little reason to be up and about early." Lady Ravensham was enthroned on a nest of embroidered pillows, resting in the great canopied bed that dominated the master suite.

"I would not want you to tire yourself by changing your habits just for me, Grandmother. You need your rest." Sarah leaned over and gave Lady Ravensham a gentle kiss on her cheek. Despite her age, her grandmother's complexion was fresh, only a few lines testifying to her years.

"We have a lot to do, launching you on London, my dear. Your Aunt Margaret and Angela will want to meet you as soon as possible, I know. I sent a note around to their Mount Street house to acquaint them of your arrival." Lady Ravensham was all eagerness to arrange a meeting, and Sarah wished she could anticipate the confrontation with her relatives with the enthusiasm her grandmother expected. For some reason she felt apprehensive, although certainly, if they welcomed her as warmly as her grandmother had, she had nothing to fear.

"And we must not forget Lucien is coming to take you for a ride in Hyde Park. I have a note here from him"—she waved to the pile of correspondence on her breakfast tray—"He suggests eleven o'clock, an unfashionable early hour, but the poor boy is so busy with his duties, we must be grateful he can spare any time at all."

Sarah bit back the irritation her grandmother's words aroused, but she could not resist protesting, "I would not want to interrupt Colonel Valentine's day. Such a nuisance for him to feel he must dance attendance upon me, just because he is such a good friend of your family."

"Have you taken Lucien in dislike, my dear? I hope

not. I am so fond of him, and our families have always been good friends. We are neighbors in the country, you know, and it is a wish of my heart we will eventually have a closer tie than friendship," Lady Ravensham hinted with gentle raillery.

No doubt her grandmother had decided that Colonel Valentine would prove to be an excellent *parti* for the eligible Angela. Arranged marriages were quite the thing in England, Sarah suspected, annoyed that the arrangement caused her regret. After all, what business was it of hers? No doubt the elegant Angela and the starched-up colonel would make a suitable pair. After all, he was the second son of an earl and a proper match for her cousin, to whom Sarah found herself already taking a dislike. Everything she had heard about that incomparable put up her hackles. No self-respecting American miss would allow such arrangements to be made for her, she assured herself. However, she could not allow her grandmother to suspect that she took Lucien in dislike. It would cause her unhappiness, and Sarah wanted to spare the dear woman any pain, since she had endured so much.

"Not at all, Grandmother. I find Colonel Valentine a very engaging man, if a trifle arrogant, but I dislike feeling like a package that must be collected and deposited. Very lowering to one's self-esteem," she teased.

"A very attractive package, if I may say so, my dear. It's probably good for Lucien to encounter some resistance. He seems to bowl over most of the young ladies, all women for that matter. He has quite a reputation." Lady Ravensham answered lightly, as if Luciens' romantic exploits were a matter of pride.

"I can imagine," Sarah answered dryly.

"It will be a novelty for him to encounter a young woman with a mind of her own. Good for him. But now you had better go off and prepare for your excursion," her grandmother said, dismissing her, as her own maid, a prim-faced woman of fifty with disapproval written all over her tight face, entered.

"Now, my lady, you are not thinking of getting up yet. You need your rest." She glared at Sarah as if she were responsible for disturbing her mistress.

"Nonsense, Evans. Sarah is just what I need to stir up these old bones, a real tonic. Plenty of time to lie abed when I had no exciting young granddaughter to give me a reason for rising." Lady Ravensham dismissed her maid's complaints with a twinkle, realizing that her longtime retainer was a bit jealous of Sarah's quick rapport with her grandmother.

Evans was not to be gains said. "That's as may be, but you must be careful. You know what Dr. Arthur said. No excitement. It's bad for you. You will get the megrims before you know it."

"Well, Grandmother, we cannot have that. I will be off and see you later, with a full report of my impressions of London." Sarah gave her grandmother another kiss and, ignoring Evans's frowns, wished her a pleasant good morning.

Chapter Sixteen

Lucien arrived promptly at eleven to find Sarah awaiting him, a lovely picture in her yellow riding dress and chip straw bonnet with matching yellow ribbons tied jauntily under her chin. Sarah scorned the languid airs of the blasé London miss. She was enchanted at the idea of riding in Hyde Park and in her enthusiasm had no intention of keeping her escort kicking his heels or fretting over his standing horses, just to impress upon him her own importance. Lucien had expected no less. He found her excitement a refreshing change from the usual London misses he squired, and her frank anticipation of the treat banished for the moment her antagonism toward the officer.

After he had handed her into his curricle, a spanking turnabout, he dismissed his tiger, obviously wishing no ears to overhear their conversation. This action reminded Sarah that it was not so much eagerness for her company that had inspired Lucien to press for the drive so soon after her arrival, as the opportunity to discuss the delivering of General Hamilton's message.

For a moment her delight in the expedition was dampened, but she shook off her chagrin. What else had she expected? In light of her grandmother's revelations about Lucien and Angela, she might have known that his only interest in her was as a courier. She watched his strong lean hands in their cream driving gloves on the reins and wondered anew at the conflict of emotions his very presence caused her. Today he was not wearing his regimentals but was dressed in a traditional, dark driving coat and kersey breeches, his top boots shining. He wore his London dress with an equal air, for Lucien did not depend on the attraction of a uniform to win admiring glances from the ladies, she was convinced.

As they entered the park, he abandoned the civilities that he had introduced and brought up the reason for their meeting.

"I could have delivered General Hamilton's note to Pitt myself, but I think you are entitled to his personal thank you for undertaking such a mission. You may find him a bit off-putting at first. He has a great deal on his mind right now—the Irish rebellion, Napoleon's obvious intention to capture Egypt, and then invade England even, all worrying affairs. Our navy, great bulwark that it is, suffers from the Commons' penchant for economy. So you can understand why Pitt does not want relations to deteriorate with America and add to his burdens." Lucien frowned as he explained the situation.

Sarah was secretly complimented that he would speak of such serious matters with her. "He has a friend in General Hamilton," she reassured him. "In fact, some believe that the general would be perfectly willing to bring our country under Great Britain's yoke again," she added critically, holding securely to her republican views, although she was now beginning to suspect the international situation was far more complicated than she had viewed it from Philadelphia.

"Nonsense. Hamilton's paramount concern is to keep the United States from fighting a war with anyone. How could he with an army of barely thirty-five hundred men and a navy whose keels have yet to be laid. Your message to Pitt will not encourage war, but possibly prevent it." Lucien's impatience with Sarah's views did not surprise her, nor did they annoy her for at least he was treating her like a responsible adult, able to appreciate the political and military implications of the current situation.

"You know, Sarah, it is quite refreshing, your patriotism. Obviously your country's fate matters to you, and your head is not stuffed with fashions and nonsense, very different from most young women your age." He smiled down at her in approval as he tooled his curricle out of Hyde Park.

Sarah had barely time to enjoy the greenery and a fleeting glimpse of impressive buildings before their equipage was skirting St. James along the Mall and entering Whitehall. Number 10 Downing Street, the modest black-doored home of England's prime minister rather surprised Sarah in its simplicity. She had expected Pitt to live in great splendour, even in a palace. She learned that the house had been designed by the famous architect Christopher Wren some years after the Great Fire, for George Downing, supporter of Charles II's Restoration although he had also served Cromwell as an intelligence officer. The small street was deserted, the entrance guarded by only one red-jacketed soldier. The original house had been encorporated with two others to the east by the orders of Robert Walpole, England's first prime minister, but it was far from a commodious mansion, having none of the outer trappings of power. Rather like the president's house in Philadelphia, she thought.

Colonel Valentine and Sarah were escorted by a manservant into the office that overlooked a garden and the Horse Guards Parade beyond. But Sarah had little time to look about her for immediately her eyes were arrested by the handsome, tall, if careworn, figure of William Pitt, who rose to greet them. Although not yet forty, the prime minister had been a towering figure in political life for more than fifteen years, and despite his touch-me-not air he exuded a sense of power and command. Colonel Valentine had prepared her for an aloof, distant man, but his charm belied that picture. His piercing blue eyes softened as he greeted them, obviously intrigued by this unlikely emissary and more than willing to make her feel at ease.

"It was very good of you, Miss Ravensham, to undertake General Hamilton's mission. Especially since I understand that you have definite republican sympathies." His tone was light and Sarah felt the gratification that was his intention.

"Not at all, sir. It was a simple assignment," she disclaimed.

"Still," Pitted insisted gravely, "Colonel Valentine tells me there was some danger attached so we are doubly grateful for your courage."

Sarah, knowing that Pitt had important matters of state upon his mind, handed over the precious message, which she had transferred to her beaded reticule. She gave him the packet with a sigh of relief. Although she wondered briefly what Hamilton had written in the secret document, her main emotion was relief at discharging her responsibility. Now she could concentrate on her personal reasons for this journey.

"Thank you, Miss Ravensham. I hope you found General Hamilton well and not too burdened with his new duties. I am sure Colonel Valentine apprised you of the significance of this communication. Hamilton is sensible enough to know that an alliance with Napoleon could not but harm your country, and he is well aware that French spies are everywhere. He was fortunate to persuade such a charming messenger to undertake his task. Now you must dismiss the whole business from your mind and enjoy your stay in England. I hope it will prove to be a long and pleasant one and that you will discover that Englishmen are not the ogres you might have been led to believe." Pitt was obviously eager to return to the vital state business that consumed him, but he was much too well bred to show his impatience.

"Thank you, sir. I am happy to have been of service to both our countries. You were very kind to receive me," Sarah spoke courteously, unwilling to leave any impression that American manners were less punctilious than English, and she had to admit that Pitt had impressed her. Here was no soft, toadying, snobbish crown minister but a man of rare intelligence and command.

Pitt shook hands with her and turned her over to the silent Colonel Valentine, whom he also thanked briefly. Lucien had watched the exchange wryly, observing that Sarah had fallen under the spell of Pitt's grave charm despite herself and her prejudices. As they were ushered out of the sanctum, Lucien smiled at her relief, her pleasure that the ordeal of delivering the packet was safely behind her.

"You have accomplished your mission, and can now relax and enjoy the delights of London. But first I wanted you to meet Pitt. He is a great man, even greater than his father, and we will need all his skills in the months ahead, I fear." Something in his tone made Sarah realize that he was worried about affairs she only vaguely understood.

"He looks very tired, a legacy of his great responsibilities, I suppose. His father was a friend of America and I must believe he feels equally sympathetic to the former colonies," Sarah said, honest enough to admit she could not condemn all Englishmen out of hand.

"He is a friend of your country," Lucien agreed, "and a man with many private worries aside from his responsibilities as prime minister. His revered father left him a load of debt, so crippling, in fact, that he felt he could not, in all honour, marry the lady of his choice, Eleanor Eden, despite her willingness. So he is denied the solace of a loving companion to lift some of the burdens of his great office from him. And he has many enemies here at home as well as across the channel."

Sarah wondered if Lucien himself thought of acquiring the solace of a loving companion and then remembered that Angela aspired to that position. Well, at least he was finally convinced that Sarah was not just one of the legion of silly women who spent their time trying to attract him. He was coming to know her and might eventually try for a real understanding. Why this was so devoutly to be wished she could not have explained.

As they walked across the narrow hall toward the door of Number 10, a tall, thin man, dressed in severe but impeccable black, hailed Lucien.

"Well, Valentine, I see you are back from your American travels," he greeted Sarah's companion, gazing at her coldly from deep-set eyes.

"Yes, and I have brought your niece with me. Sarah, this is your Uncle Ronald, about whom you have heard," Lucien made the introduction smoothly, not one whit discomposed by Ronald Ravensham's cold, questioning stare.

"It is a pleasure to welcome to you to England at long last, Sarah. My mother has been awaiting your arrival with such anticipation." Lord Ravensham's words seemed loaded with innuendo, implying that Sarah was guilty of some infraction by her visit. His chilly manner, his very presence, was far from welcoming. He continued to address her but she was barely aware of what he was saying, so affronted was she at his condescension. "I understand we will be seeing you at dinner this evening," he mentioned. "My wife and daughter are eager to make your acquaintance and will be annoyed that I have fore-stalled them. I hardly expected to meet you in such an unlikely place." Lord Ravensham's implication was clear. He did not approve of her being at Number 10 and he wanted to know the reason.

Before Sarah could marshal her defenses to answer her uncle, Lucien broke in, "I had some messages to deliver to Pitt, which could not wait, and, as I was showing Sarah some of the sights of London, I brought her along to meet the prime minister." Lucien's tone was casual, but for all his sang-froid Sarah sensed he would not entertain any criticism of the incongruity of Sarah accompanying him on the visit.

"And what did you think of Mr. Pitt? Rather impressive, wouldn't you say, Sarah?" Lord Ravensham was apparently satisfied with Lucien's suave explanation.

"Yes, indeed," she responded coolly. "A powerful advocate, I am sure, and a good friend to our country, my grandfather believes. I feel most privileged to have met him." There was something repellent about her uncle, so severe, so proper, so little warmth in his manner. She hoped his wife and daughter were easier. A chill, barely suppressed, shook Sarah. Ronald Ravensham was a rigid man, intimidating and rather frightening. Suddenly Sarah wished she were back in Philadelphia, in the comforting secure environment of Joshua Allen's house on Front Street. Sarah did not feel her uncle was at all happy to see her. What had she done, leaving the security of her home, the open free society of her country for this sophisticated milieu in which she would always feel alien?

Sensing her discomfort, Lucien took her arm in a firm grasp and bidding a curt farewell to Lord Ravensham, escorted her from Number 10. As they drove swiftly along the avenue fronting the Thames, she tried to shake off her feeling of disquiet and her companion, too, seemed ill at ease, almost angry. Lucien had evidently been as disturbed as she by the meeting with her uncle. Although he had claimed friendship with the older man, Sarah somehow believed their relationship was more complicated than that. Her thoughts turned to her unknown father. Surely he had not been like his younger brother, remote and chilling. Her mother would never have fallen in love with such a man. If Lord Ravensham was an example of her relatives, the sooner she boarded a ship for Philadelphia the better.

Lucien, noticing her silence and aware of the reason, attempted to quiet her doubts.

"Your Uncle Ronald's manner is a bit stiff and starched," he said, "but essentially he is a good man, much trusted by Pitt and a hard-working official. He has many grave responsibilities right now. I could wish you had met under easier circumstances, though."

"I don't think it would have made any difference," Sarah answered ruefully. "He would probably have taken me in dislike. I don't think he cares much for Americans."

"Nonsense. How could he help but be charmed. You will find him very different in your grandmother's drawing room tonight." Lucien then attempted to dispel her uneasiness by abandoning the topic of

131

Ronald Ravensham and pointing out the sights of Westminster and Piccadilly as they drove toward Park Street. Sarah responded to his efforts but beneath the light chat she sensed that he, too, was disturbed, but whether it was Lord Ravensham meeting his niece at Number 10 or some graver matter she could not tell.

Chapter Seventeen

Sarah, viewing herself in the cheval mirror, decided she would do. Not too overdressed for a family dinner, in her lilac French dimity embroidered with seed pearls, her brown curls caught demurely in a pearl fillet. She was convinced the incomparable Angela would be looking her best but she refused to be put out of countenance. Lady Ravensham had told her that she had invited an old friend of the family's, a retired general, Julian Apsley-Gower, who had once served with her father. And of course, Lucien would be present, not that she cared for that she told herself firmly.

"You do look a treat, miss," Polly told her, watching admiringly as Sarah clasped her mother's pearls around her slender neck.

"Thank you, Polly. I suspect Philadelphia fashions a trifle outmoded in London, but it will have to do." Sarah frowned despite the entrancing picture she saw in the mirror. Why was she allowing herself to worry about her appearance? She chided herself for her nervousness over meeting the rest of the Ravenshams.

Although her uncle had done nothing to reassure her that she would be greeted with enthusiasm, there was no reason to think that the rest of the family would be so chilly. Her grandmother had received her with warm affection, so perhaps they would be guided by her. Still, Sarah could not shake off her doubts about the coming encounter.

She descended the curving stairway prepared to meet her relatives in the spirit of a conqueror. She would not act like a naive colonial, obviously impressed with the London beau monde. Her republican soul stirred angrily at the thought of any patronage from those who might think she was encroaching.

As she hesitated in the doorway of the huge drawing room, a resplendent salon decorated in blue brocade and velvet, it seemed, at first, that the room was crowded with people. Her grandmother, elegant in deep-magenta satin with a startling array of diamonds, came forward.

"Ah, there you are, my dear," Lady Ravensham said in her soft, warm voice, rustling toward her. "Come, your relations are eager to make your acquaintance. Your Aunt Margaret, Lady Ravensham." She indicated a faded woman of indeterminate years, who was wearing a rather dreadful gown of puce crape that made her skin look sallow. Sarah curtseyed, looking into the faded-grey eyes with compassion. What a tired, unhappy lady her aunt looked.

"Delighted, Aunt Margaret, to meet you," Sarah responded dutifully to that lady's almost unrecognizable murmur. Lady Ravensham was indeed a quenched spirit, although traces of a delicate young beauty could be seen beneath the tired worn expression. That earlier attraction had long since been extinguished by the formidable Lord Ravensham, who must have proved to be a cold companion for life's journey, Sarah thought. Watching her aunt's flickering, almost fearful glance at her husband, Sarah's initial dislike of her Uncle Ronald increased. He had subdued his wife's personality, turning her into a nonentity.

"I understand you have already met your Uncle Ronald at Number 10 this morning," her grandmother continued, escorting Sarah over to the fireplace where that austere gentleman stood talking to Colonel Valentine. Lady Ravensham's words held a question that Sarah felt she must answer, but before she could say more than acknowledge the truth of her grandmother's gentle query, Lucien stepped in with an explanation.

"Yes, a fortuitous meeting. I had to stop by Number 10 and thought Sarah might enjoy being received by Mr. Pitt, in order to allay her suspicions concerning his intentions toward her country," Lucien offered, looking quizzically at Sarah.

"And may I say how charming you look this evening, Sarah?" he continued, causing that young woman to blush, to her chagrin. He himself was looking devilishly attractive in a black superfine coat and gleaming white shirt accented by an intricately tied cravat, and the obligatory evening dress breeches.

Before she could reply to his compliment, Lord Ravensham spoke, "You are a charming addition to the family, my dear. And I know your visit will prove a great comfort to Mother." Sarah smiled prettily in response to her uncle's words, although doubting his sincerity in uttering them. What a cold fish he was and quite puffed up, she believed, her prejudices of the English coming to the fore.

"And here is your cousin, Angela," her grandmother continued. "I know you girls will be fast friends."

Sarah, turning to greet the young woman who had crossed the room at her grandmother's beckoning nod, barely repressed a gasp. Angela Ravensham was indeed a vision, her mint-gold hair swept back from her classical face in a severe style that would have been trying to most women, but that set off her beautiful pale complexion and regular features to a charm. She had cool blue eyes that swept over her cousin in an appraising fashion but showed little warmth or friendliness. After the barest of greeting, she turned and laid a proprietary arm on Lucien's black-clad elbow.

"And why were you escorting Sarah to Number 10, Lucien?" Angela asked boldly, inferring that her cousin was a pushy miss who had demanded that Lucien tear himself away from his pressing duties to squire Sarah about. That young woman, accustomed to the warm informal camaraderie of Philadelphia, sensed that Angela resented her acquaintance with Lucien and would do everything in her power to establish her prior claim to that gentleman's attention. Well, she was welcome to him. Sarah could not repress a pang of disappointment, but Angela made it quite clear she had taken her cousin in suspicion and moreover would entertain no competition for the gallant officer's favours. No danger, said Sarah to herself. Unbidden came the memory of that kiss aboard the packet, but she banished it firmly.

Lucien was not one whit embarrassed by Angela's probing or her possessive hand. "I was showing Sarah the sights of London, and certainly Number 10 is among the chief attractions, as is Mr. Pitt himself, you must agree."

"Oh, quite. Well, you need not be bothered in the future. We will take our cousin in hand. I will be happy to show you about and introduce you to everyone you should meet," Angela said condescendingly. Sarah made up her mind in an instant that she would not call upon her cousin for any assistance in such matters, and in fact, the sooner she returned to Philadelphia and put all these cursed English behind her the better. Unaccustomed to being relegated to the ranks of a tiresome duty, she did not take kindly to it, or the perpetrator of such feelings. Both Angela and the gallant colonel could go to the devil. As for her uncle, she felt instinctively that he also wished she had remained in the colonial wilderness, as he probably thought of Philadelphia.

She felt more kindly toward the two remaining guests—one of whom was her young cousin, Alan, just sixteen, an endearing young man whose gawkiness had not yet enabled him to manage his height but whose open face and shock of brown hair, barely tamed into a respectable style, had much of his mother's look about him.

"I think it's jolly to have a new cousin. I am only allowed up from Eton for this weekend to meet you, and perhaps you will be here when my holidays come around and then I will show you some excitement, far better than the prosy old drawing rooms, and silly

137

routs. "Do you ride?" he asked engagingly.

"Yes, indeed. I like it above all things," Sarah assured him, warmed by his welcome and his frank, honest face.

"Alan cares for nothing but horses. He wants to go into a cavalry regiment," his sister offered in some disdain.

"Plenty of time for that," Lord Ravensham said, frowning at his heir, "when he passes his exams. He does not apply himself as he might."

Sarah felt for the young man, embarrassed by his father's displeasure. She thought he would do very well in the army, away from the stultifying effect of his father and Angela's notions of proper behaviour.

"And here is Gen. Julian Apsley-Gower, an old friend of your father's, my dear." Her grandmother drew forward a grey-haired, smiling, portly man whose upright stature and clear grey eyes showed his military heritage. Sarah thawed immediately under the kindly, admiring gaze.

"Delighted, my dear. You have quite the look of your mother," the general greeted her. Sarah felt tears rising in her eyes. Here was someone who had known the mother she had never met, who could tell her about her parents, perhaps answer those questions that had dogged her ever since her arrival in London.

"Oh, General, I am so happy to meet you. Did you really know my mother? Were you serving in America with my father?" Sarah's whole demeanour changed, all thoughts of the difficult Ravenshams vanishing in the anticipation of learning about those long-ago days.

"Yes, indeed. Elizabeth Allen was a real beauty,

and Richard the envy of most of Howe's officers. I was among those who paid her court, but she had eyes for no one but your father, lucky devil." General Apsley-Gower recalled. "We must have a long talk about her, my dear. I am longing to get to know Richard's daughter."

Much cheered by this fortuitous meeting with her father's former comrade in arms, Sarah went into dinner on young Alan's arm in a more cheerful spirit. If Lord and Lady Ravensham and their haughty daughter had not welcomed her arrival with any enthusiasm, she believed that in Alan she had found a friend. She anticipated a long chat with the general who would perhaps be able to answer the questions she was longing to ask about her mother and father. Though he could not provide the answers to those doubts about her father's treason, he could at least tell her intimate details about her parents. Somehow she had never felt easy about questioning her grandfather. The memory of that long-ago tragedy caused Joshua Allen too much pain. General Apsley-Gower, an admitted friend of Richard Ravensham, and acquainted with her mother, would be a more disinterested observer. Why, from the general she might even find a clue to the mystery behind her father's disgrace.

Chapter Eighteen

Despite Angela Ravensham's cool reception of her new cousin, she had a healthy respect for her grandmother and no intention of offending the dowager by showing any dislike for this unwelcome colonial, whose presence, in any case, hardly threatened her own plans. That young woman had too much self-assurance to consider Sarah any kind of a rival for the attentions she considered her due. She rather thought, too, that Sarah's vivacity, her wholesome delight in all these new experiences, her lack of sophistication, and her ignorance of the way to go on among London's high-steppers would soon relegate her to the wall-flower set. She was soon to discover she had made a false assumption.

After a round of modistes, milliners, and several long hours at the Pantheon Bazaar, Lady Ravensham finally decided that Sarah's wardrobe satisfied the demands of her new life and signified that she was prepared to launch her granddaughter onto the ton, with Angela and her mother's assistance. Since the season had barely begun, with most of the great hostesses still at their country estates, Lady Ravensham invited a very select group to a small rout at her Park Street mansion. Most of the guests were contemporaries of the dowager but several brought their daughters and granddaughters to meet the new arrival along with whatever sons, husbands, and brothers could be cajoled into escorting them.

Sarah, in a fashionable gown of buttercup-yellow muslin, looked demurely charming and tried to do her grandmother proud but found her spirits gravely tried by the insipid behaviour of the young women within whose circle Lady Ravensham hoped she would take a place. Angela, with one season behind her, was allowed a bit more license but it seemed to Sarah, as she sipped tea and nibbled at iced cakes, that most of the girls donned masks of insincerity and ignorance. Surely they could do better than to simper and cast down their eyes when greeting a gentleman.

Then, too, they had no conversation. In a desperate effort to elicit some response Sarah questioned two sisters, the Misses Pemberton, blond wispy girls of no particular attraction, as to what they enjoyed seeing in London. Had they visited Parliament or the Tower of London, both of which attracted Sarah intensely? Oh, no, they would find these landmarks boring. In desperation Sarah questioned them about charitable activities. Did they organize soup kitchens for the poor, teach orphaned children, try to alleviate some of poverty and grime Sarah had been appalled to glimpse behind the stately facade of the grand houses she had seen briefly on her drives? Oh, no, they gasped.

"Our mother would never allow such unseemly

behaviour," Miss Emily Pemberton informed Sarah in horror. "Why, we might catch a loathsome disease. And these people are far beneath our touch. There are poorhouses and workhouses for such unfortunates."

Abandoning this unpromising topic, Sarah tried again. "But surely, there are cultural events of great interest in this huge metropolis—theater, art, music. What opportunities to improve your mind with so much available." By this time quite a bevy of guests had gathered around Sarah and the Pemberton sisters, who were quite embarrassed to be signaled out in this manner, particularly since among the audience was Mr. Reginald Langley-Wood, whom Louisa Pemberton hoped might come up to snuff. But he would certainly never propose if he thought she had the manners of this bold, encroaching colonial.

"We do go to the opera and the theatre, of course. But we are hardly blue stockings—so unmaidenly, don't you think, Miss Ravensham, to delve into these affairs that are far better left to the gentlemen?" Emily simpered.

Sarah was now thoroughly aroused by this vapid attitude, in such contrast to the open frank discussion she was accustomed to at home. "No, I don't." She replied curtly. "Why should men be any more capable of understanding poverty, politics, or the arts than females?"

"Bravo, Miss Ravensham. Tilting at dragons again I see," said a familiar voice. Sarah turned to see Lucien Valentine had joined the group. No one had known quite how to take this colonial hornet in their midst, but now they were reassured to discover she had Valentine's approval.

"Good afternoon, Colonel Valentine. I did not expect to see you at this affair," she said sharply, not sure of her reaction to his championship.

Before Lucien could make a response, Angela appeared and grasped Lucien's arm.

"Really, Lucien, don't encourage her," she said brightly. "She sounds like that dreadful Hannah More, such an ardent reformer and advocate of women's rights. So fatiguing." Angela looked meaningfully at Lucien, her large blue eyes open wide. Sarah felt an uncommon urge to slap the smirk off her face. Their audience stood silently, hoping perhaps to see the American commit some further social solecism. Well, she would not disappoint them.

"If Hannah More is involved with affairs beyond the modistes and the tea brigade, I would welcome an introduction. She sounds a fascinating person," Sarah said, deliberately adding fuel to the fire.

"I am sure that can be arranged, Sarah, now come along," Lucien said firmly, his lips twitching with amusement. "I have something to say to you away from all these prying eyes and ears." He would not allow Angela to bait her cousin before this select group of her grandmother's guests—not that she could not handle herself. He offered her his arm to escort her to a sofa arranged enticingly in a corner of the drawing room. But Angela, piqued at his championship of Sarah, would have none of that.

"Come, Lucien, Grandmother insists on a word with you. You will have to postpone your interview with Sarah and do the polite," she said more sharply than was her wont with Lucien, whose good opinion she cherished. Angela was always careful to keep her more spiteful remarks and bad tempers within the family and not allow her legion of beaux to see her out of sorts.

"Well, let us all go seek out Lady Ravensham, then," he assented graciously.

"You go ahead, Lucien," said an officer who had been accompanying Lucien. "I will be glad to escort Miss Ravensham—after you have introduced us, that is." Sarah looked into a pair of merry blue eyes above a shock of unruly brown hair and a smile of engaging sweetness. The young man, obviously a colleague of Lucien's, was dressed in the proper afternoon costume of dark-blue superfine coat, embroidered waistcoat, and cream kersey breeches, but his stance told of military training.

"Sarah, this graceless idiot is Capt. Robert Parry, the scourge of his regiment and a stealer of feminine hearts from Bath to Brighton, so pay no attention to his murmurings," Lucien said smiling. "I'm not sure it is safe to leave you with him."

"How do you do, Captain. I am sure you are a perfectly respectable companion and I will be delighted to question you about the attractions of London so many of our guests are reluctant to discuss." Sarah smiled charmingly at the officer, half turning her back on Angela and Lucien, signifying that she had dismissed them both.

"You have your congé, Lucien, and can leave Miss Ravensham in my capable hands, now," the captain replied audaciously. Lucien had no recourse but to smile a bit grimly, bow, and walk away with Angela still clinging determinedly to his arm. Sarah, quite happy to welcome this new friend, found the captain

144

an easy relaxed companion, rather reminiscent of Brian Willing, and treated him in the same jocular open fashion, which won his heart immediately. They bantered back and forth, charmed with each other, and unaware that Lucien, across the room, attending to Lady Ravensham and Angela, watched them with narrowed eyes.

Sarah enjoyed her conversation with Captain Parry, but another of the guests that afternoon did not receive so enthusiastic a response. Her grandmother had insisted on including Moira Amberly among the guests as a gesture of appreciation for that lady's chaperonage of Sarah on the recent voyage. Mrs. Amberly had been delighted to accept for a variety of reasons, and she had been more than cordial in her greetings to Sarah. But later in the entertainment she had drawn the girl aside to deliver one of her condescending critiques of Sarah's behaviour.

"My dear, how charming you look, and I am pleased to see that your grandmother is introducing you to all the proper people in the ton. But just a word of caution from one who has your best interests at heart. It will not do to be so forthcoming with your opinions, my dear. Young girls are not encouraged to discuss matters better left to their elders. Not attractive behaviour if you wish to be acceptable to society. You would do well to watch your cousin Angela—such a pattern of propriety." Moira Amberly could not resist the temptation to let Sarah know that her own position entitled her to give instruction, but Sarah had endured enough of Moira Amberly's jabs.

"I believe I know how to go on, Mrs. Amberly and, if not, my grandmother will guide me, I am sure.

145

Now may I find you some refreshment or introduce you to some of the guests? I do not believe you know many of the company?" Sarah was ashamed of her reply, but she would not be the butt of Mrs. Amberly's remarks, now that lady's duty toward her was fulfilled.

Moira Amberly, well aware of the put-down, would have replied sharply to the hoity-toity miss if, from the corner of her eye, she had not seen one of the objects of the reason for her presence here enter the room. "Well, yes, Sarah, if you would be so kind, I would like to meet your uncle and aunt, who have just arrived." As they crossed the room to greet the couple, Mrs. Amberly tried to retrieve her position. "Please do not take offence at my strictures, Sarah," she said sweetly. "I meant it only out of kindness and because you are a stranger to our ways."

"Of course, Mrs. Amberly. No offence taken. And here are my aunt and uncle." Sarah made the introductions, wondering why her erstwhile chaperone should be so eager to meet Lord and Lady Ravensham, for she did not feel either of them would be receptive to that lady's particular brand of charm.

Chapter Nineteen

Sarah now entered a round of routs, receptions, Roman breakfasts, and dances with reluctance, her first impression of the beau monde proving, on more familiar acquaintance, to be only too accurate. She did not find the strict social code that dominated society to her taste, and she would have protested vehemently against the many invitations that poured into Park Street if she had not feared to offend her grandmother. Lady Ravensham often attended the gentler entertainments and her pride in Sarah was very heartwarming to that young woman. Sarah had hoped that Angela might yet prove a confidante and real friend, but any expectations she had nourished concerning her cousin soon withered under that cool beauty's stylized manner.

Angela, however, was clever enough not to give avid eyes or ears any reason to believe she found her American cousin a rival, neither in her grandmother's affection nor as an attractive belle able to win the hearts and hands of susceptible and eligible young men. She managed to convey delicately that only her own charity and kindly temperament allowed her to perform what must be an irksome duty. She graciously allowed the young men of her court, who vied for her favours, to pay attention to her cousin and only tardily realized that, within a few weeks, Sarah had attracted a small court of her own, headed by the personable Capt. Robert Parry, whose indulgent and relaxed companionship Sarah found very soothing in the midst of the more meretricious bucks and rakes who made up the ton. Sarah discovered that most of the young men who frequented London's best drawing rooms were shallow, vain creatures, more concerned with the turn of a cravat or the hue of their resplendant waistcoats than with matters of more serious moment.

The looming presence of Napoleon across the narrow channel aroused few members of the ton to anxiety as to that redoubtable Frenchman's plans of conquest. The possibility of the inevitable clash with the French did not seem to worry society, which dismissed the threat airily. "That upstart Corsican" would meet his comeuppance in good time and the troubled condition of Europe must not be allowed to disturb the Season. Napoleon's defeat of Italy, his subjection of Prussia and Austria, isolating England, did not seem to pose any problem for the young men so idly passing their time, when they should have been enlisting in the army, Sarah thought. Even rumors of the huge French invasion fleet assembling at Boulogne did not overset these complacent Englishmen.

When Sarah tried to discuss the possible invasion, the political implications of Napoleon's conquest of

Europe, she received short shift from the gallants who sought to amuse her. Even the officers, mostly guardsmen from fashionable regiments, who joined the train around Angela, dismissed the French problem and advised her not to worry her pretty head about boring military matters—advice Sarah found patronizing and maddening. She had never been subjected to such condescension in Philadelphia where conversation around her grandfather's dinner table ranged from politics and philosophy to military and economic problems. She had exchanged opinions with the most prominent men in the government and business world and had always enjoyed their respect. When she did speak her mind to the coterie about Angela, much to that young woman's disgust, and to the beaux' bewilderment, she was dismissed as an earnest colonial. "So fatiguing, my dear, but what can one expect?" was the verdict.

Only Lucien appeared to take her views seriously. He answered her questions and listened gravely to her opinions on America's role in the conflict between nations. His continual presence surprised her, but he seemed to have enough leisure from his military duties to squire the ladies whenever needed. He appeared at most of the functions they attended, and if Angela preened herself on such marks of attention, Sarah suspected it was no more than a courtesy he paid due to the family friendship. He treated the cousins with equal gallantry, never lacking in those niceties expected of gentlemen, but showing neither of them any evidence of the besotted suitor.

Still, Sarah was convinced Angela had some basis for believing that Lucien eventually intended to claim her for his bride. Whatever his purpose, Angela's were quite clear and she lost no time in letting Sarah know of them.

On one of their many expeditions she confided, in a rather offhand manner that did not deceive her cousin, that, although she was enjoying her second season, she expected it to be her last, as marriage was imminent. Sarah, frank by nature, found Angela's coyness excruciatingly annoying, and asked bluntly if she knew the intended husband.

"Of course, my dear cousin. You are acquainted with him, and quite well too. You may even have been slightly *épris* yourself in that direction. I know you would not be so lacking in charity or so foolish as to cast eyes on another's intended, so I thought a word would be in order. It is Lucien, of course. We have had an understanding for some time, but I am not willing to announce it quite yet, and Lucien has been so occupied with his military duties, and that trip to the colonies. That wretched Corsican has upset all our plans. I wanted another season before I settled down to being a matron. We will set the date soon," she spoke artlessly but watched her cousin carefully to see how she took the news.

Sarah, determined not to give Angela the satisfaction of realizing that the news caused her any pangs, tendered her good wishes. Not for the world would she give her cousin any notion that the thought of Lucien affianced to Angela disturbed her. She hated to think that Lucien was a practised philanderer, and he was not a man to display his emotions to the world, but what was she to believe? Well, her cousin was welcome to him. Serve him right if she did catch him, Sarah concluded, for she had seen little sign that Lucien was overcome with passion for the incomparable. Still what did she really know of him? He was clever at subterfuge, experienced at hiding his feelings. Perhaps he and Angela were well suited, and no doubt both families encouraged the match. Angela would never marry in defiance of her family. As an earl's son, if not his heir, Lucien Valentine was a prime catch.

In the future, Sarah would let Colonel Valentine know she was not available for dallying. She suspected that her cousin was not so sure of the enigmatic colonel as she claimed, but she refused to demean herself by competing for Lucien. If this was the mode of London courtship and marriage, she wanted none of it. She would make it clear to Lucien that she was no gullible colonial, available for flirtation but not suitable for such an exalted match.

The very day after Angela's confidences he arrived to take her for a drive in Hyde Park at an unfashionable early hour. Probably, he did not want any of the ton to see him escorting her, Sarah thought waspishly. Though Angela had staked her claim on Lucien, and Sarah had made up her mind to show an indifferent face to that irritating man, she had nevertheless dressed carefully for her ride, in a charming pale-blue marocain gown with white lace accents and a fetching white straw bonnet tied with matching blue ribbons. She thanked her escort coolly when he complimented her on her appearance and handed her into his curricle, ignoring his raised eyebrows at her off-putting tone.

As they moved down Brook Street and into the

park, looking entrancing in its early May guise of greenery and flowering shrubs, Lucien chatted easily of inconsequential matters.

"You have made quite an impression on London society, Sarah. I notice you have become the toast of the town, putting less fortunate ladies in the shade. I congratulate you on your success," he teased.

"For a colonial I have not done too badly, I suppose. Just the novelty of meeting a crass American and discovering her to be nothing out of the ordinary, I am sure," answered Sarah tartly, while castigating herself for her bad humour.

Lucien frowned, glancing at her in puzzlement. "You still think of us as enemies, don't you, Sarah, despite the warm welcome you have received from your grandmother and all your other relations?"

"Oh, not really. It's just that I don't fit into this artificial world. Sometimes I miss Philadelphia and Grandfather terribly. Everyone has been very kind but I feel alien," Sarah admitted.

"We try, Sarah, but you don't always make it easy for us," Lucien said wryly, searching her face beneath the bonnet.

Sarah tossed her head restlessly, refusing to meet his gaze, or believe in the warmth of his words. Casting her eyes around the park and noticing the few carriages promenading slowly about the well-tended paths, she was suddenly distracted by recognizing the phaeton of General Apsley-Gower with a woman beside him. She peered unbelievingly at the sight of the couple, in deep conversation, unheeding of all else at this unfashionable hour.

"There is General Apsley-Gower,"—she pointed out

to Lucien, glad of the opportunity to direct his attention away from her—"and I do believe he is escorting Mrs. Amberly. I didn't know they were acquainted."

"Indeed, the general has a large circle of acquaintance. But I am surprised to see Mrs. Amberly. I thought she had joined her family in the country. Have you met her since your grandmother's rout?"

"No. She paid a call, but I was not at home. I suppose we must hail them," she conceded, not anxious to see the patronizing Mrs. Amberly again, although good manners insisted she could not ignore her. As the two carriages approached each other and Lucien steadied his horses with a tight hand, she thought she saw a look of irritation cross the lady's smooth face, but it was quickly gone and both Mrs. Amberly and her escort greeted Lucien and Sarah with cordiality.

"Good day to you, Sarah. I see you are taking advantage of one of our special spring mornings, and in the company of the gallant colonel, too. How pleasant to see you both again," Mrs. Amberly greeted the pair archly. The general, steadying his horses, murmured his own welcome, but Sarah noticed his words were perfunctory, lacking his usual warmth.

Mrs. Amberly, in her ingratiating manner, referred to her pleasure at Lady Ravensham's rout some days past. As Lucien and Sarah exchanged a few brief remarks with the general and Mrs. Amberly, it was obvious the former was most anxious to be on his way, although politeness demanded he not be too abrupt. While their carriages remained stationary, a lone rider approached and stopped for a moment beside them.

"My dear Mrs. Amberly, General, what a fortuitous meeting. Now you can introduce me to the charming American who has taken London by storm," came a dulcet chilling voice. Sarah looked up into the bold, insolent eyes of the stranger whose chamber she had invaded in Plymouth. Mrs. Amberly, on the one hand delighted to be signaled out by the marquis and on the other averse to the introduction, had no choice but to make Miss Ravensham known to Theron, Lord De Lisle. Lucien gave his own curt greeting, annoyed at the encounter.

"My dear Miss Ravensham, what a delight to meet you at long last. Now that we have been properly introduced, I hope you will allow me to call, or are you too craven to know one whose reputation gives proper young women the horrors?" Lord De Lisle smiled over Sarah's hand, raking her over with those cynical all-seeing eyes, which made Lucien want to kick him.

Sarah, well aware that her escort was irritated, and always ready herself to rise to a challenge, smiled in return. "It will depend on whether my grandmother will receive you, my Lord. I myself have no objections," she answered.

"I promise to be on my best behaviour, *à bientôt*, then." He again favoured her with that surprising smile that wiped the cynicism from his face. A devilishly attractive man, Sarah concluded, and part of his undeniable appeal was the knowledge that his reputation ensured that she would receive him at her peril. But even more satisfactory, Sarah thought, cocking her head at Lucien in an appraising way, was the knowledge that the colonel was more than annoyed at this meeting. He did not approve of Lord De Lisle and that made Sarah even more determined to cultivate the man.

Bidding a curt farewell to the general and his companion, Lucien tooled his curricle away as fast as possible, his brow furrowed in anger.

"Really, Sarah, what do you mean by encouraging that fellow. Most unsuitable, and your grandmother will not be pleased that you have met him. He is not received in polite society, for his past scandals are legion." Lucien spoke with some vehemence, despite his best intentions, because he suspected Sarah would find the bounder even more intriguing now.

"What scandals? Oh, do tell, Lucien. Did he spend too long on the terrace with some unfortunate debutante, or parade his *chère amie* under the noses of respectable dowagers? I fear that his greatest sin is ignoring the first dictate of society, to be discreet and undiscovered," she challenged, knowing there was a great deal more to De Lisle's wicked reputation than these peccadilloes. It was evident in the man's world-weary expression, which did not deceive Sarah for a moment.

"You don't know what you are talking about, Sarah. De Lisle has committed infamous transgressions, which do not bear repeating in polite society. And there is another reason why you should avoid him. I am not at all sure that he is not involved in some nefarious intrigues with the French. His life style is an expensive one, and he spends a great deal of time with some very suspect *émigrés*. Not all the French you meet in London society are pathetic victims of the Revolution, you know. We are surrounded by Napoleon's spies, *émigrés* willing to commit any perfidy if they can regain their position and estates. De Lisle owned land in Anjou, which was appropriated by the government, and no doubt he would like to regain it. He is a thoroughly bad sort," Lucien spoke angrily, vexed that Sarah would not be guided by his advice.

"Well, if he is intriguing with the French, that is one thing, but to refuse to know him, just because of his reputation with women is another. Obviously half the men in London would prove undesirable acquaintances by that standard," Sarah answered reprovingly, lifting an eyebrow and implying, Lucien thought, that he was among their number.

"There are very few gentlemen you will encounter in polite society, where your grandmother will introduce you, who have the reputation of Lord De Lisle, and every bit of it deserved by De Lisle. So don't refine on affairs you know nothing about, just to brangle with me, my girl," Lucien replied, his temper further aroused by Sarah's obstinacy.

"Well, we must just agree to disagree, Lucien. Now tell me more about General Apsley-Gower. I know he was a friend of my father's and I want to talk to him at length about his time in America, but he has been strangely elusive." Sarah turned the conversation, more than willing to forget Lord De Lisle. She had only returned his greeting with more enthusiasm than she really felt to score off Lucien, which, she admitted, was wicked of her.

Lucien sighed, wanting Sarah's promise that she would heed his warning and shun that gentleman's company, but realizing that pursuing the matter would not do at this juncture.

"I realize that you want to discuss your father with General Apsley-Gower, but do you think that is wise Sarah? It can only arouse bitter memories of what happened so long ago, and I cannot believe any good will come of rooting about in the past," Lucien said gently, unwilling to give Sarah any fresh cause for anger.

"Lucien," she said stiffly. "If we are to continue friends, you must resist this tendency to tell me how to conduct my life. I am perfectly capable of making some decisions for myself, you know, and unlike the Misses Pemberton and their company, I do not believe that men are all-wise and all-superior. I do not take you to task for your way of going on . . . although I must say there is much in your manner that gives me pause," she added, remembering Angela's confidences.

"I can't imagine what maggot you have in your head now about me, Sarah, but I am perfectly willing to be taken to task by such an attractive taskmaster," Lucien replied lightly.

Glancing at her aloof countenance turned away from him, he sighed. She rebuffed his every attempt at friendship and he would really believe she took him in deep aversion if it were not for her passionate response to his kisses. He did not think she was light-minded, and her warm reaction had stirred his senses as no other woman's but lately they had seemed at cross-purposes. She opposed him on all suits out of sheer perversity. And now, encouraging a bounder like De Lisle—she could not really be attracted to the fellow.

Unused to being treated in this fashion by females, Lucien found Sarah's independent, casual air altogether maddening. Perhaps he had not treated her as she wished, but she brought a great deal of his anger on herself. Lucien tendered no more olive branches and the two continued the ride back to Park Street in icy silence.

Chapter Twenty

Convinced that Angela and Lucien were about to announce their betrothal, Sarah decided that she must put all thoughts of confiding in him from her mind. Obviously her first instincts about that gentleman were correct, and she should not have been lured into weakening her defences under his cajoling tongue and pursuit of her. She certainly did not understand the ways of London society—a feckless, insincere lot the men were and the women little better.

She must remember that her first responsibility was to try to discover some evidence that would clear her father of the false charges of treachery. And to do that she must press for that interview with General Apsley-Gower. He was reluctant to discuss the matter, she realized, but that could be because it was too painful for him. Surely, if she could face what he might reveal, he could be persuaded to give her a true picture of events. No one alive today was a better source of information and she would wrest his secrets from him, no matter how much he demurred.

Confronting the general would take her mind off Angela's budget of news. Neither her cousin nor Lucien would distract her from pursuing the truth about her father. She only hoped that whatever she learned would not bring fresh pain to her grandmother. She had come to love and understand Lady Ravensham for the confidence and affection she bestowed on her.

After several postponements the general at last consented to grant Sarah the private interview she demanded. From the beginning she had been impressed with his kindly bluff manner, and she hoped that his aversion to causing her any discomfort would not prevent him from answering her blunt questions honestly. She had supposed him to be a fairly uncomplicated straightforward military man, whose career had progressed steadily from one success to another until he had achieved respect and honours. But on consideration she believed that was too simple an assessment. Either the rigours of his military life or some personal disappointment had undoubtedly aged him beyond his years. A contemporary of her father's, he could not be more than fifty, yet his snow-white hair, and the lines in his face testified to a far-from-easy life.

Finally a day was agreed upon and he arrived at Park Street at the appointed hour. Lady Ravensham and Sarah received him over the teacups and chatted of trivialities until Lady Ravensham excused herself. Sarah knew that her grandmother did not approve of Sarah quizzing the general, that she could see no benefit from reviewing past events. Sarah loathed causing her grandmother pain but she would not be moved from her determination to learn all she could from the one man who might give her some clue.

Sarah lost no time in introducing the topic which consumed her. "I understand, General, that you and my father were close friends from school days and served together through many postings, including our Revolution."

"That's true, my dear. Your father was a bit younger, but we struck up a friendship at Eton that lasted until the end. He was an unusually gifted young man, head of his form, a terror on the cricket field, and more than adequate in his studies. Quite put my poor efforts to shame, not that I took this in bad part. But he was a very pattern card of honour and bravery, which made the final judgment of him so much more surprising. But then we never know a man, or woman for that matter, completely. Who can thoroughly understand even an intimate friend's ambitions and motives? I thought I was as close to Richard as anyone, except your dear mother, and yet I had no conception of what he contemplated." The general gazed with apparent candour and sorrow at Sarah, obviously upset at confirming the view that she refused to accept.

"I find it very difficult to believe," Sarah insisted obstinately. "He had everything to lose, and not a great deal to gain by turning traitor."

"That's true. Howe regarded him as one of his best officers. He outshone us all in every department. That is what made his defection all the more puzzling and unexpected," the general confided sadly. "I think you must just accept it, however painful, my dear."

But Sarah would not accept his judgment of her

father. "Who, do you suppose, laid the accusation against him with his commanding officer?"

"None of us knew, and Richard was never able to discover the name of his accuser. The charge came from the War Office in London. It is difficult to conceive that your father had any enemies, but it is possible some disgruntled official at home may have laid information due to jealousy. It's hard to believe, for he was a very popular officer," the general spoke sympathetically, but his eyes dropped from Sarah's candid questioning gaze.

"The imputation," he continued, "that your mother had anything to do with his suspected treason was ridiculous. A gentler, more lovely lady never lived. We all were fond of her, but she had eyes for no one but Richard."

"Exactly what was the basis of the accusation that he betrayed his country?" Sarah persisted.

"I am not really sure, but I believe he was accused, under the influence of your mother, of approaching Tench Tilghman, General Washington's aide-de-camp, with the plans for Howe's juncture with Burgoyne, the date of his evacuation of Philadelphia. Of course, as a member of Howe's staff, he was privy to all the details of the projected campaign. Although Philadelphia was generally conceded to be Tory-minded, there were many who sympathized with the rebels and others who played a waiting game. Look at Benedict Arnold. It was rumoured that Major Ravensham, persuaded by your mother, cajoled him into betrayal, because she wanted him to remain in the colonies after the war, perhaps. I find that difficult to accept."

"So you really have little to tell me, beyond what my grandfather has already explained," Sarah concluded sadly.

"I am afraid so. I was still with Howe when Richard was transferred to General Burgoyne and really knew little of the actual charges."

"Of course, I never knew my mother," Sarah said, "but my grandfather assured me she took little interest in the rights and wrongs of the colonial cause. Her only concern was my father and she loved him deeply. His death under such circumstances completely overcame her. My grandfather, of course, made enquiries about the whole affair."

"And what did he discover?" the general asked, surprising Sarah with his sharp tone.

"Very little more than we have discussed. As you said, the charges came from London and, although Howe himself was reluctant to pursue the matter, he had little choice. There must have been some evidence, because my father's own family believed the accusation unequivocally," Sarah answered. "I do not believe my mother persuaded my father to neglect his duty."

"Elizabeth Allen was a very beautiful woman. It is possible that your father would have gone to any lengths to win her," the general said gently.

"Not betray his country," she insisted. "And how Lord Ravensham could have believed such charges against his son amazes me. My grandfather was appalled at such a canard. He never accepted that my father was capable of treason, and he certainly was not blinded by the affection he felt for them both."

"Lord Ravensham had a great deal of influence

163

with the War Office, with Lord George Germain. The evidence must have been convincing or he would never have accepted it. He was a harsh man, but a just one. You must not continue to let that long-ago affair trouble you, my dear. There is nothing you can do, although I completely understand your desire to vindicate your parents."

Sarah felt the general was impatient with her insistence on continuing the probing conversation, so thanking him for his willingness to discuss the matter, she bade him good-bye. He seemed eager to leave. To him, too, the interview must have been disturbing, if he were such a friend of her father. Sarah felt despair overcome her. Would she never discover who had betrayed her father and caused the termination not only of his brilliant career, but of his very life? He might have died in battle but certainly he would not have exposed himself recklessly to danger if he had not been desperate. His accuser was his murderer and Sarah for the first time wondered if the villain had not desired such an outcome. What could have been his motive?

Suddenly Sarah recalled Lucien's explanation of the Ravensham family. Although, when her father had left for America, his elder brother was still alive and there was seemingly little chance of her father's inheriting the title, might that slim possibility have provided a motive? Sarah hesitated to suspect her Uncle Ronald. She did not like his aloof harsh air, but she could not imagine that he hated his brother so deeply that he would arrange such a vile deception. No doubt her uncle was ambitious, but did he desire the title so fervently that he would arrange to betray his own brother? And was he in a position to do so? Sarah shuddered. She might not admire her uncle but she could not accept that he would behave so.

Perhaps a fellow officer, from jealousy or some other pressing need, was responsible. But the general had assured her that Richard Ravensham had been genuinely admired and respected by his colleagues. She wanted desperately to discuss the situation with Lucien, whose cool dispassionate views would help her come to some resolution. But Lucien was unavailable. Angela had made it quite clear that Sarah's attachment to him must cause him embarrassment and hold her up to ridicule.

How could she attempt, alone, to overturn the verdict that had caused her parents' deaths? The man who laid the charges was probably dead or at least was so protected by the twenty years since the event that he had covered his tracks beyond any discovery.

How would she ever discover the truth when there were no clues to help her and no sympathetic listeners? Sarah realized that the general, for all his tact and kindly manner, did not doubt for a moment the justice of the verdict. And if he, who had been so close to her father, did not doubt, what hope had she? Her only recourse now was to ask her grandmother for her recollection of those accusations, and she dreaded reviving those painful memories. How could she even suggest her Uncle Ronald as the perpetrator? How could she endanger the loving rapport she felt with her grandmother, who had suffered so much already?

Sarah sighed. The burden was almost too much to bear, but a stubborn refusal to accept that past treachery would not be denied. Somehow she would get the truth. She threw off her disquiet and went to reassure her grandmother with a heavy heart, dismissing the annoying feeling that somewhere in the general's conversation was a clue to the mystery she was trying so valiantly to solve.

Chapter Twenty-one

Baffled, an uneasy Sarah could not escape the feeling of impending disaster that loomed over her. Her visit was providing far more problems than she had anticipated, although she knew that the search for the vindication of her father would not be easy. She had not expected the complication of her reaction to Lucien, which, despite her most valiant efforts, continued to plague her. Her suspicions as to the perpetrator of her father's fall from grace centered increasingly on her Uncle Ronald, although she had no evidence to support her feeling. As she observed him more closely, she found him cold, unfeeling, and ambitious. His whole interest concerned his career in the Foreign Office. Certainly his family did not attract his affection, if he were capable of entertaining such an unlikely emotion. He acted as if his wife bored him, and, although he must have had some pride in his son, he did not treat him in a manner that inspired affection or trust in return. Still, cold-bloodedly plotting his brother's disgrace would indicate a callousness of conscience almost beyond contemplation. An unsympathetic and unlikeable character was no reason to accuse him of such diabolical behaviour. She must have evidence, and how was she to ferret out the facts needed to buttress her suspicion? Then, too, there was her grandmother, Lady Ravensham, who had suffered enough from the family's false pride and antique idea of honour. How would she feel if she knew Sarah was delving into the past with the intention of discrediting her only living son.

Oh, dear, Sarah reproved herself. She must not be faint-hearted. Somehow she would prove her father's innocence, and, in the meantime, the dilemma kept her mind from the immediate problem of Lucien and his ambiguous treatment of herself and Angela. Just when she had steeled herself to think of him as a heartless womanizer, a deceiver, and a false friend, he confounded her with his gentle understanding, sympathy, and obvious admiration. She vacillated between hatred and a dangerously opposite emotion. Whether she liked it or not, he had become a major figure in her life, and the only way to dislodge him was to return to Philadelphia, and that she was strangely reluctant to do just yet.

Returning from a morning ride in the park one day, Sarah was astounded to find the hall massed with roses, and Peverel, Lady Ravensham's butler, looking both distracted and disapproving. He lost no time in apprising her of the reason for his dismay at such a turn of events.

"These bouquets have been arriving for you all morning, Miss Sarah, and almost an equal amount of violets for her ladyship. We are running out of vases in which to display them. Here are the cards that have accompanied them." He tendered a pile of stiff white pasteboards, trying not to evidence any interest in the sender, but obviously curious. Sarah, averse to opening the cards under his watchful eye, asked him where her grandmother could be found.

"Her ladyship is in the morning room. Will you be joining her there for chocolate, Miss Sarah?" Peverel asked.

"Yes, of course. Thank you, Peverel." Sarah took one more look at the floral display and escaped to discover in private who could have been so extravagant. Somehow she was not surprised to find across each of the dozen or so cards, "*À bientôt*, De Lisle." Really, what was that cynical libertine thinking of, bombarding her with flowers in this reckless manner? And did the "*À bientôt*," refer to an imminent meeting? She rather feared it did.

"Well, Sarah, you continually surprise me. How in the world did you ever meet a man like Theron De Lisle?" Her grandmother seemed more amused than shocked at this turn of events, when Sarah had kissed her good morning and shown her De Lisle's calling card.

"Well, it is a peculiar story, Grandmother, and not entirely to my credit, I am afraid." Sarah related the circumstances of her heedless entrance into De Lisle's chamber at the Plymouth inn.

"He wants to call upon you here and very properly asks my permission, reminding me of the friendship that existed between me and his own grandmother. Actually, I had quite a fondness for him when he was younger. I know his reputation is disreputable, but he might have been expected to pursue such a ramshackle life, considering the tragedy of his parents, poor boy." Her grandmother never ceased to surprise her with her tolerance of human transgressions. According to Lucien, Theron De Lisle was everything despicable, a deep-dyed sinner incapable of redemption, but obviously her grandmother did not share this view.

"But I understand from Lucien that he is beyond the pale, not accepted in any proper drawing room, and a menace to properly reared females?" Sarah queried lightly.

"Yes, well, Lucien may have some reason for expressing himself so strongly, but I cannot totally agree. No matter how appalling Theron's actions, there are very few hostesses who would turn him from the door, for he is wealthy beyond belief, his title an old and respected one, and he is a bachelor. If any of the season's mothers thought he could be brought up to scratch in the marriage stakes, they would receive him in a minute. It has been *his* decision to shun polite society for more notorious company. He was a nice and lovable young boy, who adored his flighty mother, one of the beauties of her day. She had been married off in her first season by her avaricious parents to De Lisle, some twenty years her senior— not a happy union. Then, when Theron was at Eton, she ran away with a young guardsman and they were killed when their carriage overturned on the way to Dover. Theron's father took out his anger and humiliation on the boy. A rather dreadful legacy for Theron, who in his own unhappiness got up to every wild caper, was expelled from Eton, denied a commission in the army, which might have helped him, and was rejected by his childhood sweetheart, who made a more advantageous marriage. In those days the De Lisles were not as wealthy as he is today, a fortune made at the gaming tables, I believe. My husband, of course, would never allow him in the house, but I have always had a soft spot for the boy."

"Yes, I can quite see how he would behave recklessly. London society is quick to condemn, the sin is being discovered, and discretion can mask the most despicable behaviour as long as propriety is observed," Sarah agreed a bit bitterly, thinking of her father.

"In his note to me, along with this huge budget of violets, he asks if he may call. I have no doubt the attraction is you, Sarah. What am I to reply?" her grandmother asked.

"Oh, why not," Sarah replied naughtily. "I would rather enjoy cocking a snook at society. And it will certainly annoy Lucien."

"Your relationship with Lucien seems to be very volatile, Sarah. In your effort to score off him, do not be lured into actions that later you might regret. But then, advice in matters of heart from the older generation is never appreciated." She had been observing the several passages at arms between Lucien and Sarah with much interest. Now she saw the colour rise in Sarah's cheeks.

"We're not discussing my heart, and it is not at issue here," Sarah said sharply, annoyed that her grandmother may have noticed her preoccupation with Lucien, a situation she found embarrassing in the extreme.

"Well, we will receive Theron and only hope he does

not provoke any untoward reaction from your various other beaux," Lady Ravensham observed with a twinkle. Sarah suspected she was quite enjoying the prospect of Theron De Lisle shocking her circumspect guests with behaviour unacceptable to society, and in her drawing room, too.

As it turned out, Lord De Lisle was a very pattern card of respectability when he called that afternoon while Lady Ravensham and Sarah were entertaining Captain Parry, Angela, and a few other friends.

Bowing low over Lady Ravensham's hand, Lord De Lisle murmured to her, "This is very kind of you, ma'am. I am sure I owe your charity to your deep friendship for my grandmother, now, alas, no longer with us."

"Yes, I was quite disturbed to hear of Elizabeth's death last year. So many old friends are leaving us. But it was not entirely for her sake, Theron. I am quite curious as to why you should be so anxious to renew contact and go to such lavish lengths. Your bouquets were quite excessive." Lady Ravensham, while thanking him prettily, kept a shrewd eye on his bland face.

"I believed I needed all the persuasive powers possible to gain your approval and acceptance. I have no doubt you are well aware of the reason," he replied, raising one eyebrow in questioning fashion.

"Yes, Theron, but be warned. I will not have you using your wiles on Sarah. She is very dear to me, and her happiness is of the utmost importance. You are not to trifle with her, casting out lures one moment, and then turning away, indifferent to any suffering you may cause," Lady Ravensham said sternly, her

172

normally kindly nature aroused as she delivered her warning.

"I suspect I may be the victim rather than the perpetrator in this instance, dear lady. Be assured. I will do nothing to disturb your ewe lamb," Lord De Lisle replied wryly. "And now I will make my obeisances, if I may." He turned away, to cross the room to Sarah's side where she sat demurely on the ivory brocade settee talking in a desultory manner with Captain Parry. She had been aware of Lord De Lisle's presence since his entrance and in fact could not be unaware of it as Angela and her mother both barely repressed shocked gasps and two or three other ladies of her grandmother's circle seemed equally taken aback.

"Good afternoon, Miss Ravensham." De Lisle looked down at the picture Sarah made in her *eau de Nile* muslin gown designed to highlight the titian glints in her chestnut curls and set off her topaz eyes. "What an enchanting afternoon it is too," he continued suggestively.

"What a surprise to see you here, Lord De Lisle," Sarah responded, an imp of mischief gleaming in her eyes. Then she turned to Captain Parry at her side and added, "Do you know Captain Parry, my lord. Robert, this is Lord De Lisle." She had a great deal of difficulty subduing her laughter as Robert Parry stiffened and bristled, obviously in two minds whether to acknowledge De Lisle or not. Good manners and the knowledge of what he owed his hostess, however, carried the day. "Your servant, sir," he said but made no move to surrender his place by Sarah's side. He seemed determined to protect her from any

173

untoward advances by this libertine, and disapproval was writ all over his honest face. Sarah feared her composure would be finally overset, but De Lisle was more than equal to the occasion, as he would be to most contretemps, Sarah concluded. The three of them talked stiffly for a few moments, and then Robert, unable to outface De Lisle, reluctantly abandoned the struggle and made his way across the room to Lady Ravensham to discover her reaction to this invasion of her drawing room. De Lisle, seizing his advantage, sat down and turned to Sarah.

"I see you are surrounded by admirers and I must make a push to engage your interest before I, in turn, am turfed out of my position," he said suavely, amused at her confusion, for every eye in the room was riveted on them, much to Sarah's embarrassment.

"No doubt you are more than capable of repelling any such attempts," she replied. "Your audacity is only surpassed by your address, my lord. But I am forgetting to thank you for your extravagant gift of flowers. We are quite inundated. You have transformed my grandmother's rooms into a bower."

"No more than you deserve, my dear. Although I welcome your grandmother's kind reception of me, I find this occasion very daunting to conversation with you. May I hope you will allow me to escort you on a ride about the park in my phaeton, perhaps tomorrow, if you are free," De Lisle responded gently, aware of her discomfort at their being the cynosure of all eyes. Since he was so composed, Sarah suspected he found the fact that he was conducting a gentle flirtation in Lady Ravensham's very proper drawing room an amusing diversion. It was a change from his usual haunts, but one in which he was equally at ease. Before she could refuse his invitation—which she had every intention of doing, not wanting to become involved with this dangerous lord—their tête-à-tête was interrupted by a steely voice.

"I do not think Miss Ravensham would find an afternoon in your company to her taste, my lord." Lucien Valentine glared at the two seated on the sofa.

"Oh, good afternoon, Lucien. Are you acquainted with Lord De Lisle," Sarah said blithely, ignoring Lucien's angry gaze. De Lisle, looking over his adversary, continued to appear amused, but beneath that bland manner Sarah sensed antagonism, an emotion she was inclined to share. How dare Lucien take that proprietary air, when his responsibilities lay elsewhere. Why wasn't he attending to Angela?

"Yes, I know De Lisle, and I know he is not a fit person to be received in your grandmother's drawing room or for you to know," replied Lucien, his fury overcoming his good manners. For a moment Sarah actually feared the men would come to cuffs right before her, but, if Lucien had lost his temper, De Lisle was too old a hand to put himself at such a disadvantage.

"I really feel that is Lady Ravensham's decision, Valentine. And as she has seen fit to welcome me, I cannot see that it is your business to interfere. Is there some reason that Miss Ravensham should be guided by your notions of behaviour?" he challenged, a nasty look in his eye.

Before Lucien could reply and cause the scandal Sarah feared was brewing, she intervened, feeling rather like a bone fought over by two snarling dogs.

"I really do not see what business it is of yours, Lucien. You take too much upon yourself," she reproved, flushed and irritated to be the center of dispute. Her displeasure did not seem to touch Lucien who, determined to oust De Lisle, barely glanced at her.

"Good afternoon, Lucien." Angela suddenly joined in. "What are you about, standing here glaring in that ferocious way. Not the conduct my grandmother favours, I fear." And, tucking her hand proprietarily in Lucien's arm, she smiled sunnily at the trio as if to say "come children, enough of this, remember your manners."

Lucien had no recourse but to greet her politely, and Sarah to make the introduction of Lord De Lisle to her cousin. Sarah heartily wished the whole company would disappear and vowed she could not decide whom she most wished to perdition, Lord De Lisle, Lucien, or her cousin. But Angela's interference had cooled both gentlemen's tempers, and she succeeded in luring Lucien away from what would have undoubtedly been a most scandalous confrontation.

Sarah turned to De Lisle, who had a smile of contempt on his face, and said crossly, "My lord, I feel you enjoyed that, but let me tell you I do not like being the object of such attention. You have seriously embarrassed me."

"Please accept my apologies, if that is true, and let me atone for it by escorting you and your grandmother to the theatre one evening if you will not oblige me with a tool about the park. I abjectly crave your good opinion, Sarah," De Lisle pleaded with every evidence of sincerity, and then spoiled the effect by smiling devilishly and continuing in the same even tone, "I fancy your grandmother would not be best pleased to learn of our initial encounter, nor would the very noble Colonel Valentine, I vow."

Sarah gasped at his effrontery, "Are you blackmailing me, my lord?"

"Alas, I hope I will not be forced to descend to such depths in order to secure your company, my dear," he acknowledged wryly, but Sarah felt he would have no such compunction.

Outrageous as his suggestion was, Sarah could not help but be flattered at his efforts to persuade her into accepting his invitation—which naturally she would not do. Despite his threats, his cynicism, and the world-weary air he displayed, she did not believe for one moment that he would betray her. Actually, though, Lord De Lisle might serve her purposes well—to annoy Lucien. A libertine and a rake De Lisle might be, but he did have a certain fascination, and she rather enjoyed the flurry his arrival had caused among the starched and hypocritical beau monde that condemned him. She was loath to admit her motive, but De Lisle's pursuit of her would irritate Lucien. It was time that arrogant officer learned she was not the simple little fool he thought her, content merely to follow his orders and grateful for any casual and insulting favours while he paid serious court to her cousin.

Chapter Twenty-two

Her resolutions were put to the test the very next day when Lucien Valentine arrived and took her to task for flirting with the marquis. She did not appreciate being raked down, especially in front of her cousin, Angela, who was clinging to his arm. This last did nothing to soothe Sarah's temper. It was obvious that Lucien believed the very worst of her, and, despite her grandmother's attempt to soothe the atmosphere, they came to daggers drawn immediately.

"Really, ma'am, you cannot allow Sarah to be seen around town with De Lisle," Lucien exclaimed furiously to Lady Ravensham. "Any credibility she has gained will be ruined by the association with a man of his reputation—all of which is deserved I might add."

"I feel you are a mite harsh, Lucien," Lady Ravensham reproved, rather amused by Lucien's black expression. "Theron's grandmother was a bosom bow of mine, and I am convinced that he intends no insult to Sarah. If he is prepared to mend his ways and reenter society, we must not reject him. He has done all that was proper."

"Really, Grandmother, you cannot believe Lord De Lisle is acceptable. Sarah's credit would be quite overset if she spent time in his company," Angela contributed, further infuriating Sarah, who was now up in the boughs, whatever initial good sense she had intended to apply toward the problem.

"I wish you would stop discussing me as if I were not here," she said hotly. "I am not a member of the nursery set, and I am quite capable of deciding whom I should see." Her cheeks flushed and her hands clenched with the effort of hanging onto her control.

Lucien gave her an icy look. "Well, my girl, if you are going to act like a child, you must expect to be treated like one. You know little about De Lisle, but you should have sense enough to realize he would ruin you if given the opportunity. Your grandmother's protection would avail you nothing, then."

Before she could round on him and tell him just what she thought of his own duplicity in making up to her while he was all but engaged to Angela, Peverel appeared at the drawing room door and in a sepulchral tone announced, "Lord De Lisle."

Theron marched into the drawing room on his heels, very fashionably attired in smooth cream kersey britches, gleaming top boots, and a midnight-blue coat styled by Weston's master hand. He raised a questioning eyebrow at the trio facing him, all of them obviously aroused by some heated emotion.

"Good afternoon, Lady Ravensham, Miss Ravensham, Colonel Valentine, and Sarah," he greeted them suavely, content to ignore the charged atmosphere.

"What are you doing here, De Lisle?" Lucien demanded coldly.

Theron De Lisle's dark eyebrows rose derisively. "I don't believe I am accountable to you for my actions, Valentine, but, since I am in charity with the world today, I will tell you I have come to escort Sarah on a ride about the park."

If Sarah's senses had not been in such a turbulent state, she would have been amused at both Lucien and Angela's reaction, but she was so irritated with the two of them, she rushed heedlessly ahead into the very situation she had previously determined to avoid.

"How kind of you, Lord De Lisle, I would be delighted. If that is all right with you, Grandmother," she turned belatedly to Lady Ravensham. Inwardly, she was delighted to have the opportunity to score off Lucien and get away from the hateful sight of her cousin and the colonel.

"Of course, my dear," Lady Ravensham approved, a twinkle in her eye. "It is a lovely day. Enjoy yourself."

"Then if you will excuse me, Lord De Lisle, I will just go put on my bonnet." Sarah smiled more provocatively than was wise at her escort and left the room. For a moment Lady Ravensham feared for the decorum of her drawing room, but engrained politeness came to both gentlemen's rescue and the talk turned to less dangerous topics. Sarah returned in a trice, her chestnut curls peeping out deliciously from a froth of straw and green ribbons, and the two departed with any more ado.

Behind them they left a bewildered trio. Lucien, still at the mercy of his anger and disgust, could barely observe the conventions of polite behaviour. Angela, annoyed at his obvious interest in Sarah's reputation, wanted to rail against her cousin but experience told her that gentlemen disliked females who ripped one another up. She must present a picture of sorrowful charity at her cousin's misguided attitude. Fueling her jealousy further was the knowledge that De Lisle had hardly given her a glance, a treatment to which she was not accustomed from any man. Lady Ravensham, on her part, was convinced that Lucien's loss of control sprang from motives she was eager to encourage, and she mused to herself that events were shaping up nicely. However, she kept her suspicions to herself and chatted amicably to the pair for the remainder of their short visit.

The couple in question had no doubt that their abrupt departure was providing plenty of speculation in Lady Ravensham's drawing room. And in the park, too. For at this hour of the afternoon most of the ton took the air, to see and be seen. Ignoring the avid looks and craning necks, De Lisle gave an expert flick to his reins, keeping the spirited pair of matched greys in good order, and looked at Sarah with a quizzical eye.

"I think the honorable colonel wanted to plant me a facer, and, if the scene had been elsewhere, I would obviously have had to parry some blows. Perhaps he will call me out, yet," he remarked wryly.

"Do not call him the 'honorable colonel.' He is far from that. The argumentative, arrogant busybody. He takes entirely too much upon himself," Sarah fumed, still filled with righteous indignation.

"Oh, I don't know. I believe I understand and almost sympathize with the fellow," De Lisle returned. "He is jealous, my dear, of anyone supplanting him in your affections. And does he have cause, I wonder?" He spoke lightly but his dark eyes searched hers, attempting to breach the defences she had raised.

"That's ridiculous. I am not the object of his affections. He is just being critical and aggravating, because he believes I do not know how to conduct myself, that I am a naive colonial. He wants me to behave like my cousin, Angela." Sarah was surprised to find herself confiding in Theron De Lisle.

"I can't see why. A very unexceptional, boring female, in my opinion," he soothed. Sarah, pleased with this but realizing how mean-spirited she was, decided to turn the conversation by querying De Lisle's own motives.

"And just why are you showing me this attention, my lord. I am not your usual style, I suspect. Are you trying to reform?" Sarah asked mischievously.

"Perhaps. Quite time I did, don't you think, and what better companion for my reformation," he replied, not one whit discomforted. "I am sure to do a good deed and bring me back into respectability challenges you, Sarah."

"I doubt that you will ever be respectable, my lord," she bantered. "But of course, I am quite willing to make you my charity of the week." They continued on their way, chatting easily, impervious to the stares and speculation of the fashionable throngs who found in the libertine De Lisle and the innocent young colonial an enthralling item of gossip.

Theron De Lisle's continued pursuit of Sarah remained the *on dit* of the moment, and more than a few eyebrows were raised at his attentions to a female so out of the way of the charmers who normally caught his eye. Granted the audacious American was a novelty, more than attractive with a frank and engaging air, so removed from the blasé beauties, affected and boring in their sameness. Provocative and out of the ordinary Sarah Ravensham might be, but she was too young, too respectable, and too inexperienced to engage De Lisle for long. Such was the opinion of the more knowledgeable arbiters of the ton. Certainly he would not offer her marriage, even though wagers were laid down in White's betting book as to that possibility, and even De Lisle, accomplished seducer that he was, could not tender Lady Ravensham's granddaughter carte blanche. Yet no outrageous behaviour was beyond him.

The ton watched, considerably entertained by the spectacle of a famous rake tempering his actions to the demands of propriety. Ambitious and impecunious parents ground their teeth in rage at the thought of Sarah carrying off such a prize. Surely, if he were hanging out for a wife, their own daughters should be the object of his regard. For years his name had been anathema in polite circles, but, if he was indeed ready to renounce his former habits, there were many who would welcome him into their ranks, all past transgressions forgiven. His ancient title, his large rent roll, and his handsome countenance appealed to not a few of the season's incomparables but they sighed after him in vain.

Several of De Lisle's cronies were tempted to ask him what he really intended toward Sarah, but a tentative question in Brooks one evening after several bottles of wine had been broached brought a steely snub, and it would be a brave man who ventured further. De Lisle had five times bested his man in a duel with both pistols and rapiers and not many were eager to meet him in the field.

Lucien Valentine was the exception, but within a day of the confrontation in Lady Ravensham's drawing room, he was called out of town on those mysterious military duties that Angela found so vexing, and even Lucien at times would have liked to ignore. This was one of the times, but he had no choice but to follow the trail of a French provocateur to Devon, where the *émigré* was suspected of smuggling messages to his countrymen from a remote seaside hamlet.

Sarah found De Lisle's company a stimulating distraction from the several problems that confronted her. She suspected that Lucien's absence meant he had washed his hands of her. Although she at one time had devoutly hoped for this circumstance, now she felt strangely unhappy at his desertion. Angela, taking advantage of the opportunity, was quick to apprise Sarah of the reason for Lucien's disappearance from the scene. Naturally, she implied, she was in his confidence and he had told her why he left London, which in reality she had learned from her father.

The cousins continued to see more of one another than either wished, but family circumstances enforced this intimacy, for neither wanted to upset Lady Ravensham. In her presence they both behaved if not with enthusiasm, then with tempered good will. Sarah treated her cousin kindly because she disliked rancour and because she did not want her grandmother disturbed by family animosity. Angela's motives were less charitable and more selfish.

Sarah had yet another reason for spending time with her cousin. It enabled her to learn more about her Uncle Ronald, whom she still suspected of planning her father's downfall but she had not discovered any evidence to buttress this belief. If only she could discuss her fears with Lucien. Despite his treatment of her, she trusted him in matters not connected with affairs of the heart. For a time she thought of confiding in De Lisle, but some unexplained emotion prevented her. She tried to corner General Apsley-Gower for more confidences, but he refused to take her investigation seriously, implying she was wasting her time following a will-o'-the-wisp, and might be laying up more tragedy for herself and her grandmother.

All in all, the weeks following her interview with him, despite De Lisle's distracting attentions, were not satisfactory ones. Sarah could not decide how now to approach her mission, but soon new evidence would appear to alter her indecisive mood and spur her into action.

Chapter Twenty-three

Lady Ravensham, who had followed Theron De Lisle's pursuit of Sarah with tolerance, even amusement, now began to be worried. Fond as she was of the scapegrace lord, he was not her choice of a husband for Sarah. From the time of her granddaughter's arrival she had wished that Sarah might find a young man with whom she could settle down, make her home in England, and not be parted from her grandmother. Lady Ravensham admitted her desire was a selfish one, but Sarah had shown no evidence of leaving her heart behind her in Philadelphia so there was reason to suppose she might make her choice in the land of her ancestors and thus remain within Lady Ravensham's orbit.

Almost from the first day of her visit the dowager had believed Sarah's choice might settle on Lucien, which Lady Ravensham would have endorsed enthusiastically. Lucien, too, had seemed more than attracted to the young American despite their heated passages at arms. Lately, however, Lady Ravensham had observed a cooling-off between the two. Sarah did not confide in her grandmother, but obviously a serious quarrel had occurred, greater than the normal sparring that each had enjoyed and that had not really disturbed Lady Ravensham.

Lucien, dear boy that he was, had a tendency to be autocratic, a quality Sarah would find offensive, and he needed a set-down. What he did not need was some meek submissive wife who would obey him blindly, nor could he find happiness with a simpering town miss whose world consisted of balls, fashions, and gossip. Sarah would make him an ideal wife, and he would be the perfect husband for her granddaughter, but now her hopes seemed unlikely to be realized. Lucien had disappeared, off on some military mission at the worst possible moment, when he should be on hand to ward off the persistent attentions of De Lisle.

Unlike many of the beau monde Lady Ravensham did not believe De Lisle had designs on Sarah's virtue—but he might win her heart, and she doubted if he intended to offer her granddaughter marriage. Rather Sarah provided amusement, a chance to thumb his nose at the society that he had rejected. In this she might be doing him an injustice, but in any case she worried. Sarah might suffer, and this she must try to prevent. She really believed her granddaughter had too much sense to fall for Theron's ploys, although he had a definite attraction—especially as Lucien was behaving in such a stupid fashion. Lady Ravensham hesitated to question her granddaughter, so, although distressed, she watched the affair while keeping her own counsel.

The season was now in full swing with gaiety of every description distracting Sarah from the several problems that concerned her. If she had known of her grandmother's agitation over her friendship with Theron De Lisle, she would have reassured her, but the thought never occurred to her. She did not take him seriously, but her sensibilities, wounded by Lucien's defection, were soothed by De Lisle's flattering attentions. As a companion he proved amusing, light-hearted, and devoted, a dangerous combination of qualities. Very tempting also was becoming the object of the ton's curiosity and an incomparable herself that quite put Angela in the shade. Sarah was human enough to enjoy her cousin's irritation at her own popularity, although she had no illusions about the cause for it.

This evening should prove entertaining, for the Ravenshams were attending the Devonshires' ball. Lady Ravensham did not really approve of the duke and duchess who lived in great amiability with each other and Lady Elizabeth Foster, an outrageous *ménage à trois*, which no longer shocked any but the strictest doyennes of society. No doubt the Devonshires were scandalous, but they gave bang-up entertainments and few refused their invitations because of scruples over their morality. Lady Ravensham had tactfully told Sarah of her own objections to the trio, but admitted they were exceptional hosts and their balls not be missed for they were top-of-the-tree entertainments.

Sarah found the situation all of a one with her views

of the hypocrisy of London society, but realized astutely that she could only make herself ridiculous by objecting to a life style she would never embrace for herself. Sarah smiled ruefully when she found herself rationalizing her position. Her grandfather would certainly take her to task, but then he would not want her to offend Lady Ravensham's feelings. There was little danger of sensible Sarah adopting these loose standards for her own. He had trained her too well.

Devonshire House was in full fete for the evening, every window of the imposing mansion blazed with light, the courtyard off Piccadilly crammed with carriages inching their way up to the imposing entrance. The Ravenshams, who had come in one carriage, crowding the ladies rather badly, stepped out into the magnificent throng and slowly progressed up the stairway to where the duke and duchess were receiving guests.

Until she saw the duchess, Sarah had been quite pleased with her own appearance. She wore a gown of gold tissue over white satin highlighted by the topaz and diamond necklace her grandmother had insisted she wear. But Georginia, Duchess of Devonshire, although now past her fortieth birthday, outshone all her guests in a lavish dress of gossamer blue silk and lace and aglow with the spectacular Devonshire diamonds. Her delicate features of rare translucent beauty showed little effect of the passage of time, but Sarah noticed that the speedwell-blue eyes glowed with a feverish light and darted back and forth while her hands clutched at one with a frantic nervousness.

Poor lady, Sarah mused as she passed beyond the reception line into the huge ballroom. She had heard her gambling debts were excessive and that the duke had recently paid more than £60,000 to rescue her from queer street. Could the gambling be her respite from the strange relationship imposed upon her by the constant presence of Lady Elizabeth Foster? Sarah sighed over the foibles of the great peers of English society. Their wealth and imposing houses, jewels and exalted position did not assure them happiness.

Both Sarah and Angela were surrounded on their entrance into the ballroom. Sarah had now become the rage, the object of every young buck's desire, brought into fashion by her apparent subjection of Theron De Lisle. Angela, her usual impeccable self in a dazzling white gown studded with crystals and pearls, her blond hair dressed in a complicated style *à la Grecque*, frowned momentarily as she saw Sarah's coterie of beaux exceed her own, but she quickly erased the frown. No one must believe she did not enjoy her cousin's success. Soon De Lisle had elbowed the importuning suitors from Sarah's side and swept her away for the first country dance of the evening.

Sarah, although not unaccustomed to the glittering throng and frenetic pace of these great balls, found this evening even more crowded and lavish than usual. Few great houses were decorated with the style of Devonshire House, and few could hold the hundreds of guests now disporting themselves under the lustrous Venetian chandeliers, whose myriad candles reflected the sumptuous jewels, the silks and satins of the fashionable dancers as they glided through the intricacies of the dance. As Sarah whirled from one partner's arms to another's, she could barely absorb the picture of all this magnificence. After several dances she pleaded a respite and, sending one of her cavaliers for a cooling drink, sat down by her grandmother's side on one of the delicate gold French chairs lining the silk-damask-covered walls.

"Enjoying yourself, my dear, I am glad to see. And wise, too, not to dance more than twice with Theron. You must not offend the chaperones, you know," her grandmother advised kindly.

"So many silly rules, Grandmother. Do you really think my virtue will be damaged if I dance three or four times with Lord De Lisle in full view of the company?" Sarah scoffed.

"No, I don't, Sarah, but it does not to serve to rebel against standards of conduct, no matter how foolish they appear," Lady Ravensham demurred. "You would be shunned and gossiped about, and I should dislike that, if you would not be concerned yourself."

"Never fear, Grandmother. I will behave. But what a crush! I am exhausted by all this glittering assembly. The Season is more tiring than anything imaginable." Sarah watched the dancers, spying Moira Amberly stepping through the intricacies of a gavotte with her Uncle Ronald. How surprising to see them together. Sarah had momentarily forgotten introducing the two at her grandmother's rout some weeks ago. Had Mrs. Amberly followed up on that initial meeting and why had Sarah not been aware of it?

"I did not realize that Mrs. Amberly would be here, Grandmother, and isn't it odd that she is dancing with Uncle Ronald?"

"I believe she and your Aunt Margaret have become quite intimate in the past few weeks," Lady Ravensham replied. "I can't understand it myself, for they would seem to have little in common."

Sarah raised her eyebrows at her grandmother's ingenuous answer. She suspected that Moira Amberly had cultivated Aunt Margaret for reasons that had nothing to do with that colourless woman's appeal. Sarah frowned, realizing that she had discounted Mrs. Amberly as merely a socially ambitious woman with a shallow grasping character. Perhaps she had underestimated her. She would have to keep a more careful eye on her erstwhile chaperone.

After her brief rest Sarah was again involved in the gaiety, her hand solicited for every dance. She welcomed De Lisle's escort to the supper room with relief. Her feet in their delicate satin slippers were aching and she yearned to settled down for a while and rest. The menu was as lavish as the rest of the entertainment, lobster patties, plover and quail eggs, turbot, York ham, spun-sugar delights, and a profusion of jellies, a truly rich and indigestible feast. Sarah often wondered how much of such prodigal display was discarded, extravagantly thrown aside, while on London's mean streets scores of women and children went to bed hungry. Such revolutionary ideas did not provide appealing table talk at ton parties, Sarah had discovered. She could say what she thought to De Lisle, however, and did so as they settled down at a small table in the supper room.

"Do you ever wonder, my lord, at what happens to all the food that is not eaten after these entertainments?" Sarah asked.

"No, I cannot say I have ever concerned myself with kitchen politics. No doubt the scullery maids, cooks, and waiters carry it home to their families," he replied, amused as usual by the drift of Sarah's conversation. She continually surprised him. What English miss would worry about leftover food? Only this rare republican American.

"I certainly hope so, or perhaps the poor will benefit. I worry a great deal about the poverty and filth I see in London's meaner districts. We have none of this in Philadelphia," she said proudly.

"You are a very loyal revolutionary, Sarah. I quite commend your defence of America's more equitable social distinctions, but surely you have the poor there as well. I understand the poor are always with us," he replied sardonically in his usual cynical style, which he did more to stir Sarah into argument than because he cared one way or another. Although Sarah was not unaware of his motives, her passionate concern would not be stifled.

"Theron, you deliberately try to arouse my indignation," she exclaimed. "Well, I will not disappoint you. I find the aristocrats of London arrogantly indifferent to the needs of the mass of the citizenry, a shocking state of affairs in a wealthy country to let any of its people go hungry while others suffer from an over-

193

abundance."

He flicked a speck of dirt from his dark evening coat. "So fatiguing, my dear, all this passion to do good. You must guard yourself against the tendency for reform. It's not attractive to your beaux, you know."

"Since I do not consider you a beau, and I do not believe you are as unconcerned as you appear, I will ignore that, Theron," she retorted, undismayed by his attitude.

"I am truly wounded that you do not consider me a devoted courtier when I have gone to some pains to give that impression. We must pursue this further as it is far more interesting than Continental politics. You are such a fierce little colonial, I surmise you would like to see the whole assembly here carried away to Madame Guillotine. All this impassioned republicanism is not very encouraging to dalliance, I fear," he teased.

Sarah wrinkled her nose at him. "Don't be ridiculous. I think the excesses of the French deplorable, but I do wish members of the aristocracy here, who have so much, would spare a thought and a groat for those less fortunate. I suppose you are not all completely steeped in the selfish round of pleasure, which seems to be your chief preoccupation, but you certainly do not seem to be concerned with the pitable condition of the poor."

"Come, stop glaring at me so angrily. The dowagers will think I have made an improper suggestion to you, and then we will both be in your grandmother's bad graces. Let us walk in the garden and you can finish ripping me up in private." Theron smiled at her, daring her to brave the stares of the company and leave the ballroom with him. Sarah, always quick to accept a challenge and eager to continue their discussion, took his arm, and they sauntered from the supper room, ignoring the curious and disapproving glances that followed them.

Chapter Twenty-four

The balmy May evening had lured other couples from the overheated ballroom, and Sarah noticed many guests strolling casually along the formal pathways, edged with massive shrubbery. She was determined to discover if Theron De Lisle was more than the frivolous creature he seemed, as she had long suspected. He was a master at masking his feelings and playing the ton's game of the bored and blasé man of the world. Disillusionment and rejection had pushed him into portraying the cynical libertine who had tasted all of life's temptations, but Sarah believed this was but a pose to protect himself from further pain. In this analysis she was more astute than she knew. Theron De Lisle had discovered in Sarah a surprisingly fresh and honest companion who threatened to shatter the defences he had so carefully built up through the years. He was rather irritated that she did not take his attentions seriously. He did not know exactly how he felt about her, but he wanted her trust and her admiration, and he feared he had neither.

He steered her to a wrought-iron bench, cleverly

placed to offer some privacy behind a huge privet hedge, and indicated that they might sit and relax for a few moments. Sarah, distracted by the arguments she had been pursuing with him, had forgotten appearances, the construction that would be placed on her leaving the ballroom with such a partner by many of the company. Suddenly proprieties were remembered.

"Really, my lord, we must return. My partners will think badly of me, cutting their promised dances in this rude fashion," she objected, preparing to rise and return to the brightly lit salon. She had been foolish to come into the garden with De Lisle.

"Not so fast, my girl. I have been trying to lure you into just such a situation for days, and well you know it," De Lisle said, rising and restraining her from moving away. Before she could demur she found herself in his arms and enduring his kiss. Experienced and far too clever to force a response, De Lisle's lips were gentle and persuasive. Sarah found the kiss in no way repulsive, but neither did it stir her blood and inspire her to return it with ardour. She did not struggle but remained passive within his arms, and, recognizing her lack of warmth, he soon released her, saying wryly, "Are you going to slap my face and tell me what a cad I am now, Sarah. I have given you the perfect opportunity."

"Don't be foolish, my lord. I only regret I have given you the impression that I would welcome your kisses. The fault is equally mine," she answered coolly, patting her hair composedly.

"A well-deserved set-down, Sarah! You are certainly wounding to my consequence. I must study to make you take me in less dislike. Come let us return to the ballroom. I can see that I have blotted my copybook enough for one evening," he responded, rather annoyed at her nonchalant reception of his advances, accustomed as he was to quite a different response from the ladies.

"You go ahead, my lord. I believe I will stay here for a moment and enjoy the evening while I recover from your advances," Sarah said, smiling to take the sting from her words. He bowed and walked off, his air of wounded pride amusing Sarah. He probably had rarely met with such indifference to his faultless technique. Sarah did not believe he had been inspired by any real desire, certainly not by love, and she wondered why he had kissed her. No doubt he could not resist the occasion to practice his skills. How off-putting and hurtful to be so apathetically received.

Sarah rather enjoyed sparring with Theron De Lisle and was human enough to enjoy the stir his attentions had evoked, but his was not a character that would ever attract her. His longtime career of self-indulgence and loose living did not disgust her as much as his complete disinterest in aught but his own desires. She had little sympathy with his world-weary pose and little faith that his reentrance into society heralded a real reform of his temperament. Granted he had a devilish attraction, a wicked sense of humor, an ability to see through cant and hypocrisy, but Theron De Lisle must look elsewhere for a gullible female to lure within his net, whatever his intentions, honourable or not.

Sarah dismissed the intriguing marquis quite quickly from her thoughts, which would have caused him considered annoyance if he had been aware of it. She could not help but compare him to Lucien, who had wrung a far different response from her, and the remembrance of those embraces threatened her composure. She must not indulge in useless dreams about the colonel, for she had no patience with females who yearned after unattainable men. Her idle musings were suddenly interrupted by voices drifting into her consciousness from the other side of the high hedge. Surely the man's tone was familiar and then, hearing more, she quickly came alert.

"My dear Mrs. Amberly, I am honoured that you wish to confide in me, but may I suggest the proper object of your confidences should be your husband?" The terse, austere tones of Ronald Ravensham were unmistakable. Sarah could hardly believe what she was hearing. Why were Moira Amberly and her uncle rendezvousing in the Devonshire gardens?

"But alas, my husband is thousands of miles away, and I must seek the advice of a strong and decisive man who can advise me. We poor females are so unaccustomed to making decisions for ourselves. Will you not help me?" Mrs. Amberly's cooing voice brought a *moue* of disgust to Sarah's face, but she held her breath to hear more.

"My dear Mrs. Amberly, I can only advise you to return to the country, rejoin your children, whom I am sure miss your guiding hand, and try to forget about the war. I promise you that His Majesty's government has matters well in hand and you must not be disturbed by all this careless talk of invasion," Lord Ronald replied curtly. He was not at all impressed by his companion's flattery, Sarah thought and was pleased to learn he had the good sense to see through Mrs. Amberly's wiles. Why was that woman trying to lure him into indiscreet talk? Sarah had no compunction about eavesdropping on this strange conversation, but her uncle evidently had had enough.

"If you have recovered from your temporary indisposition, Mrs. Amberly, let us return to the ballroom," he said impatiently. "Lady Margaret will be looking for me. Perhaps, if you are still feeling unwell, I can summon your escort to see you home."

Sarah smiled to herself as she heard the couple walk away. Her erstwhile chaperone had received little change from Uncle Ronald, not a man to succumb to the seductive promises of any woman. Whatever was Mrs. Amberly's motive? Surely she was not stupid enough to think Lord Ravensham could be persuaded to reveal state secrets by appealing to his senses. Really, that woman was becoming a nuisance, Sarah thought in disgust, parlaying her slight acquaintance with the Ravenshams into a closer relationship and ignoring their obvious disinclination to accept her tenders of friendship. That could only mean she had some ulterior reason.

Sarah rose to her feet, still considering what Mrs. Amberly's words had meant, but, coming to no conclusion, she wandered back to the ballroom. Really, the devious motives of much of the beau monde was beyond her. Lucien, De Lisle, Uncle Ronald, Angela—all of them playing games, none of them what they seemed, masking their real feelings and intentions. She was weary of the whole lot, and, if it were not for an instinctive sense that somehow she was approaching the solution of her father's betrayal, she would have boarded the next packet back to America.

Chapter Twenty-five

If Sarah was confused and aggravated by the maze of deceit and mystery that she was struggling to penetrate, her own behavior was causing equal dismay in the hearts and minds of both her grandmother and Lucien Valentine. While Lucien had been absent from London on a special intelligence mission in Devon, he had spent more time thinking about Sarah's sudden aloofness than the matter at hand. Of course, he had no idea that Angela had put a spoke in his wheel with her artless disclosures to her cousin. He would have been gratified to learn that Sarah had reacted with jealousy to Angela's possessiveness, but such a suspicion never crossed his mind. He concluded ruefully that he had handled the hotheaded Sarah badly.

Perhaps he had been too confident that he could override her prejudice against Englishmen and win her regard. She had more than won his, and he reluctantly admitted to himself that he was jealous of De Lisle and furious that she had disregarded his own warnings about continuing that relationship. He should have learned by now that the least opposition set her back up and made her determined to thwart him on all suits, and he in turn reacted like a spoilt and callow youth. Well, he would just have to change his tactics if he wished to bring her around, and he knew, however many disclaimers he made to himself, this was exactly what he wanted.

As for his mission in Devon, he learned what might have been the reason for De Lisle's visit to Plymouth. He had no real proof, but he was satisfied in his own mind and thought he could lay enough doubt before his superiors to satisfy them that De Lisle merited closer investigation. Valentine astutely surmised that the rakish lord's sudden desire to be reinstated in the society he had so long spurned was motivated by more than a sudden attraction to Sarah or a yearning to reform his licentious ways. Traveling posthaste back to London, Lucien made up his mind that Theron De Lisle posed a threat not only to Sarah's future but to the country's security, and in neither case must he be allowed to succeed. As Lucien covered the long miles, he prepared his strategy.

In London, Lady Ravensham, too, was making a decision after long hours pondering over her beloved granddaughter's future. Sarah possessed a pride to equal Lucien's and no doubt pride had contributed heavily to their misunderstanding. However, she believed there might be other factors contributing to this recent estrangement. Lady Ravensham may have appeared wrapped up in her sorrow and submissive to her husband, but long experience of hiding her thoughts while watching those around her had made her a shrewd if kindly observer of human nature.

Sarah's father, Richard, with his winning, outgoing

personality, his charm, and his physical courage, had always been her favorite of her three sons, and she had never ceased to mourn his death or the circumstances surrounding it. Sarah, a delight in herself, reminded Lady Ravensham of Richard in so many ways, and she was determined that her granddaughter would not suffer from society's judgments nor be forced into a marriage that might bring her unhappiness. Not that Sarah would take kindly to interference in matters of the heart. Obviously she would make her own decision about a husband, and her choice might not be Lucien. Nor would it be De Lisle, Lady Ravensham hoped. Perhaps, Sarah was adroitly fending off proposals from eligible Englishmen because her real interest was fixed on a young man in Philadelphia. She had shown no evidence of this, never had hovered about waiting anxiously for the post, and the only letters she did receive from America were undoubtedly from her grandfather.

Rather, her whole attention seemed devoted to unraveling the mystery of her father's betrayal, and, although for the moment those efforts had been balked through a lack of evidence, Lady Ravensham did not believe for one moment that Sarah had forgotten what was obviously her chief reason for making this journey. If Lucien had scoffed at her investigations and her passionate belief in her father's innocence, that might explain her anger with him, but somehow Lady Ravensham was convinced he would not be so unfeeling or insensitive. No, she must look elsewhere for the cause of their estrangement, and she rather thought she need look no further than the family circle. If that were the case, she would soon sort it out, she vowed.

Sarah, at her wit's end to know how she must proceed to discover more about her father's imputed treachery, had been brooding over her conversation with General Apsley-Gower. She felt sure there had been a clue in his confidences that she had missed. Certainly he was averse to continuing any discussion about those long-ago days in Philadelphia, and Sarah thought he avoided her, although his manner was always pleasant when they met at various social functions. She shrank from discussing her misgivings with her grandmother because she wished to spare her the pain of recalling those days, but she knew that eventually she must question her.

While she mulled over her next move, weighing her suspicions about her uncle and deciding whether to confide those in her grandmother, Lucien Valentine returned from Devon and called at Park Street, determination in every line of his bearing. He would not be fended off with excuses. Today Sarah would listen to him, and their recent estrangement brought to an end.

Peverel discovered Sarah in the morning room, sitting and dreaming before an open window where the light air of a perfect May morning had distracted her from her brooding. She had been writing to her grandfather, but the letter remained unfinished on the table, as she watched a stubborn robin wrestle with a worm on the green lawn. Dressed in a simple jonquil muslin frock, her hair tied back fetchingly with a matching ribbon, she appeared as carefree and lovely as the morning itself.

"Miss Ravensham, Colonel Valentine has called and is awaiting you in the library," Peverel intoned.

"Lady Ravensham is still resting and suggests that it would be perfectly suitable for you to receive him alone." Sarah smiled at the butler brightly, although she was far from happy to hear his news, and agreed to join Colonel Valentine in the library. Now what could Lucien want? Surely, having been away from the social scene for several days, he should be dancing attendance on Angela and repulse his many rivals, who, encouraged by Angela, had no doubt taken advantage of his absence to press their suits. Playing games again, Sarah thought angrily, and she decided to give the arrogant colonel a set-down.

Lucien eyed her warily as she entered the library. She looked very alluring, but the light in her topaz eyes and the set of her chin did not auger well.

"Good morning, Sarah. I hurried around to see you immediately upon my arrival in town, for I have quite a budget of news for you. Besides, I thought you might not have known of my duties calling me away for a spell, and were wondering what was responsible for my deserting you." He spoke carefully, aware that her reception of him veered on the chilly side.

"Angela told us of your departure," she answered, not meeting his gaze.

"I wonder how she knew. I suppose her father told her," he said cheerfully, relieved to see a softening in Sarah's features. "Now what have you been up to while I have not been at hand to keep you out of trouble?" Lucien inquired lightly.

"*You* keep *me* out of trouble?" Sarah scoffed. "Much more likely to get me into it, I vow." But she could not restrain a slight smile which Lucien did not miss. "Anyway I have been a very pattern card of propriety and, if you don't believe me, ask Grandmother," Sarah said airily, aware of a niggling remembrance of De Lisle's embrace in the Devonshires' garden. Why should she be embarrassed by that? She owed no explanation to Lucien.

"I believe you, Sarah. I know how much you value honesty, one of your most endearing qualities," Lucien said seriously, coming close to her and taking both her hands in his. "Come, let us sit down, for I have an important matter to discuss with you."

For a moment Sarah's heart pounded so hard she thought he must surely hear it. Could he be about to propose? She seated herself on the velvet-covered divan, leaving plenty of room for Lucien to settle beside her. He still held her hands.

"I know you have been quite annoyed with me lately, Sarah, because you think I have been unjust and dictatorial about your friendship with De Lisle. But I now have reason to believe I was correct in my judgment of that lord's reversal in his conduct. I went to Devon to investigate rumours of smuggling near Plymouth, not that the army is too concerned about the odd case or two of French silks and brandy. We leave that to the excisemen, but those same smuggling ships also carry suspect characters from France—not all of them *émigrés* escaping Napoleon's butchers, either. And I found evidence that De Lisle is implicated in this cargo of spies. It does not surprise me, not just because I find the fellow offensive, but because the government has wondered for some time how he supports his extravagant life style. He has already run through one fortune, and his funds must be coming from somewhere." Lucien had put his accusations most carefully, determined not to antagonize Sarah by arrogantly laying down the law about her preference for the marquis and the danger that association could pose.

Whatever Sarah had expected, this revelation did not so much shock her as disappoint her. Carefully she removed her hands from Lucien's warm grasp. He must never suspect what she had for a moment thought he might say. How could she have been so foolish? She lowered her eyes, refusing to meet his gaze. He must never imagine she had expected an avowal of love. Her pride came to her rescue, and she replied calmly, "Of course, I cannot dispute what you say, Lucien. I dislike thinking that Theron would betray his country, and I find it difficult to contemplate. Then, too, I have some experience of false accusations of treachery being laid against innocent men. Theron has been a good friend to me. He has not misled me about his intentions, and I enjoy his company. Naturally I will be influenced by your investigations and would not be so small-minded as to dispute the sincerity of your statements."

Lucien had rather expected Sarah to fly up in the boughs, defend De Lisle, or rail against him for his accusation, even accuse him of jealousy. This cool reception of his news set him aback, and he was nettled by her reference to her father. Would she never put that tragedy behind her? And would she never learn to trust him. He sighed. She was a prickly, maddening female, quick to judge him, and eager to suspect his motives. However, he refused to surrender to the anger that he felt at her reaction.

"I am relieved to see you take this so calmly, Sarah.

Naturally what I have told you is in confidence. The War Office will conduct further investigations. We do not want to falsely accuse anyone, but you must admit that De Lisle is a complex and confusing character, open to suspicion."

"Of course, I shall regard your news as confidential, and I appreciate your telling me. Now, if that is all, I must attend to some errands for Grandmother." Sarah rose, eager to dismiss him, her manner distant and aloof.

Lucien struggled with an overmastering desire to shake some sense into Sarah but restrained himself for really she had given him no cause. If only she would treat him honestly, return to the open, vital girl he had once believed could never indulge in the devious behaviour she was now exhibiting. How could he break through these barriers she had erected between them and find the warm, winning Sarah he had once known?

"I wish I knew what foolish ideas you are harbouring in that lovely head of yours now, Sarah, for I feel you are hiding your real feelings from me. Surely you know that I have your best interests at heart, that I would do nothing to cause you unhappiness." He spoke gravely, trying to hold her gaze with his, but she dropped her eyes, refusing to return his look.

"You are very kind, Lucien, and I am grateful for your concern, but now I must really leave," Sarah answered and, before he could demur, whisked out of the room, leaving him prey to a welter of emotions, chief among them bewilderment at her reception of his news and her apparent unwillingness to endure his company.

He had intended to ask her to go driving with him, but somehow he felt she would have turned down his invitation. All his expectations of breaching her reserve and probing her real feelings had come to naught and he must now study a new approach to win her regard. He left Park Street without more ado, damning all females and particularly this independent colonial who was causing him so much disquiet.

Chapter Twenty-six

Sarah convinced herself that she had not revealed her disappointment to Lucien, pleased that she had accepted his friendly overtures with the proper combination of politeness and indifference. She was loath to admit that his explanation of De Lisle's incongruous behaviour might be correct. If Theron's attentions were flattering, his company amusing, and his kisses pleasant, he did not stir her heart as Lucien was capable of doing. She was honest enough to admit that she would have welcomed a declaration from Lucien, for somehow, despite their passages at arms and antagonism toward the English, he had managed to win her love. There she had confessed it to herself, no matter how she had hidden it from the world. She cared for Lucien Valentine and much good it would do her. He felt nothing but a brotherly regard for her. Angela held his heart and she must just accept that, no matter how bitter that knowledge might be.

Pride came to her rescue once again. She would concentrate on her real mission here and forget Lucien Valentine, Angela, Theron De Lisle, and all the other distractions of London life. Determined to come to grips with the one problem she could control, she marched into her grandmother's boudoir.

"Good morning, Grandmother. I hope you are feeling well this lovely morning," she greeted Lady Ravensham brightly.

"Yes, indeed, Sarah dear. I am just being lazy, which is why I did not dress to receive Lucien. I suspected he really wanted to see you in any event. Did he have any exciting news?" Lady Ravensham asked, not entirely deceived by Sarah's cheerful manner.

"Perhaps, not so much exciting as disturbing," Sarah replied. "He believes Theron De Lisle is a traitor. This is all in confidence, Grandmother, but I think Lucien would want you to know, and I am sure you can keep a secret. On his trip to Devon he discovered some evidence that Theron might be involved in smuggling French spies into the country. I find it hard to believe, but Lucien is convinced that the marquis is up to some nasty practices." Sarah sat on her grandmother's bed and regarded her with a troubled expression. She was surprised to see that Lady Ravensham accepted this horrifying budget of news without protest.

"Yes, well, Theron has a bad reputation and a penchant for trouble. I dislike thinking he might be a traitor, but his actions are liable to misinterpretation, and, until recently, he has done all he could to incur the disgust and contempt of polite society. Still, treachery is a serious accusation. How do you feel about Theron yourself?" Lady Ravensham asked, really hoping to discover how Sarah felt about Lucien, but wise enough not to put that question to her granddaughter.

"That old adage about where there is smoke, there must be fire might apply," she said thoughtfully, "but Theron is apt to stir the pot out of pure mischief-making. Still Theron's behaviour is not my problem, unhappy as these suspicions make me. What I really want to talk to you about, Grandmother, is some of the facts General Apsley-Gower has told me. I know this is a painful topic for you, and I am reluctant to quiz you, but I have been brooding over his conversation with me and feel I must discuss it with you." She spoke carefully, knowing she must cause her grandmother sorrow.

"Julian Apsley-Gower is an old and trusted friend, Sarah, and among the few people who knew Richard well. He would make every effort to put the best face upon Richard's actions possible. Indeed, it was his acceptance of the evidence against his old comrade that was so damning to my husband," Lady Ravensham sighed, recalling the bitter past.

Sarah hesitated. She realized that her suspicions about her Uncle Ronald would only cause her grandmother further unhappiness, but she felt she must probe more deeply into his past actions. Before she could form the question that trembled on her lips, her grandmother voiced her own uneasiness.

"Sarah, you must not continue to let that tragedy distress you so and cast a cloud over your visit. Believe me, my husband examined every bit of evidence at the time. He did not accept the verdict of his son's betrayal calmly, you know. He was proud of Richard, as I was, and expected him to attain a high rank in his chosen career. We were both disappointed when he went to America with General Howe. He was not convinced that we should attempt to coerce the colonies, but his duty led him. Many officers shared his feelings. Some generals refused to serve in America, you know, because they doubted the justice of our fight there." Lady Ravensham frowned, remembering the folly of that brutal argument between the two countries.

"He may have doubted the justice of the cause but, I am sure, once he accepted the necessity to go, he would not have betrayed his country and his family's honour," Sarah insisted stubbornly. "Nothing I have heard of him allows me to believe that."

"I agree with you, Sarah. I thought I knew Richard well, a more open, warm-hearted boy never lived. He had nothing of his brother's austerity, or hardness in his nature. Everyone loved him," Lady Ravensham recalled sadly.

"Was Uncle Ronald jealous of my father?" Sarah put the question tentatively, unwilling to voice her suspicions of her uncle to his mother.

"Well, I suppose he was, a bit, but only because Ronald, perhaps, would have liked to be more genial, more outward-looking. He was very like his father," Lady Ravensham conceded.

"I know it is not my business, but why was Lord Ravensham so stiff and unbending, unwilling to give Father the benefit of the doubt. How could you care for such a man?" Sarah asked gently, not wanting to criticize her grandfather to his wife.

"My husband was a very proud man, very concerned with his family honour. Ours was an arranged match, you know. We were not in love, but our marriage was successful on the whole, especially after I provided the heirs he so ardently desired. Your grandfather was not a man to reveal his emotions, but we rubbed along together very well, and I had my children. I never suspected two of them would be taken away so tragically." Her faded blue eyes darkened as she remembered those dreadful days. "The death of our eldest, Harry, was a terrible blow. My husband never recovered completely, which made Richard's defection, so soon after, a double tragedy."

"I understand from General Apsley-Gower that the accusations came from the War Office here," Sarah pressed. "Surely Lord Ravensham had enough influence to insist on learning the name of his son's accuser?"

"He tried, but Lord Germain was adamant about secrecy. He would only say the evidence was irrefutable. A very arrogant and peculiar man, George Germain, but the Sackvilles are all odd," Lady Ravensham recalled.

"Is he still alive?" Sarah asked hopefully.

"No, no. He died a few years after the peace, I believe. You know he was dismissed from his army career in disgrace, although never court-martialed. I believe that made him resentful and even more toplofty, unwilling to bow to anyone."

"If he was unjustly accused, he should have been more sympathetic to father's plight. Where are the records of the affair, I wonder?" Sarah's determination rather appalled her less resolute grandmother, who would never have approached the authorities herself, having been trained to believe such affairs should be left to men. "I wanted to enlist Colonel Valentine's assistance in my search, but . . ." Sarah's voice dwindled as she remembered Angela's warning.

"Yes, about Lucien. I am sure I have noticed his interest in you, my dear, but you seem to be very cool toward him. Has he offended you in some way?" Lady Ravensham asked, eager to change the direction of the conversation and discover what really lay in Sarah's heart.

"I am sure that my opinion of Colonel Valentine is of no moment. I understand he has already made his preference clear," Sarah answered in a stilted voice, furious at the warmth she felt rising in her cheeks.

Lady Ravensham, now convinced she understood Sarah's recent attitude toward Lucien, would not accept her granddaughter's dismissal of the subject. For some days now she had suspected that Sarah had misunderstood the relationship between Lucien and Angela.

Lady Ravensham had few illusions about her other granddaughter. She had watched Angela since her youngest days in leading strings, a beautiful child always, but willful, spoiled, not sweet-natured, unlike her brother Alan. As she grew to adulthood she had learned to hide from the outer world her real character, but to the family circle she often appeared cold, vain, and grasping, rather like her father, Lady Ravensham conceded ruefully. She had tried to love Angela, if she did not completely like her, but that haughty miss did not inspire affection since she had little to offer. She was inclined to pity the man who eventually claimed Angela as a wife for she feared he would find little comfort in her. Now her brother,

Alan, was a dear lad, who resembled his gentle mother but with more spine.

Lady Ravensham had wondered if Angela had put a spoke in her cousin's budding romance. If she wanted Lucien herself, she would not be above it, and, even if she did not, Angela would not look kindly on any deviation by one whom she considered to be in her own train. Certainly Angela would not brook being supplanted in Lucien's affections by her cousin. Until Sarah's arrival on the scene Lady Ravensham had rather expected that Angela and Lucien would eventually make a match of it and had endorsed the idea, accustomed as she was to arranged marriages, unions based on alliances of property and status. Such a marriage might do for Angela but never for Sarah, whose warm heart and independent spirit would not allow her to settle for such a cheerless marriage of convenience. No, reluctant as she was to meddle, she must relieve Sarah of her mistaken notions.

"If you have been led to believe that Lucien has asked for Angela's hand, my dear, you are quite wrong. At one time there may have been a possibility of such a match but I am sure whatever *tendre* he may have felt for your cousin has long since disappeared under the force of a stronger emotion. Your loyalty is commendable, Sarah, but Lucien is not committed to Angela," Lady Ravensham stated decisively.

"Well, whatever his intentions, they do not concern me, I assure you, Grandmother. I am too involved in searching for proof of my father's innocence to worry about the posturings of London beaux. And I do not think that Lucien is sympathetic to my investigations," Sarah answered, refusing to admit that Lady

217

Ravensham's explanations had raised her spirits. She had her share of Ravensham pride and would never play the lovesick forlorn maiden for the ton's amusement.

"Well, I think you are misjudging Lucien, Sarah. He is not some fribbling fashionable buck playing games with young women. Still it will all sort itself before times, I vow," Lady Ravensham concluded, now a bit tired by the coil of emotions she had endeavoured to unwind. Sarah, seeing that her grandmother had had enough conversation for the moment, bade her a loving good morning and retired to brood over this latest news in privacy.

Chapter Twenty-seven

Mulling over the latest information she had learned from her grandmother, Sarah decided that one option was open to her. She could approach General Apsley-Gower again, this time requesting that he use his influence with the War Office to allow her access to the records. There must be official transcripts of the accusations laid against her father, and, since the affair was now some twenty years old, there could be no opposition to releasing the pertinent documents. Somehow this sensible reasoning did not convince Sarah that it would be that simple. But surely, with so many of the principals dead, it could not matter if the records were examined now. George Germain, the chief stumbling block to access, had long ago stuck his spoon in the wall, and what possible difference could it make to the present head of the ministry, Henry Dundas, a Scot who cared more about India than the war in Europe?

She would have preferred to discuss the whole business with Lucien, but their present strained relationship made that impossible. Much as she wanted to believe her grandmother's explanation of Lucien's indifference to Angela, she was not completely convinced that he did not care for her cousin. Then there was the imbroglio over Lord De Lisle. No, she must persuade the general to assist her, awkward as that might be.

Not one to postpone unpleasant tasks, Sarah dispatched a note to General Apsley-Gower's rooms, requesting that he call upon her as soon as convenient on a matter of some import. Her messenger would wait for his answer. He replied that he would wait upon her that very afternoon and was her obedient servant.

Happily this gave Sarah the excuse to refuse De Lisle's invitation for a ride in the park that afternoon. She did not want to face that sardonic gentleman, in view of Lucien's revelations, until she had time to decide on how to treat him. Not clever at dissembling her feelings, Sarah was certain she would blurt out her suspicions or behave in some other manner certain to bring about an ugly situation with the marquis. After all, to accuse a man of treachery on the unsupported word of another was the outside of enough, and he would have every reason to berate her, an uncomfortable position she must avoid at least until she had armed herself with some irrefutable evidence.

How maddening of Lucien to place her in such a dilemma and arrogantly expect her to obey his orders about the marquis. Well, she had no intention of surrendering to his commands. Besides the whole affair may have been blown out of context. Theron De Lisle had as much right to be in Plymouth on personal business as Lucien, and he need not explain his presence there either. Lucien was an overbearing autocrat, certain that he knew best, and expecting her to heed his demands, no matter how outrageous.

It did not occur to Sarah that Lucien's objections to Theron might be based on jealousy. She had never been a conceited girl. Her grandmother's explanation of Angela's intriguing had not completely satisfied Sarah, for her cousin had sounded so sure, so smug, so certain that she could have Lucien for the lifting of a finger. She must have more than wishful thinking on which to base her faith in Lucien's love. Oh dear, all this tortuous weighing of motives had brought on a headache. And she must be in good fettle to tackle the general.

By the time that distinguished officer arrived at Park Street that afternoon, Sarah had succeeded in working herself into an agony of doubt and indecision. She had wanted to prepare a careful campaign of persuasion so that General Apsley-Gower would plead on her behalf at the War Office, but instead, when actually facing her father's old comrade, she blurted out her request, in her impatience unable to practice any subterfuge.

"You see, General, I am convinced those papers will give us some clue as to the real culprit. I suspect little investigation took place at the time, with Howe's evacuation of Philadelphia coming hard on the heels of the discovery, and the War Office nabobs having much more important matters to decide. But nothing is more important to me than to clear my father's name," Sarah pleaded.

The general frowned, considering her argument, then his blue eyes softened, for he was not impervious to her distress. Still he could not allow her to continue in this unhappy quest.

"My dear, I would do all in my power to assist you, be assured of that, but I cannot see how dragging all this up again will result in anything but gossip and trouble. Neither your grandmother nor your uncle will appreciate being the butt of London scandalmongers, you know. They have already endured the humiliation of your father's treachery once. It would be cruel to put them through it all again, and for no reason. Your uncle's brilliant career at the Foreign Office might even be endangered by the brouhaha. Believe me, I applaud your defense of Richard and your desire to see him acquitted, but I do not think it possible," he argued gently, watching her closely.

"Yes, I understand your reluctance, General, but does that mean you will not help me? Believe me, if you refuse, this will not alter my determination, even if I have to call on Henry Dundas myself and put my case." Sarah tilted her chin in defiance.

"Have you discussed this with Valentine or your grandmother?" General Apsley-Gower asked, noting the stubbornness in her flushed face.

For a moment she was tempted to lie, but she could not bring herself to such a deception. "No, General, I have not. This effort to remove the stain from father's reputation is my responsibility. I do not want to involve my grandmother, and Colonel Valentine shares your feelings that only pain can arise from continuing to delve into the past."

"You would best be guided by him, my dear. I am sure he has your best interests at heart. Still, if you are determined on this course of action, I have no recourse but to aid you. I cannot have you storming into the War Office and causing embarrassment. You are a valiant fighter, Sarah, and I can see I must become your ally. You will be wise to keep this conversation secret, for I think neither your friends nor your family would approve of your reckless actions. It will be our secret, agreed?" he asked, anxiously watching her, for he had discovered that Sarah, in her passion for justice, was heedless of her reputation or that of anyone else.

"If you promise to do your utmost to bring me a copy of those papers, I will not breathe a word to anyone. I quite agree that our investigations must be confidential," Sarah concurred, willing, now that she had achieved her objective, to soothe the general's sensibilities.

He bade her a cheerful farewell, commending her stout-heartedness, and counseling patience. She felt she had enrolled a useful confederate in her struggle to acquit her father. The general, well schooled in hiding his emotions, kept his expression of kindly concern firmly in place until he reached the street, where he gave vent to a few hearty curses. This was indeed a coil, an unexpected development for which he was unprepared, and arising at the worst possible time. Still he must allay Sarah's fears and cooperate with her on this hunt for the evidence that would vindicate her father. For the moment he must put aside other more vital interests and satisfy her that the verdict of twenty years ago was the only possible one.

Sarah, satisfied that she had now put in train all she could do for the moment, tried to subdue her impatience and concentrate on her grandmother. Lady

Ravensham decided that her health had improved so much that she might plan a more elaborate entertainment in honour of her granddaughter, now that the Season was well advanced. Sarah, who would have been perfectly content to forgo such an honour, realized that her grandmother anticipated the event with real pleasure. She seemed to blossom under the arrangements for a great ball in the Park Street house, which was well suited to such a lavish evening. The servants, too, were not loath to expend effort on readying the mansion for an influx of several hundred guests.

Sarah did her utmost to spare her grandmother the more exacting chores like addressing invitations and calling on caterers and musicians, but she could not really throw herself enthusiastically into preparations while awaiting the outcome of the general's request from the War Department. Chiding herself for her irritation, she tried valiantly to show her grandmother how much she appreciated the pains she was taking for her enjoyment, but it was an effort, and one not made easier by Angela's resentment over the June ball. That young woman complained at some length that her grandmother had not seen fit to honour her in such a fashion at her come-out and had to be taken to task by her mother and Lady Ravensham for her fit of sullens.

As for Lucien, Sarah could not understand that enigmatic gentleman's attitude. He continued to turn up with regularity at Park Street to escort her on rides in the park, to routs and other festivities, often competing with Lord De Lisle for her company. Whatever the reason for his antagonism to the marquis, he had decided to ignore their past passages at arms and treated De Lisle with cool courtesy when they met, confusing Sarah and causing De Lisle considerable amusement. Since Angela was so often a member of the party, Sarah at last concluded that Lucien was still interested in her cousin despite her grandmother's views to the contrary. All in all, the days following her interview with General Apsley-Gower were not comfortable, but she tried to keep her anxiety at bay as best she could.

Chapter Twenty-eight

The projected ball soon involved the whole household in preparations. Sarah feared the elaborate plans would exhaust her grandmother, but Lady Ravensham seemed to thrive on all the bustle and arrangements. The servants, who might have been expected to take such a flurry of activity in annoyance, on the contrary threw themselves into the undertaking with enthusiasm, for Sarah had early won the approval of the servants' hall. Despite her colonial upbringing, they considered her a true lady, her frank and open manner winning their hearts.

Such longtime family retainers as Peverel, the butler, and Mrs. Hopkins, the housekeeper, knew of the estrangement between the American branch of the family and the inmates of Park Street and the Hall, and had prepared themselves to reserve judgment on this colonial miss who had appeared so dramatically in their midst. But Peverel, for all his starched airs, was no proof against Sarah's appealing ways and Mrs. Hopkins succumbed to Sarah's avid questions about her father's boyhood, for he had been a favorite of hers. The enchanting politeness with which she responded to what were only normal domestic services was yet another point in her favour. Belowstairs the attention that Colonel Valentine had paid Sarah had not gone unnoticed, and Mrs. Hopkins confided to Peverel over a cup of tea that she hoped the two would make a match of it. Angela Ravensham had never been a favorite in the servants' hall, for her manner was haughty and patronizing.

If the staff at Park Street had decided that Lucien and Sarah were destined to be shackled, the two principals remained in ignorance of the fate decreed for them. Despite his best efforts, Lucien found Sarah even more distant after their abortive interview concerning De Lisle and, since that gentleman continued to haunt Park Street, the situation did not seem likely to improve. On the surface all was politeness and mannerly deportment, with Angela complicating affairs by her own ploys. Angela was now taking great pains to prove her claims.

As the cousins were often paired at the various festivities of the season Sarah had ample opportunity to watch Angela's overtures toward Lucien. She flattered, simpered, cajoled, and hung on his every word and on his arm, even rebuffing many of her ardent suitors in favour of his more restrained attentions. Always polite toward Angela and realizing a bit belatedly that he might have given her cause to think he wanted her as a wife, Lucien was embarrassed by her stratagems and uncertain how to disabuse her of the notion. Now that he was pursuing Sarah in earnest, much of his usual adroitness with the ladies seemed to have deserted him, and Angela unnecessarily complicated affairs. Of course, by making her own feelings plain, Sarah could have instantly depressed her cousin's intentions, but she was too proud to show a preference that might not be welcomed.

Sarah's *amour-propre* could not help but be soothed in this taxing situation by De Lisle's attentions, which continued to be constant, whatever his real aims were. Doubtless he had not decided himself. If Sarah had been a different sort of female, he would have lost no time in making the improper suggestion expected by the women he hunted during his normal round of pleasure. Sarah had at first intrigued him as a novelty and then had served as a useful excuse for his reentrance into a society he had heretofore scorned. Whether he was prepared to settle down into domesticity at long last was a question avidly asked by most of the ton, and he did nothing to assuage their curiosity. One of De Lisle's chief attributes in Sarah's mind was his complete indifference to Angela, who had tried to lure him with her flirtatious ways and received a cool set-down, just another score added to the long list of grudges she was compiling against Sarah.

In the days just before the ball, the tension among the two couples heightened, but this time Lucien remained in control, determined not to send Sarah into one of her tempers by criticizing De Lisle. De Lisle never showed any emotion but sardonic amusement toward the world and a gentle raillery toward Sarah. This unsatisfactory state of affairs seemed destined to continue indefinitely, and Sarah felt helpless to alter events.

Just when she had despaired of General Apsley-

Gower ever coming to her assistance, she received an unexpected call from him. If he noticed her tension and the rather drawn, pale expression on her face, he gave no sign of it. He appeared troubled himself and was almost brusque in his approach, far from his normal benign and kindly attitude.

"My dear, I am still trying to wrest those papers from the War Office. Bureaucrats are apt to be tediously slow in answering any request, as I am sure you understand, but another development has arisen that I hesitate to bring to your attention. If I had not promised to give you all possible assistance in this matter, I would not do so," he said in a manner calculated to depress rather than raise Sarah's spirits.

"Please go on, General," Sarah responded. "I am anxious to follow any avenue that will enable me to clear my father's name."

The general sighed in resignation, obviously loath to raise her hopes. "Quite by chance I have run across an old soldier, a veteran of our regiment, who served under your father, not only in Philadelphia, but also later with General Burgoyne. He remembers your father with great affection and did not believe the charges against him. If you wish to see this Sergeant O'Toole, I can make the necessary arrangements, although I do not approve of the idea and am reluctant to abet you in this fruitless quest."

"Oh, General, I am so grateful to you. Of course I want to interview Sergeant O'Toole. Even if he has little real information, it would gladden my heart to talk to someone who knew my father in those days." Sarah's mercurial spirits rebounded at the thought that at last she was making some progress. She remained deaf to the general's warnings about the inadvisability of this meeting and urged him to make the arrangements with all speed. After a few more half-hearted demurs he agreed to set up a meeting with the sergeant, explaining that she must be prepared because the location of his lodgings was not what she was accustomed to visiting, undesirable in every way, and again stating his objections to the whole project.

His hesitation only whetted Sarah's determination to proceed, and she turned aside his opposition with blithe assurances as to her complete trust in whatever he decided. Although she was eager to leave immediately to see this sergeant, she was forced to agree that the general must have time to make suitable arrangements for the visit. He promised to put events in train as soon as possible and would contact her before too long.

Sarah, while expressing her gratitude, wondered to herself about his reluctance to escort her immediately to the interview but decided his old-fashioned chivalry balked at the notion of taking her into a poor and squalid neighborhood. Now that she had some prospect of action, her spirits rose and she countered all his objections with enthusiasm, which the general realized he could not dampen. Upon parting, he cautioned her again to keep their negotiations secret as neither her friends nor her grandmother would approve of such an outing.

Sarah, overcome with excitement at the notion of finally proving her father's innocence, had difficulty in behaving calmly. She was certain her grandmother must note her state of seething anticipation, but Lady

Ravensham, usually so attuned to Sarah's moods, had become so immersed in preparations for the ball that she became distrait if other concerns intruded. Sarah tried to compose herself to await developments with patience but it was as well the general contacted her within a few days. He sent her a message by his batman, the brevity of which was explained by his plea of a sudden illness.

My dear Sarah,

If you can accompany my man on receipt of this note, he will escort you to O'Toole's lodgings. The sergeant has agreed to an interview and will tell you all he can remember about those long-ago days. I am sorry I cannot accompany you, but I am laid low by a reoccurrence of an old fever, which has completely overcome me.

Your obedient servant,
Julian Apsley-Gower

Sarah, thanking the fates that had intervened to allow her to leave without parrying questions from her grandmother, who had gone to the mantua makers, rushed from the room to secure her bonnet and shawl. In her haste she threw the general's missive onto the library desk where it was retrieved, once she had departed, by the general's man and placed in his pocket with a sigh of satisfaction. In her excitement and haste Sarah had not really noticed the messenger, a rather grimy and uncouth individual, who certainly did not have the upright stature and countenance of a proper gentleman's servant. Peverel, however, had not been so remiss, and as the two left the Park Street house he wondered, in some distress, where Miss Sarah was going with such an unlikely person. He watched from the entrance hall as they climbed into a shabby hackney and the horses were whipped away.

Once in the carriage, however, Sarah looked at her escort more closely. He certainly was not a man to inspire confidence and seemed a brutal type to be in the general's service. Stocky, with a lined face and protruding eyes that returned her glance with effrontery, he had little of the bearing of a military man. A shudder of apprehension shook her as she realized she had put her safety in this man's hands, a prospect she now hailed with some uneasiness.

Chapter Twenty-nine

As Sarah and her unprepossessing escort bowled out of sight, their progress was noted by Theron De Lisle, whose phaeton had pulled up behind the hackney just as Sarah had entered the carriage with the general's man. Raising his eyebrows at the sight, De Lisle frowned. Where was she going with such unseemly speed and in such company? Perhaps he had best follow and keep an eye toward the goings-on. Sarah was capable of who knew what folly and he had not liked the brief glimpse he had caught of her companion. The route the hackney and its trailing phaeton followed was circuitous, passing down Piccadilly and crossing behind the theatres of Drury Lane into the stews beyond Covent Garden. As they penetrated deeper into a section of London Sarah had never visited but which De Lisle knew intimately from his excursions into the seamy world of brothels, gin mills, and gaming halls, his frown deepened. Only trouble could come from Sarah penetrating this vice-ridden area. What was she seeking? At last the hackney came to a stop in a dark alley, overshadowed by grimy dilapidated buildings whose stench was noxious. Sarah, alighting from the hackney, wrinkled her nose in disgust but steeled herself to enter the tenement facing them. Her escort grasped her arm in a firm grip, determined not to allow her to escape.

"Surely, this cannot be the lodgings of a respectable sergeant in His Majesty's forces," Sarah demurred, trying to remove her arm from the man's tight grip.

"No questions, Missy. Just do as you're bid and it will be the easier on you," he growled, dragging her through the door that was opened by a blowzy woman, whose brassy-hued hair and painted face would have proclaimed her profession to any but an innocent such as Sarah. Now thoroughly frightened, Sarah eyed the woman with trepidation. Was this the sergeant's wife? Taking her courage in hand, she asked with all the firmness she could muster, "Where is Sergeant O'Toole? I understand he is expecting me."

"Ho, aren't we a fine one? We can certainly use her in the kip shop. Now come along, dearie, and don't give me no trouble or it will be the worse for you." The woman loomed over Sarah in a menacing fashion.

Wrenching her arm away from her captor, Sarah turned to flee but was pushed back against a wall by the woman, whose fetid breath and sweaty body turned Sarah sick with disgust and some other unnamed terror. But Sarah was no coward and she determined not to let these two mean persons see her increasing fear.

"How dare you treat me thus! Where is Sergeant

234

O'Toole? Let me go immediately or it will be upon your heads when the general finds out that you have abducted me!" she spoke scornfully although her limbs were trembling.

"I likes a little spirit, but we will get that out of you before long, dearie," leered the woman. Both the woman and Sarah's erstwhile captor were concentrating so hard on the girl they held at their mercy they did not hear the door open.

"I think not, Lil. You have made a mistake that could easily land you in the cells," came De Lisle's smooth, mocking voice, but the steel in his eye was evident, and the pistol he held in his hand reinforced his command of the situation. "Come, Sarah, let us leave this hell. It is obviously no place for you."

If she had not been so overcome by fright and so relieved, Sarah might have laughed at the expressions on the faces of her two unwholesome adversaries. Never had De Lisle seemed such a welcome sight. Evading the woman who stood before her in shock at the unexpected intrusion, she darted beneath her outstretched arm and hurried to De Lisle's side. His suave manner had not altered a jot, but he moved her carefully behind him as he noted the man who eyed him sullenly.

"We meant no harm, Governor, just a little mistake. You wouldn't hold it against us now, just out for a bit 'o fun," whimpered the man, not at all reassured by the look on De Lisle's face.

"There's a mystery here, Sarah, that I would dearly like to solve, but I feel you might be happier out of this stew. My phaeton is in front. Let us depart and leave these two to their nasty ploys. But be warned," he turned to the two miscreants, raking them with a baleful glance, "Forget whatever evil deeds you had in mind concerning this young woman, or it will be the worse for you. As it is, I am tempted to haul you before the magistrate and have you transported for life." Faced with his threats, delivered in that icy voice, all the starch went out of Sarah's captors and they cowered before De Lisle's intimidation.

Without more ado he bundled her into his phaeton and they made all speed away from the wretched streets and its unsavoury citizens. Sarah, still recovering from her ordeal and feeling more than a little faint, tried to behave with a sang-froid to hide her giddiness.

"I cannot thank you enough, my lord. I am sorry to be such a pea goose but I really cannot seem to order my wits about me," Sarah apologized tentatively, uncertain how to explain how she had found herself in such a hideous dilemma. She did not for a moment believe De Lisle would be turned off with some specious excuse.

"Yes, my dear, you have some explaining to do, but we can postpone that for the nonce until you are in more command of yourself. I sincerely hope you do not fully realize what danger you were in. That unsavoury woman is a notorious brothelkeeper and had no doubt intended to add you to her stable of impures," De Lisle spoke harshly, himself upset at the nearness of Sarah's horrid plight.

Sarah, in the first flush of relief at her rescue, wanted to explain to De Lisle how she had become embroiled in this disastrous adventure, but second thoughts produced caution. She could not accuse the general of luring her to a brothel, of exposing her to a ruinous fate, if he were innocent. Perhaps he would have an explanation, but certainly it would have to be convincing to excuse the traumatic experience she had undergone. At all costs her grandmother must not hear about how nearly her beloved granddaughter had been forced into slavery of the most disgusting sort. Sarah could not repress the shudders and the near faintness she felt when she contemplated her future if De Lisle had not rescued her. She owed him an explanation, but she must choose her words carefully.

"Theron, I will be forever grateful to you for saving me from that dreadful house and those horrid creatures. I do not understand what they intended, but, before I can reveal how I came to be in such circumstances, I must do some investigating. It would never do to accuse anyone of planning such a fate for me, if he were innocent. And my grandmother must never know. The shock might send her to her bed for days. I could not have that on my conscience. Promise me you will not tell her," Sarah pleaded.

"No more than you would I wish to upset Lady Ravensham, Sarah, but you must promise me to take care. Obviously you have an enemy who intends grievous harm toward you. If you will not confide in me, I cannot force you, but be warned that whoever it is might try again. You may be a courageous, independent colonial, but you are not equipped to deal with the scoundrels who would treat you so," De Lisle said seriously.

Under other circumstances Sarah would have been amused at disturbing his imperturbability. She did not think he was easily shocked, but she was in no case to analyse his state of mind, her own being in such turmoil. She still felt sick at the thought of what those vile creatures had in store for her, but as they neared Park Street she regained some of her composure and only hoped she could reach the safety of her room before her grandmother returned. She needed time to order her thoughts and restore her nerves. She must plan how to deal with the general. Surely he could not be the enemy Theron suggested.

The marquis escorted her to the door of her grandmother's house and bade her good-bye with admirable restraint, considering he must be concerned and eager to question her more fully. Sarah was profuse in her thanks but gave no explanations.

After ordering her abigail to bring her a bath, Sarah undressed and sat down to decide on her next move. She felt soiled and unstrung by her horrible experience, but she decided that at least she had flushed out an enemy and traitor. Whoever had arranged for her kidnapping must believe she represented some sort of threat, which meant her suspicions were correct. Also, her assailant must be among Lady Ravensham's intimate circle, and he would stop at nothing to protect his secret. It could be the general but it might be her uncle. She refused to consider Lucien as the culprit. She could not bear to think that he was her enemy, that he had tried to disarm her by making love to her. However, her first responsibility was to quiz the general and his explanations had better be convincing or she would expose him for all to see. Despite De Lisle's warning, now that she had emerged unscathed from her experience, Sarah's natural courage and determination to solve the mystery was undaunted.

Chapter Thirty

While Sarah was plotting her next move to unmask the traitor in their midst, Lucien was making plans of his own. His attempts to break through Sarah's reserve, her refusal to treat him as more than a casual acquaintance, her preference for De Lisle's company hurt and angered him. Had she really taken him in dislike? Her earlier passionate responses to his embraces led him to think differently. He could not believe that Sarah would bestow her favours so casually. She was not a light-minded flirt. Frustrated and unhappy over her rebuffs, he threw himself into the many pursuits London offered an eligible and attractive bachelor, intent on banishing the maddening female from his mind. He spent entirely too much time over the tables at White's and at Gentleman Jackson's boxing salon where he worked off some of his impatience on the bucks who turned up daily for hard sparring. Too disciplined and fastidious to join his comrades in tasting the offerings of the fashionable impures whose attractions did not compensate for their avaricious tastes and shallow minds, he drank too much and gambled more than his wont, seeking relief. Finally accepting that Sarah could not be banished from his heart and mind by such distractions, he decided to enlist the advice of Lady Ravensham. He chose a time when Sarah had accompanied Angela on a trip to Hookum's Lending Library and the delights of the famed confections at Gunter's.

"Lady Ravensham, I must crave your indulgence on a matter of great importance to me." Lucien hesitated, but the dowager's kindly expression and obvious sympathy encouraged him to continue.

"As you may have noticed, I have become very fond of Sarah and, until recently, had some hopes that she returned my regard, but lately she has rebuffed any efforts I have made to seek her company. I know she tends to think of the English as arrogant, puffed-up popinjays, sworn enemies of her country, but I think I have somewhat disabused her of this notion. Have I in some way offended her that she is now out of charity with me?" Lucien's sincerity was obvious and Lady Ravensham smiled slightly to think that such a courageous military officer should fear to put his chances with her granddaughter to the test. Since a match between them was among her dearest wishes, she hastened to lay his anxieties at rest.

"I believe Sarah had been overset by this business of her father's treachery and the interview she had recently with General Apsley-Gower, which did little to encourage her hopes of proving his innocence. Also she is missing her grandfather but I do not think that natural nostalgia is responsible for her attitude toward you." Lady Ravensham realized that, in order to secure Sarah's happiness, she must put the question of Angela to the rout. "Could it be that she thinks your interest is fixed elsewhere and that you are merely flirting with her?" she hinted.

"I am not a man for the ladies in the usual way, as I am sure you understand. My military career has engaged all my energies and left little time for the dalliance many of the London bucks pursue. Compared to De Lisle, I am almost a Puritan, although I do admit to the usual escapades." Lucien frowned, remembering his several romantic encounters with Sarah. Did she not realize he was serious, those interludes more than just casual flirtations?

"Yes, I know that, Lucien. You are certainly not a rake or philanderer, but Sarah, loyal and honest as she is, may not see it that way. I suspect, too, that she has been warned off you by her cousin. Just what were your intentions toward Angela?" Lady Ravensham asked boldly, tired of skirting the issue.

Lucien, abashed, reddened slightly. His instinct was to deny any interest in Angela, but his honesty impelled him to tell Lady Ravensham the truth.

"As you know, dear lady, my father is quite anxious for me to marry. My brother, Alistair, his heir, has been shackled these four years and no sign of a child. Father has looked upon my army career as a necessary evil, quite fitting for a second son, but he does not want the land or the title to go to Cousin Osbert's line, a ramshackle bunch as you will agree. Since the Ravenshams and the Lenminster land marches in Hereford, he led me to believe it would solve several problems if I offered for Angela. Not that she would have me, incomparable that she is," he concluded modestly.

"Oh, I think you are way out there, Lucien. An earl's son, even a second son, is no mean catch, and she is not to everyone's taste, you know. She has had some eligible offers, I believe, but she rather enjoys being a toast of the town. Lately, though, I suspect she has come round to Ronald's view that she must settle, and I believe she would take you in a flash," Lady Ravensham spoke wryly, but unwilling to criticize Angela too harshly.

"We have always been friends, but I certainly have not led her on, Lady Ravensham. I do not believe her heart is engaged in any way, and, since Sarah's appearance on the scene, she should have no doubt where my affections lay." Lucien was finding this conversation very trying. He disliked laying his feelings out for even as kind a lady as this one, to make mock of, although he acquitted her of attempting to tease him.

"I think Angela believes that your childhood relationship was ripened into a more mature feeling. She knows your father, and hers, would be in favour, and she is prepared to accept a proposal from you." Lady Ravensham's tone was firm, far different than her usual soothing manner. She was reluctant to tell Lucien that Angela may have hinted to Sarah that their engagement was to be announced momentarily. Angela deserved a set-down for her meddling, but her grandmother wished to spare her embarrassment if possible.

"Come now, Lady Ravensham, can you see Angela following the drum? I am not about to give up my army career to play lap dog to a society beauty, you know. She would be most put out about at having to hide her talents in some rugged army post, aside from the fact that our natures do not suit in any way." Lucien spoke with more frankness than tact, annoyed that Angela might have spoiled his chances with Sarah.

"While Sarah, on the other hand, would take to the life like a charm, pouring tea to generals' wives, and seeing to the comfort of the troops, as well as yours. That's not good enough for her, you know, to be judged on her adaptability to army life," Lady Ravensham demurred.

"If Sarah insisted, I would even give up the army, although I don't believe she would ask that of me. There is no comparing the two. Sarah is superior in every way, surely you have noticed that—her frankness, enjoyment of life, her courage, even her stubbornness. I find she completely captivates me. I want her and no other for a wife, and I am sure I could make her happy, despite her fierce American independence. I would not want to alter her in any way. I just hope I am the man to win her, that she is not pining for someone in Philadelphia or involved with that rake, De Lisle." Lucien's sincerity was obvious, all trace of reserve and arrogance banished by the strength of his feeling.

Lady Ravensham, her fears at rest, answered with equal frankness. "No, I can set your mind at rest there. No beau across the Atlantic claims her allegiance. And I believe she is using De Lisle as he is her, to hide her real feelings, which she may not want to admit, believing you to be promised elsewhere. She is sensible enough to see that Theron would never do as a husband, even if he offered. You must put your fate

to the touch. Sarah is a loyal little soul and may have
been led to think Angela is your choice. She would not
poach, you know. And I think Angela is not above
meddling. She may be responsible for creating mischief. Ask Sarah, Lucien, don't wait too long or her
pride will force her to return to Philadelphia. Your
rival is not so much another man as her devotion to
her grandfather and her preoccupation with this affair
of her father's disgrace. I am sure you can deal with
that."

"Oh, yes. I could wish she would put that tragedy
behind her but she is a stubborn little miss. I admire
Joshua Allen and would never separate Sarah from
her grandfather. At any rate, I believe I may be sent
back to America before the year is out. Relations
between our two countries appear a bit better than
they have been and I am determined they will remain
so. Fortunately, Mr. Pitt is of a like mind," Lucien
spoke resolutely. Now that he had Lady Ravensham's
approval, any obstacle such as the devious Angela, De
Lisle, or Sarah's own sensibilities could be overcome.

"As you know I am giving a ball for Sarah in a se'n-
night preceded by a small dinner here. That might be
the occasion to put your destiny to the touch, if you
can control your impatience. I will leave that up to
you, not wanting to tell you how to go about your
wooing," Lady Ravensham smiled. How foolish Sarah
and Lucien were to deny their feelings because of
jealousy and pride.

"I will take your advice and, if all turns out well, I
cannot thank you enough for your understanding and
encouragement. You need not mention this conversation to Sarah. I am man enough to do my own

courting, I think," Lucien replied a bit grimly. "That maddening little miss will soon have her defences breached, I promise."

"She is not a redoubt to be taken, a battle to be won, Lucien," Lady Ravensham reproved whimsically.

"The most difficult adversary I have ever faced, I fear, but I am a good strategist and will win the day," Lucien grinned confidently, buoyed by the interview. He had his campaign well in mind now and intended to carry the day.

Chapter Thirty-one

Lady Ravensham, much cheered by Lucien's confession, could not help but notice Sarah's distrait manner although she had no idea what caused her granddaughter's preoccupation. Having been convinced that Sarah cared for Lucien, she now began to have doubts. Could Sarah be falling in love with De Lisle after all? He continued to pursue her, serving to keep Lucien at a distance, but was Sarah's acceptance of Theron's attentions a ploy to soothe her pride, convinced as she was that Lucien had been dallying with her affections? Lady Ravensham longed to put the question to Sarah, but she had promised Lucien not to interfere, and she would not force her granddaughter's confidence. How she wished Sarah would abandon this quest for her father's betrayer. Much as Lady Ravensham would like to see her son's innocence established, after all these years would it be possible to restore his reputation? She sincerely felt that Sarah was just storing up much unhappiness for herself in this fruitless search for evidence of his loyalty.

Sarah waited a few days to see if the general would

contact her. When he did not, she wrote to him, again requesting he call upon her. She had looked for the note he had sent with that ruffian but had been unable to find it. She had even questioned the servants, believing it might have been thrown out when one of them was tidying the library, but they had no knowledge of the incriminating message. She felt her hand would have been strengthened in the coming interview if she had had that evidence, but its loss did not deter her. When the general finally appeared, she made no effort to hide her anger, and he faced a stern and unyielding countenance that would not be assuaged by small talk.

"General, I am somewhat dismayed that you have made no effort to discover the outcome of my expedition to see Sergeant O'Toole, which you arranged for me three days ago," she began, her manner very cool and astringent.

"I just assumed that it had not been very successful, as I warned might be the case. What did happen?" he replied, apparently bewildered by her manner.

"Your man arrived to escort me to the sergeant's lodgings but instead took me to a disreputable house behind Drury Lane where he and a vile woman intended to force me into a house of ill repute. I cannot believe this was what you had in mind," she stated, her tone ironic.

"My dear, I am appalled. Certainly I sent my man with a message for you, explaining that I was down with a fever and that I would be unable to escort you to O'Toole's. What can have happened?" he said, his kindly face full of distress.

Briefly Sarah explained what had happened, confused by the general's surprise. Could his note have been intercepted and his man have been waylaid? The general appeared to be sincerely horrified by her tale and eager to get to the bottom of the deception.

"I regret that you had this dreadful experience, Sarah, and I will discover just what happened, you can be sure of that. I cannot understand why my man did not tell me that he had been attacked or obstructed in some manner. Perhaps he was bribed by an enemy intent on causing your downfall, but he has been with me for years. I trust him implicitly. I will delve into this matter at once. But, my dear, this should serve as a warning to you that you are interfering in dangerous concerns that may lead you into serious harm. Please abandon this search for evidence of your father's innocence. No good can come of it," he urged, his face suddenly drawn and haggard, at the thought of what she had escaped. Somewhat disarmed by the general's apparent shock at her news, Sarah was still not prepared to abandon her search for the culprit.

"Perhaps I might talk to your batman myself and ask him if he was approached or threatened by some stranger. He might be reluctant to tell you, afraid of losing his position," she urged, anxious to take matters into her own hands.

"No, I do not think that will serve, Sarah," the general demurred. "He is a stubborn stoic soul and would only be embarrassed if, in some way, he was at fault, and he would refuse to answer your questions. I will deal with him."

"Well, I want an answer. And I am not deterred by

this attack. I will find out the truth, as now I am sure there is a basis for my investigations. Have you made any progress with the papers from the War Office?" she pressed, unwilling to be soothed by platitudes.

"Dundas has promised to look into the matter, but I cannot badger him too closely," the general answered. "He is completely engrossed in the Irish and India businesses as well as the conduct of the war. We will just have to be patient."

Although Sarah disliked being fobbed off in this manner, she had to accept the fact that the general would proceed in his own fashion and would not be cajoled into further action. He did not like her probing, that she recognized and she wondered why he was so reluctant. Surely, as an old comrade of her father, he was as concerned as she was in securing a reversal of the sentence against him. She could not repress a feeling that he was hiding some important evidence from her, protecting someone who would be endangered by any revelations. Certainly, she knew now, some unknown enemy wished her ill and was determined to stop her efforts.

Sarah's original view of the general as a kindly devoted officer of impeccable reputation suffered a sea change during this interview. She wondered about his motives and if that bluff hearty manner concealed some damning secret. She would watch him carefully in the future, for she felt dissatisfied with his explanations and uneasy at his reassurances. He was all too eager to leave her presence, and he left her with a great deal of food for thought.

Since her interview with the general posed more questions than it answered, Sarah pondered her next move. She did not know where to turn, for she felt surrounded by suspicion and betrayal. Whom could she trust? Could her Uncle Ronald have hired someone to waylay the general's man and plan such a despicable fate for her? He had seemed his usual self when they had met after her encounter in the stews of Drury Lane—not surprised to see her or particularly interested in her at all, for that matter. She was tempted to chance her hand and tell Lucien the whole story, but some innate caution held her back, and that left De Lisle. He already knew so much, could she safely reveal to him the whole story? Her grandmother inadvertently pushed her toward a decision when she informed her that after the ball, in three days' time, they would be going down to the Hall.

"We will need a respite after the crush of the Season, and then, too, I want you to see the home of which your father was so fond. Ronald has suggested we accompany them when they leave, and you will be seeing it at its best right now," her grandmother insisted. She hoped that Lucien could be persuaded to take some leave and visit his own father's estates at the same time, and in the less distracting country environment Sarah might look kindly on his suit. Of course, Sarah, although she yearned to see her father's childhood home, could not embrace the plan wholeheartedly. She suspected that her Uncle Ronald, if he was indeed the villain, would have much easier access to her in the country in case he intended further harm. Well, she would just have to be vigilant and perhaps force a resolution of events. She responded somewhat tepidly to her grandmother's idea, which led that lady to think again that it must be because she was loath to leave London and De Lisle.

While Sarah continued to fret over her dilemma, hearing nothing from the general, and harassed by all the preparations for the ball, the two gentlemen who had her welfare at heart met at White's one afternoon. De Lisle, despite all his wild escapades, had never resigned from his clubs and now that he had reentered the society to which he rightfully belonged spent time reacquainting himself with the amenities. White's, the most exclusive of the lot, its membership almost entirely aristocratic, possessed the famous bay window that overlooked St. James Street, where passersby received a severe scrutiny from the nobs who spent their leisure gazing critically upon the motley. The political cast of the eighty-some members was decidedly Tory and the chief entertainment consisted of games of chance. Rumour had it that the manager, George Raggett, had made a pretty penny just by sweeping up the counters on the floor after a night's deep play.

De Lisle, entering the sanctum intent on whiling an hour or two away at the whist table, saw Valentine sunk in an armchair and contemplating his boots with some gloom. A nearly emptly bottle of madeira by his side told its own tale. De Lisle, sitting down across from him and receiving no more than a muttered greeting, suggested they broach another bottle, to which Lucien agreed. Although De Lisle was not his choice of drinking companion, his lowered spirits welcomed any respite and the two chatted casually for a moment or two before De Lisle was convinced that his companion was not too far gone in wine to listen attentively to his story.

"I know you do not think too well of me, Valentine, and I must agree that you have good cause, but let me assure you I intend no harm to a lady whom we both revere. It has never been my intention to cast a rub in your way, although I must confess I have enjoyed tweaking your consequence a bit, but now that matters have become more serious I think I must confide in you," De Lisle said, aware that he had Lucien's full attention and that, however much wine the colonel had imbibed, he was in full possession of his senses. The keen glance with which Lucien raked his rival proved that. Without more ado De Lisle told Lucien of Sarah's recent adventure from which he had rescued her. Lucien, at first horrified and then angry, questioned him closely.

"Who could have lured her to such a dive? And why would she have gone without protection? Damn the stubborn chit, has she no understanding of the dangers involved in such heedless behaviour? It's this ridiculous notion of hers that she can prove her father's innocence. She needs a good spanking, and I am within an ace of giving it to her," Lucien fumed, half out of his mind at the picture De Lisle painted of the peril in which Sarah had stood.

"I take it you know some reason why she would have gone jaunting off with the ruffian whom I found her with?" De Lisle asked, amused but not surprised by Lucien's reaction.

"Yes, only too well, and I suppose I am at fault for not trying to help her solve the wretched affair, but I never imagined she would go so far in her efforts," Lucien replied. He was not altogether willing to confide in the marquis, but somehow the devil had become involved with Sarah and had fortunately been on hand to effect her rescue, which, Lucien conceded, irritated him beyond measure. Now she would be grateful to the bloke for playing Sir Galahad, yet another star in his crown. How he wished he had been the one to wrest her gallantly from her attackers. Her gratitude might have forced her to relax that hoity-toity air she had been displaying toward him.

De Lisle, who had no difficulty in surmising the tenor of Lucien's thoughts, gazed at him with some amusement, his suspicions about the gallant colonel enhanced by his reaction to the news of Sarah's near brush with horror.

"I think it might be wise, in the lady's own interest, of course, if we pool our information." De Lisle continued. "But before you call me out, let me assure you, I feel nothing but the most brotherly affection for Sarah. Grant you, she is a most entrancing young thing, but hardly my style and I am quite occupied elsewhere. I admit I have used her for my own purposes, not the act of a gentleman, I agree, but harmless. She is not *épris* and, I suggest, has her own reasons for encouraging me, the minx. I take it you feel more deeply, and I wish you all the luck in the world. Also, I believe we share certain concerns about the recent influx of French *émigrés*, which should ensure our cooperation on events now rising to a climax. You have had your suspicions of me, I know, and I have done little to dampen them, for other reasons. In case you have any doubts of my fidelity, I suggest you ask Dundas. He knows what rig I have been running," De Lisle said, now all intent on impressing Lucien with the gravity of the situation.

The two continued their conversation in soft murmurs, causing raised eyebrows among their fellow members, who found the sight of a careless libertine like De Lisle and a steady soldier like Valentine strange companions. Although the club clientele wondered about their whisperings, it was accepted that interruptions would not be welcome, and they were not disturbed. Finally De Lisle rose and wandered across the hall, looking for a game, while Lucien hurried from the club, eager to challenge Sarah on her latest disastrous meddling.

Chapter Thirty-two

Sarah faced Lucien in her grandmother's drawing room with a bravado she was far from feeling. Her obvious reluctance to grant him an interview only exacerbated his emotions, a welter of anger, pride, and a desire to protect her from her own folly. He noticed, too, her rather fine-drawn aspect, a result no doubt of her horrifying experience and the constant remembrance of how nearly she had come to grief. No doubt she had been sleeping badly, prey to nightmares, and served her right, he concluded callously. His own worry and frustration at her attitude provoked the very quarrel he had been determined to avoid.

Sarah had received him with some wariness. "And to what do I owe the honour of this visit, Lucien?" she asked, striving for an easy tone. "We have not seen much of you lately," she said and then flushed. She would not want him to think his absence had bothered her.

"You know perfectly well I have been absent on army business, and I had not noticed that you were so eager for my company," he answered, concealing his pleasure that she had been aware of his dereliction.

"We are always pleased to see you. Grandmother has been asking about you," Sarah responded coolly, implying an unconcern over his lack of attention.

"Well, you will not be pleased to see me today, I warrant. I have just been having a most informative chat with your latest cavalier, the Marquis De Lisle, and he gave me quite a budget of news." Lucien eyed her angrily. "Damn it, Sarah, the minute my back is turned you are up to all sorts of rigs, casting yourself heedlessly into a situation that could have led to a terrible tragedy for you. What were you thinking of to rush off with some disreputable fellow in search of God knows what? You have no idea of the peril you so thoughtlessly exposed yourself to. But then that is your style, your damned independence forcing you to behave in a manner no decent girl would consider for a moment."

"I hardly think it necessary for you to swear at me, Lucien," Sarah said, trying to assume a casual haughty manner. "I am surprised that Theron told you of my experience, and I agree I was most fortunate he was on hand to rescue me. But I had good reason to believe I was at last making some progress in my attempts to solve the mystery of my father's accusers. And how could I know that the general's efforts would lead me into that dreadful place?"

"You are fortunate my gentlemanly instincts—which I admit are sorely tried at this news—prevent me from doing more than swear at you," Lucien returned. "I never heard of such a foolish, childish behaviour. What would your grandmother feel if she knew you had exposed yourself to such a fate?"

Sarah pressed her hands together in her lap, furious at herself for feeling a bit frightened by Lucien's demeanor and his barely leashed anger.

"Perhaps I did not think it all out as carefully as I might have," she said with as much dignity as she could manage, "but the general had found this man who had served with my father, and I believed the sergeant might have some valuable information. Then, too, how could I know that the man who appeared with the general's note was an imposter?"

"Yes, well, I want to know all about that. I cannot think that the general would deliberately entice you into danger. I want you to tell me exactly what happened," he demanded.

Sarah sighed. It would be a relief to explain the whole distressing matter to Lucien, but not if he were to merely scoff at her conclusions. He would probably jeer at her reasoning and not understand her desperation to discover some lead to her father's innocence. Taking a deep breath, she launched into a recital of the general's discoveries and her own determination to interview the sergeant. On describing the general's own reasons for the mix-up she realized how thin his justification appeared, and she could not deny the whole story sounded very suspect. She confessed all but her own suspicions of her uncle, and she felt a huge relief to have transferred the burden onto Lucien's shoulders, no matter how angry he was.

"This tale of the general's man sounds very spurious to me, and I intend to get to the bottom of it. But, Sarah, please believe me, I have only your welfare at heart. If you think I am unsympathetic about your efforts to exonerate your father, believe me it is only because I want to protect you from disappointment and sorrow," Lucien said sincerely, wondering if he should go further and admit that he wanted to take on the job of protecting her for the rest of his life.

Softened by his obvious concern, Sarah looked at him mistily, her tears barely controlled. Looking into her troubled face, Lucien cast his own control to the winds and took her in his arms, prepared to tell her at last what she had come to mean to him and to ask her to trust him with her future. He kissed her gently, and would have continued if they had not been interrupted rudely by the door opening.

Angela stood in the entrance, eyeing the two narrowly, not unaware that her presence was unexpected and unwanted but deciding to ignore the intimate scene before her.

"Good afternoon, you two. I do hope I am not interrupting but, Sarah, had you forgotten we are expected at Lady Montfort's rout? Mother and Grandmother are awaiting us. And we mustn't let the horses stand too long," she spoke brightly, concealing her fury at the sight of Lucien and Sarah in what she suspected had been a close embrace.

"Not at all, Angela," Lucian answered quickly for Sarah. "Sarah and I were just conducting some personal business, which can wait. I will not delay you any further. Your servants." Lucian bowed and stood between the two women, allowing Sarah, whose reactions were much slower, to gather herself together. He had not liked Angela's tone and could not deny her appearance had been most inopportune, for Sarah's reaction to his scold and his attempt to make her trust him had been received much more happily than he had expected. If Angela had not intervened, he was convinced Sarah would have given him the answer he sought. But Lucien, accustomed to exercising patience in the pursuit of his ends, thought that he would have another opportunity before long, and, now that Sarah's defences had been breached, he would not allow her to hide behind her pride and stubborness.

He bade them both adieux, admitting to himself ruefully he was abandoning Sarah to her cousin's questions but unable to see any other possible behaviour. Certainly Sarah was capable of turning aside Angela's probing. He left them prey to both hope and frustration.

"Really, Sarah, what are you thinking of, luring Lucien into a tryst? Your colonial manners will not do here, you know. I am sure Grandmother was not aware you were abandoning all notions of propriety by receiving him alone. And I have warned you not to be beguiled by his inability to refuse the lures of an attractive female," Angela said snidely, barely hiding her chagrin. Just how far had matters progressed between Lucien and her cousin? She would not countenance Sarah casting a rub in her way, and she had now quite decided to claim Lucien for her own.

"You refine too much on a private conversation I was having with Lucien, Angela." Sarah answered tartly. "And it is not your business. Come, if you are so eager to depart, we must not keep your mother and Grandmother waiting, and don't forget the horses." She had had quite enough of Angela's insinuations and was almost convinced her cousin's interest in

Lucien was not returned, although he had seemed inordinately anxious to leave the scene after that interrupted embrace, Sarah thought with annoyance.

Raising her eyebrows in disdain, Angela flounced from the room, leaving her cousin to follow. Sarah shrugged her shoulders at Angela's display of ill temper. She doubted it would be a pleasant afternoon.

Chapter Thirty-three

If Lucien had not been successful in securing from Sarah the response he so ardently desired, he could at least assuage his impatience by facing the general. He had not been impressed with Sarah's explanations of the general's excuses for the confusion of messages. Having known the general all his life and been aware of that officer's close intimacy with the Ravenshams, he could not believe the general himself intended Sarah any harm, but his story was puzzling in the extreme. And surely, by now, having learnt of Sarah's misfortune, he must have made some push to discover the villain who had lured her from Park Street into the stews beyond Covent Gardens. Marshaling his arguments, Lucien rode directly around to the general's room in Clarges Street.

Lucien eyed the general's batman, who admitted him, and was forced to conclude that this man in no way resembled the varlet who had conveyed Sarah on the false visit to one Sergeant O'Toole. He might question the man later, after he had said his piece to the general. That officer, who was relaxing before the fireplace in his sitting room, greeted him with all amiability and seemed distinctly pleased to see him.

"Ah, Lucien, my boy," the general said jovially, waving him to a seat. "To what do I owe this pleasure? I confess I am not feeling quite up to snuff and have been idling away here by the fire. A touch of my old nemesis, the dratted fever, has been dogging me. Old bones, I fear, the result of too many campaigns, but you do not have to worry about that yet."

"Sorry to hear you are indisposed, sir. That explains why you have not followed up on this distressing affair of Sarah Ravensham's abduction, I suspect," said Lucien adroitly.

The general frowned. "Ah, she had told you that miserable tale, I see. I admit I am all at sea over it, but I have quizzed my man closely, and he has admitted that he stopped by his pub and had a few too many that day. I feel he may have been doped, for he normally has quite a strong head. He was with me in the Low Countries, you know, and is the soul of loyalty and discretion. Someone has it in for the delightful Miss Sarah, I perceive, although I cannot see why such an unexceptional young woman should have aroused such enmity. She has been burrowing away at that old affair of her father's. Could that be the cause of this latest affair, I wonder?" The general seemed sincerely distressed and obviously in some pain.

Lucien found it difficult to believe that his reaction was feigned, but his story did not ring true. The general's open guileless face betrayed no emotion other than bewilderment and sorrow at Sarah's near brush with disaster. Accustomed to considering

Apsley-Gower as an officer of impeccable honour, Lucien could not imagine that he would become involved in such a vile attack on his old comrade's daughter. Then, too, what would be his reason? Her disappearance would certainly arouse her friends and family, and the outcry would eventually lead to discovery. What could the general gain from an investigation, if he were the culprit, but disgrace and the odium of his acquaintances? His long distinguished career would be tarnished beyond hope and he would have to leave his comfortable life and flee abroad, not a prospect to be contemplated with any enjoyment while Napoleon ruled across the channel.

Perhaps he needed money, but, looking around the quiet luxury of the general's rooms, Lucien found that difficult to believe. Accustomed to the avarice and strange passions of men, Lucien had long ago learned not to be surprised at the motives that urged them into treachery, but, in all the years he had known the general, he had never seen him behave meanly or greedily. He had achieved his success through dogged courage, obedience to orders, and an ability to cooperate with those in authority. Lucien had always considered him an officer, if not gifted with unusual talent, at least patriotic and dependable. There was no conceivable reason that he would abandon the habits and beliefs of a lifetime, jeopardize all he had achieved in order to remove Sarah Ravensham from the world.

While these thoughts were running wildly through his head, no sign of his disturbance showed on Lucien's countenance. Skilled at negotiation and questioning enemy prisoners, his quiet manner and self-assurance had always stood him in good stead in the past. Now, when it seemed most important, he was not about to lose his ability for wresting information from those unwilling to reveal it, but, with all his experience guiding him, he was at war with his own longtime knowledge and respect for Apsley-Gower and did not know quite how to proceed and waited for the general to continue.

The general, eyeing him carefully, seemed to understand his dilemma. If he was angry that Lucien could suspect him of causing Sarah harm, he did not show it.

"I realize this story sounds a bit vague, almost unbelievable, Lucien, but I assure you it is the truth. Sarah Ravensham for some reason has made a dangerous enemy. You, who know her so well and who perhaps had some occasion in the colonies to learn about her political contacts and allegiance, might know better than I do why she has attracted this undesirable attention. She seems to be an open, honest girl with more than the usual London miss's penchant for independence, but I cannot believe she is involved in any treasonable activity against His Majesty's government, which might embroil her in perilous situations." The general's tone was ruminative. Had he placed a doubt in Lucien's mind about Sarah?

Lucien quickly disabused the general of Sarah's duplicity, but that officer's words had given him some uncomfortable ideas. He trusted Sarah, even if she did infuriate him with her precipitate rash behaviour. What concerned him about the general's remarks was that she might have given that officer the impression that she was or had been involved in some conspiracy. No one must know about the Hamilton-Pitt negotiations, even such a loyal soldier as the general. He bade the general a restrained farewell, not entirely satisfied with that officer's explanations, but now an additional problem was added to the budget of worries he already carried.

Before leaving the general's rooms, Lucien stopped for a brief talk with the batman who had admitted him. The man sprang from the breed of soldier devoted to their superior officer, taciturn, unschooled, but well-trained. He did not like being questioned by Lucien, but his master had indicated that he must cooperate so he gave grudging answers to Lucien's queries.

"Do you remember who you encountered in the pub where you stopped off on your way to deliver the message to Miss Ravensham?" Lucien asked.

"Can't say that I do, sir, it was not my usual pub, and I was only there for the one noggin," the man answered, but he was not an accomplished dissembler, and Lucien felt convinced he was lying.

"Well, just tell me exactly what happened after you ordered your drink." Lucien persisted.

"I exchanged a few words with a bloke standing next to me about the weather. You know how 'tis, sir. Nothing of no account, 'twere. I had the note in my pocket, but I cannot rightly see how he stole it without me seeing it, or even how I came not to notice. The next thing I remember I came to, with my head on the table, feeling groggy like. I asked the pubkeeper what had happened and all he said was that I came over faint and the cove nearby helped me to a table, to have a sit-down. He didn't seem to notice much else. 'Twas a busy tavern, off Piccadilly." The man rattled off his explanation as if he had learned it by rote. Lucien was convinced he was lying but felt he would not shake him while the general stood by.

"I'm not sure this fellow is telling us the whole story," he said to the general, "but he's your man, and you will have better luck getting the real tale from him. I'll leave you to it, for I am sure there is more to it than this Banbury tale." Lucien bid the general a curt farewell, uneasy at the tenor of the interview although he could not quite say why.

With less than two days before the ball, Sarah found all the distraction she needed from her pressing personal problems. Accustomed to much less extravagant entertainments, she had been amazed from her first appearances in the London beau monde by the elegant and splendid festivities provided, each one more lavish than the previous gala, as if the jaded appetites of London's elite must be tempted ever more diligently. She had thought the Devonshire's ball had reached an apogee, but obviously her grandmother felt impelled to rival that occasion. Lady Ravensham excused the expenditure and intricate preparations by explaining that she had not entertained in such a manner for years, not even when Angela had made her come-out, so it behooved her to go the whole way and ensure that the Park Street house present its best face on the evening in question. More to the point, Sarah saw that her grandmother really was enjoying herself and not endangering her health.

In readiness for the grand affair, the great chandelier in the ballroom was lowered and cleaned painstakingly, before glistening new wax tapers were inserted in the hundreds of holders. The parquet floor was polished under Peverel's direction with a special recipe of beeswax and linseed oil. Even the gilt chairs surrounding the huge room had been refurbished, awaiting the stylish guests who would sit out the dances and eye the revellers. Lady Ravensham threw herself with animation into every detail of the arrangements. Invitations, menu, flowers, wine, music, they all received her personal attention.

She insisted that Sarah buy a startlingly beautiful new gown for the occasion, although Sarah felt her wardrobe was already crowded with enough gowns to clothe several females. But Lady Ravensham prevailed, and escorted her to the most fashionable modiste of the day, Mme. Charles, whose prices made Sarah gasp. After inspecting countless designs in the *Lady's Magazine* and mulling over bolts of silver gauze, French dimity, satins, crepes, and laces of delicate hues, they finally settled on a simple design of rich figured gauze over apricot silk, as the best complement to Sarah's colouring and chestnut curls. Lady Ravensham had definite ideas as to the style and design and, although she conceded that young girls traditionally wore white for their presentations, felt Sarah would shine to best advantage in a less insipid shade. Sarah, bemused by the profusion of materials and patterns, bowed to the wisdom of her grandmother's choice. If the gown selected had not been entirely to her taste, she might have argued, but Lady Ravensham's choice could not be faulted.

Sarah was human enough to find all this frenzied preparation in her honour exciting and distracting so that she did not brood over her various problems. She heard from Lucien that he had been forced to rush down to the coast again on army business but would be back in plenty of time for the ball and he would then tell her the results of his interview with the general. In the meantime, he wrote, she was to stay out of trouble since he would not be on hand to extricate her, and he might remind her that they had other unfinished business to discuss. She also had his permission to go driving with De Lisle as he and the Marquis had come to an understanding over the latter's attentions to Sarah. Lucien had chuckled when he wrote this last line to Sarah, knowing how she would bristle at his taking over her affairs in this arrogant manner, but he admitted there was little to laugh about in the current situation, redolent as it was with suspicion, betrayal, and danger for her.

In the past several days, Sarah had perforce spent more time with her cousin than she would have preferred. Her cousin, whose nose was quite put out of joint by Lady Ravensham's obvious preference for Sarah's company and her delight with that young lady's success with the ton, tried to put a good face on the affair. But she did not like sharing her beaux' favours, nor could she compete with Sarah's pretty manners.

Angela had been especially piqued by the Marquis De Lisle's interest in Sarah, for she would not have minded attracting that gentleman to her own train, despite his reputation as a libertine and womanizer. The coy flirtatious glances and brittle conversation, which Angela cast to such good effect with less experienced men of the beau monde, made no impression on De Lisle, who plainly was indifferent and outright bored. Tossing her head, she confided to one of her friends that she found him too blasé and scandalous for her taste. Her cousin was welcome to him, although she might find her reputation would be ruined. It never occurred to Angela that Sarah and Theron might be enjoying a chaste friendship, in which neither of their hearts was involved deeply. Angela did not think of hearts or the warmer emotions. Her interest lay in rent rolls and titles.

She did, however, feel quite satisfied that she had put a stop to her cousin's attempts to draw Lucien into her net. She herself intended to shine so brilliantly at the coming ball that Lucien, among others, would be so dazzled that a mere untutored colonial would be quite put in the shade. Angela had decided that the ball would serve her purposes well. She would secure Lucien's promise that evening and depress her cousin's pretensions in that direction once and for all. It never crossed her mind that the gentleman in question might have other ideas.

Chapter Thirty-four

Finally the evening of the ball arrived. Lady Ravensham had insisted that Sarah spend some of the afternoon resting in preparation for the gala evening, a restriction Sarah found taxing. It left her too much leisure to fret about Lucien's intentions. She could not fathom his attitude toward herself. One moment he was a teasing, forthright companion, brotherly in nature, the next he behaved like a jealous lover, protective and upset over other men poaching on his preserves. At their last meeting, she felt certain he would have confessed his feelings if Angela had not interrupted them, but maybe in a cooler moment he was grateful for that interruption. She could not decide if he were playing with her, or if he were really sincere. She had admitted that her own heart was seriously involved, however she might be forced to hide it from Lucien himself.

Indeed, her grandmother's insistence on a rest period during the afternoon of the ball created more nervousness than if she had been allowed to take a brisk ride in the park or to busy herself with the preparations, as she would have for a similar entertainment at home in Philadelphia. But then, nothing about her life in London resembled the simpler pleasures of her former home, and not for the first time Sarah wished she could close her eyes and awaken in her own fourposter in Joshua Allen's red-brick solid house on Fourth Street.

Despite all her worries, the unresolved questions weighing on her mind, Sarah still felt an anticipatory thrill at the thought of the ball being given in her honour that evening. She had her share of female vanity, although her grandfather had often chided her for it, and the notion that London's elite would be flocking to the Park Street as a signal of their approval of the Ravenshams' American cousin was a heady one.

As the hour drew near for the first guests to arrive, Sarah pirouetted before the mirror, deciding that she looked quite the thing. Her abigail, Polly, round-eyed, assured her, "You will be the prettiest lady at the ball, miss," a compliment Sarah took with some skepticism. She had to agree, though, that the new apricot ball gown did bring out the gleaming lights of her chestnut hair, which had been dressed more intricately this evening in the Grecian style, and her complexion glowed with the healthy flush of anticipation and excitement. From her cream slippers to the pearls woven in her coiffure she looked every inch the finished, sophisticated product of fashionable London, but inside she knew she quivered with the nervousness of a small girl at her first party. Chiding herself for viewing the ball with such apprehension, she tripped off to join her grandmother who was waiting to greet the guests.

Quite a splendid company gathered in Lady Ravensham's drawing room that evening before the ball proper began. Two-dozen favoured guests had been invited for dinner, an interesting mixture of personalities supplementing the family. De Lisle was among those favoured, and he looked his usual impeccable self, but with a decided gleam in his eye, which Sarah thought might be connected with the luscious creature on his arm. He introduced his companion, noting with amusement Sarah's comprehensive glance at the stylish woman, a ravishing brunette with the indubitable air of a chic Parisian.

"Sarah, I want you to meet one of my French cousins, Comtesse Aimée de la Frontons, who has only very recently escaped the rigours of Napoleon's court to join us. Ma chère, Mademoiselle Sarah Ravensham."

Sarah, noting that De Lisle spoke to the comtesse in the intimate pronoun, was not one bit surprised to see the lady return his affectionate glance with one of almost smouldering promise. Naturally the Frenchwoman was of good family—even De Lisle would not introduce a member of the demimondaine to her grandmother's guests—but it seemed evident their relationship was deeper than one of cousinly affection. Sarah found herself both amused and relieved. Although she had quite enjoyed De Lisle's attentions, she had never been in danger of losing her heart to that controversial gentleman, nor did she think that he fancied himself in love with her. Whatever his reasons for playing the devoted cavalier, a sincere and deep affection was not among them. Still, he had proved an amusing and fascinating companion, and she owed him a deep debt of gratitude for rescuing her from the hideous fate her unknown enemy had planned.

Escorted into dinner by Lucien, she found herself seated between him and the impressive Lord Grenville, whose espousing of union with Ireland had caused such a commotion. A bit shy in the presence of such an august lord, she contented herself with unexceptional conversation, hoping to avoid making a gauche remark and allowing Lord Grenville to expound his political theories without argument. He found her an attentive audience through the elaborate collation of turtle soup, turbot, and saddle of mutton. The daunting eye of Angela, who was seated directly across from her, did little to put her at ease. But Lucien, aware of her agitation, did his best to soothe her and under his skillful handling during the host of removes that followed the mutton, she almost regained her normal blithe spirits.

"Lady Ravensham has done you proud this evening, Sarah. A distinguished gathering to toast your official entrance into society. Not that you don't deserve it. I have never seen you looking more charming," Lucien remarked lightly. He did not mention the general or his conversation with that officer, who was seated at the right of Angela but close enough to prevent his becoming the object of their conversation. At any event this was not the moment to discuss his call on General Apsley-Gower with Sarah. He did not want to distress her on this occasion, which he hoped would be one of enjoyment and felicity for her.

"Yes, she has quite outdone herself, and I wish she

had been a bit more restrained. I believe more than six hundred have been invited to the ball." Sarah was annoyed that Lucien's admiring gaze and compliment had put her in such a pother.

"Well, I am sure you will be overwhelmed with admirers once the music begins, so I will take advantage of the opportunity to plead for the opening dance and however many more you can spare and prevail upon you to let me take you down to supper." Lucien smiled engagingly at the lovely picture Sarah made in her finery.

Sarah, who had been warned that she must not accept more than two dances with any one gentleman, was a bit surprised.

"Isn't that a bit excessive, Colonel?" she riposted.

"Not a bit of it. I must fix my attention with you before too many rivals appear to whisk you off. You will be beseiged, I am sure," he answered with his usual aplomb.

Angela, prevented by social nicety from displaying her avid curiosity as to the tête-à-tête across the table, narrowed her eyes and frowned slightly. Lucien was paying entirely too much attention to her colonial cousin, but she was helpless to intervene. As the long meal continued she could not help but be aware that Lord Grenville had very short innings with Sarah, whose response to Lucien's practised ardour seemed excessive. When the ladies arose from the table, leaving the gentlemen to their wine, Angela intended to remind her cousin that she was making a cake of herself.

Finally, at her grandmother's nod the ladies rose to withdraw, Sarah in a bemused state from Lucien's compliments and gentle raillery. Certainly he was making every effort to charm her and she was finding it increasingly difficult to resist.

Lady Ravensham, aware that Sarah might find the company slightly intimidating to her granddaughter, claimed her company in the drawing room, involving her in comfortable chat with one of her own bosom bows, a sprightly matron of her generation who looked kindly upon Sarah, and showed none of the disdain that some members of the ton were wont to display when faced with a colonial. Angela drifted casually over to join the group on the sofa.

"What a delightful evening, Grandmother," she said, insinuating herself into the conversation. "Sarah, you are fortunate to be honoured with such an entertainment and such interesting dinner partners. I do think, Grandmother, you might have found me someone more exciting than that dull old general and Lord Brigham." Angela's complaint was voiced in her most dulcet tones, but Lady Ravensham was not deceived. What a spoiled shrew Angela was becoming, jealous of any attention paid to others. But Lady Ravensham was skilled in soothing annoyances of that sort and not about to be criticized.

"Not at all, Angela. I find Lord Brigham a most delightful young man, and of course Julian Apsley-Gower is one of our family's oldest friends," she chided.

"Quite so, but not a very stimulating conversationalist. Still, once the ball begins, I have no doubt I will have more entertaining companions. Poor you, Sarah, having to stand in a receiving line for hours, while I am free to enjoy the dancing." Angela's barbed remarks continued despite her grandmother's obvious warning tone.

"Not at all. I am looking forward to meeting all the delightful company Grandmother has bid to the ball," Sarah returned coolly, a bit amused at Angela's attitude. Her cousin was obviously displeased and made no attempt to hide it.

"Well, I believe I will give my first dance to Lucien, although there will be many competitors for the honour, I am sure," Angela preened.

Before Sarah could reply, her grandmother intervened, "Wait until you are asked, my girl. Getting a bit above yourself. Not pretty behaviour."

Angela, taken aback by her grandmother's rare criticism, was about to protest, but she was interrupted by the arrival of the gentlemen, and she noticed that Lucien made directly for their group. Which one of them was he so eager to secure she wondered and not for the first time conceded that that gentleman's intentions were capable of several interpretations.

Chapter Thirty-five

Angela was correct in advising Sarah that she would spend a tedious time receiving the countless guests Lady Ravensham had invited to the ball. As the fashionable horde streamed up the grand staircase to greet their hostess and her granddaughter, Sarah felt her smile become fixed and her hand grow limp from the procession of society's most distinguished company. Her grandmother, looking relaxed and regal, in magenta silk and diamonds, did not seem to find the ordeal in the least taxing, welcoming each newcomer with a gracious word and presenting them to Sarah with pride. At last Sarah was dismissed to find Lucien hovering to claim the promised dance. Several importunate gentlemen, including Captain Parry, had already solicited her hand and her dance program was filled with scrawled initials, but she had saved the first quadrille and supper dance for Lucien much against her better judgment.

The movements of the dance prevented any serious conversation. Still Sarah was aware of his every glance and the firm pressure of his hand as he led her through the intricate movements. Despite herself her cheeks flushed and she blossomed under his admiring gaze whenever their eyes met.

"Sarah, I have a matter of great import I wish to speak to you about and you have proved strangely elusive lately," Lucien said as they came together.

"Is it about your conversation with General Apsley-Gower?" Sarah asked hopefully.

"No, it is not. Are you so preoccupied with your recent experience you have no thoughts for other matters? I admit you endured some terrifying moments but you must put that ordeal behind you now. At a more opportune time I will tell you what transpired between the general and myself," Lucien promised, annoyed that Sarah's mood did not seem propitious for his wooing. Could he have been mistaken? Did she really care only for establishing her father's innocence and nothing for her own future? Or was that future already decided and not to include him?

Nervous and unsure of herself under his searching gaze, Sarah's volatile temper rose. She must protect herself, for her mortification at the thought he might suspect how much she cared about his opinion of her made her adopt a cloak of indifference. Doubting his sincerity she answered with an air of self-possession she was far from feeling. "Of course not. I do appreciate your involvement in my affairs, Lucien, and your approaching the general, but it is only natural that I wish to get to the bottom of the matter. There are so many unanswered questions."

"I quite agree, but your safety is my paramount concern and I still feel you are exposing yourself to unnecessary danger and sorrow, my dear," he said gently, unwilling to give her cause for anger, but piqued that she could think of no other reason for his requested interview.

"I am still absolutely certain that Father was betrayed by someone who knew him well, and it is nigh driving me to distraction for I know I have missed the vital clue, either in General Apsley-Gower's recital of events or somewhere," Sarah conceded, loath to believe that Lucien might wish to ask her a more personal question.

"The general certainly knows as much about that affair as anyone, and I agree he has not been as forthcoming as he might have been. There is a strange odour about that message," Lucien agreed, frowning. He realized that until Sarah solved the problem surrounding her recent abduction and the general's role in it, she had little time for more personal concepts. A good set-down to his consequence, he conceded sardonically. Even if he were not the man to win her, he cared enough to put his own desires aside and help her achieve some resolution of the affair. At the end of the set, his impatience could be held in check no longer. Her next dance was with Robert Parry, but he prevailed upon her to walk outside, onto the terrace, for the night was balmy and the ballroom stuffy under the myriad of candles that shone from the glittering chandeliers.

Sarah hesitated, knowing it was rude to cut her next dance, but she was anxious to talk to Lucien. She had to discuss her concern with someone and Lucien was her first choice. She felt confidence in his opinion even though he did not believe there was reason to reopen the investigation. And if Lucien's attitude toward her was ambiguous, at least she could trust his judgment. She could not deny Lucien's integrity in matters of duty or patriotism, or his ability to take charge. It was only in matters of the heart she found him deficient. The feelings he evoked in her she banished, not wanting to confess he had routed all her defences.

Their progress onto the terrace did not go unnoticed and there were several raised eyebrows from the more conservative dowagers whose suspicions about "fast" American girls were confirmed. Lady Ravensham, on the other hand, smiled, confident that Lucien was about to put his fate to the test with her granddaughter, and not at all displeased with the notion. Aware of the impropriety of Sarah's cutting her dance with her next partner to accompany Lucien, she was prepared to ignore the breach of etiquette if the result was felicitous.

Angela also had been keeping an eye on the pair and could barely restrain her chagrin. Although looking her best in a cerulean silk gown that set off her flawless complexion and smooth blond hair and beseiged with partners, she had not seen Lucien among them, to her great annoyance. And now he was leaving the ballroom with Sarah. Only long training and a belief in her own superior attractions prevented her from exhibiting her anger. She would not allow her upstart cousin to put a spoke in her wheel. Masking her irritation, she smiled graciously at the beaux who surrounded her before the next set began but inwardly determined to thwart Sarah's blatant attempts to lure Lucien into a compromising rendez-vous.

Sarah, unaware of the speculation surrounding her action, was intent only on confiding her worries to Lucien, whose own reasons for desiring an interview she could not fathom.

"Lucien, when I talked to the general a few days ago, I had the definite feeling he was not telling me all he knew. So many of the people involved in that long-ago treachery are dead. Lord George Germain, the key to the whole business, for one. I understand General Howe is in Newcastle in command of troops in the northern district. I wish I could talk to him. Would he see me, do you thing?" Sarah asked.

"Probably, but you would get little satisfaction from him. He has probably forgotten the whole affair." Lucien said, thinking he would not allow this opportunity to pass without stating his own intentions. But first she would listen to her confidences, pleased that she trusted him enough to put faith in his advice. "Howe is naturally of an indolent disposition," he went on, "loath to put himself out for anyone and inclined to indifference toward the affairs of his junior officers. He has always tended to ignore trouble of any sort." Lucien spoke critically, for Howe had not endeared himself to the men who served under him. He was a coarse man of dubious morality, and Lucien did not want to expose Sarah to his lewd approaches.

"Well, I am going to try to seek an interview with him, just the same. I must get to the bottom of this affair, and I know there is much more to learn," Sarah insisted stubbornly.

"Sarah, please listen to me. I want to help you, to set your mind at rest over this affair, but, more important, I want to shield you from any unhappiness, from this and any other torment." Lucien grasped her strongly by both arms, the fierce light in his usually dark, enigmatic eyes evidence of this impatience. "Forget Howe, Apsley-Gower, forget it all and hear me out. Despite all our differences, you must be aware of the attraction between us. I have known from the first sight of you on the steps of your grandfather's house that you had been sent to disturb my life. Come, admit you return my feelings." Lucien, for the first time in his life, was in danger of losing control under the passion of his emotions, beguiled by Sarah's candid, tawny eyes and seduced by her closeness. Before she could summon her defenses, he rained kisses on her hair, her brow, finally her lips, without giving her time to demur. Completely lost in the blissful sensation his hard warm lips evoked, she surrendered totally to her clamouring senses, unaware of all but the passionate response Lucien's caresses evoked.

"Lucien, you really must behave more sensibly," Angela's cool, patronizing voice cut across the idyll, bringing both Lucien and Sarah out of their bemused state. "Anyone could see you, and it is quite unfair to put Sarah in such a compromising position. I understand you might be carried away by the situation and the romantic night, and Sarah is looking entrancing, but do give a care to her reputation."

Sarah, her hair tousled and her cheeks red from the ardour of Lucien's kisses, did not at first take in the sneering words of her cousin, but she tore herself from Lucien's grasp and turned to face her adversary.

"My dear Sarah," Angela continued, "do not make a cake of yourself. I warned you but you would not listen. Grandmother would be disgusted at your loose actions." Angela was enjoying her cousin's discomfort and ignored Lucien, who, as distracted as Sarah, more quickly controlled his features and assumed his usual aplomb.

Sarah, completely overset by her emotions and throbbing from the desires Lucien had aroused, was totally confused. She could not look at Lucien and avoided Angela's scornful eye, believing that her cousin had every right to reprove her for her loose actions.

"I'm sorry. It was all a mistake," she muttered in a turmoil of embarrassment and, before Lucien could say a word in rebuttal of Angela's accusations, she fled from the terrace, seeking sanctuary from her traitorous emotions and her cousin's baleful, disdainful stare.

Skirting the edge of the ballroom, conscious of being the focus of critical eyes, she rushed into the library to regain some composure and face her grandmother's guests with an armour of indifference. Gasping, unable to restrain the tears that poured down her cheeks, she sank into a chair and tried to settle her tumultuous emotions.

How could she have allowed Lucien to kiss her like that, knowing that he was only playing with her? She had been warned. And the fact that Angela had discovered them in that fervent embrace only added to her unhappiness. Well, let Lucien explain to Angela how he had been carried away, had yielded to an unexplainable impulse. How right she herself had been to elude him, to suspect his attentions. Whatever he felt for her was no more than tepid friendship, and a desire to score over her. From the beginning of their relationship she had known he might cause her heartache. Sarah tried to summon righteous anger at his taking advantage of her vulnerability, of allaying her antagonism with sympathy. Could he be so conceited, so accustomed to getting his way with women, that he was lost to all propriety? What did he want of her? A passionate interlude, a brief flirtation, or a foil to make Angela jealous? She would not be used so. Even De Lisle, with all his lecherous reputation, had not treated her in such a heartless fashion. She hated him. She hated him.

But despite her shame and anger Sarah could not deny that the fault was not his alone. She had responded so ardently to his kisses. She had not believed herself possible of such an upsurge of passion. What a villain he was to practice his seduction upon her. She would not allow him any further liberties. She would put the memory of his advances from her mind and remember only that he was promised to Angela. Never, never would she allow herself to surrender again to his cajoling embraces. Still, she knew that no matter how sensible the arguments, she would find it difficult to put Lucien from her heart.

Sarah straightened her chin resolutely. She was not some fainthearted silly fool to be toyed with in this insulting manner. She would return to the ballroom, keep her head high, flirt and dance the evening away, and that would show both Lucien and Angela just how little she cared. Pride came to her rescue. She smoothed down her curls and decided that she must repair to her bedroom to put herself in order. But before she could leave her sanctuary, she heard the door opening, and voices heralding the approach of some guests. How could she explain her presence here? Scrunching down in the commodious wing chair she hoped they would not notice her, before she could retire with some casual greeting.

Then she recognized the voice of Gen. Julian Apsley-Gower and his companion, Moira Amberly, and was taken aback by the tenor of their conversation. All intentions of declaring her presence disappeared, and she listened avidly, hardly daring to breathe in case they discovered her.

Chapter Thirty-six

"Really, Julian, need you have dragged me away from the company in that cavalier way?" Moira Amberly's fretful tone signified her displeasure.

"It doesn't signify and no one will notice our absence. We can be quite private here, and far safer from observation than a rendezvous in the park. I am not pleased with you, my dear." General Apsley-Gower's low harsh intonation was a far cry from his usual kindly speech. Sarah, who would not normally listen to a conversation not meant for her ears, had no compunction about doing so now. There was a note to the general's tone that sent a frisson of fear and excitement through her, and she cowered lower in her capacious chair. This alliance promised to answer some of her most pressing questions, she was convinced.

"You failed miserably in your task aboard ship. I thought perhaps you had not received my instructions in time, but now I can only conclude you made little attempt to carry them out. You did not find the document Hamilton sent to Pitt. I wanted that paper badly, and so did our masters." The general's tone held a threat that sent a cold chill down Sarah's spine.

"I know, Julian, but it was not for lack of trying. I searched Colonel Valentine's cabin very thoroughly. I pretended seasickness and no one suspected me although I was frightened half to death. I even made a push to go through Sarah's things, but she is such a ninny, I do not think he would have given her the message, the annoying chit. Surely, now that I have done what you commanded, I might have my letters back. It was not my fault the message was not in their effects," Moira cajoled.

"Perhaps Valentine did not have the packet. There must have been another agent aboard, for my information could not be faulted. You have forced me into action that might endanger my whole career, and I do not look kindly on that. But that is behind us. I arranged for you to chaperone that chit just so you could be available for that mission and you failed me. You have not been more successful with Lord Ravensham. You were directed to approach him and wrest from him the secrets of the Foreign Office, and in that too you have proved a disappointment," he said, listing her ineptitude impatiently.

"He's a cold fish. I doubt if any woman, no matter how alluring, could work her wiles on him. He isn't interested in women. It was not for lack of trying, believe me, and I have endured enough humiliation. When can I have my letters? If my husband learns of my liaison with Comte Vergennes, I am lost. Surely it is not to your advantage to break up my marriage. That would avail you nothing. Think of my children,"

Moira pleaded.

"Neither your brats nor your husband, dreary clod that he is, concern me. But it is true he would be unhappy to learn his pattern card of a wife had an affair with that popinjay Vergennes. Very rash of you, my dear, to trust that *émigré*. He may be a more skilled lover than Amberly, but he is an opportunist. I had no difficulty in wresting those letters from him," the general continued coldly.

"You are an evil brute. Not only willing to betray your country but persecute a poor woman to secure your treacherous designs, and everyone convinced you are a kindly courageous officer," Moira sneered.

"You are no better, my dear. We both need money and your greedy little hands are no cleaner than mine. Now I expect results from Ravensham. He is privy to all that goes on at the Foreign Office and Pitt confides in him. I want to get my hands on those secret memos." The general was unmoved by Moira's tirade.

"I won't prostitute myself. I will get those letters back somehow," Moira spoke desperately.

"Little good if you did. I have confided all in a diary, which will be published if anything happens to me. I doubt if you have the courage to do me in no matter how fervently you desire my end. I have too much at stake to let your foolish vapourings stand in my way. Either you cajole Ravensham into revealing Pitt's plans toward the Frenchies or your letters will be given to your husband. That's my last word." The general had not raised his voice but the icy threat in his tone left no doubt to Moira, or to Sarah, that he meant exactly what he said.

"I will try, Julian. I must have those letters," Moira wailed.

"You must succeed, my dear. I will give you another few weeks. Time is pressing. My French masters are very demanding. They pay only for results. You have quite as much at risk as I do, remember. And remember too that I am a dangerous man to cross. I have not played this game all these years to come a cropper now. We had best return to the ballroom separately. I don't want the Ravensham's suspicions aroused about our relationship, and that wily devil Valentine is up on every suit. He must notice nothing," the general ordered brusquely.

Sarah then heard the door of the library shut gently. So appalled was she at the revelations of the traitors that she barely heard Mrs. Amberly's muffled sobs. On one thing she was decided. Somehow she must turn this overheard conversation to her advantage. She could not afford to hesitate. If General Apsley-Gower had betrayed his country once, he would do it again. She must discover more, and while Moira Amberly was so vulnerable, she might be able to wring some valuable information from her.

Not for a moment did Sarah consider the anomalous position in which she had placed herself, nor the possible danger if she revealed what she had overheard. She rose from her hiding place to confront an astonished Moira Amberly. She presented a calm facade to her adversary and said in a guileless voice.

"Good evening, Mrs. Amberly. I don't believe you knew there was a witness to your conversation, but I will not apologize since your interview with the general has given me several strong cards to play, and I intend to use them."

Moira, overset by Sarah's appearance and words, was in no condition to marshal her forces against this unwelcome witness to the damning conversation that had just taken place. Curse the girl! She had been trouble since the minute she had laid eyes on her, and she must be prevented from revealing the indiscretions she had heard.

"Sarah, how unfortunate, and how devious of you to spy on a private conversation. You should have made yourself known. Not the manners I would expect from a gently reared girl." Moira attempted to put a bold face upon what had occurred but knew she was at a disadvantage. Sarah was no gullible, silly miss who could be cozened into thinking her relationship with the general was anything but reprehensible, no matter how she wished otherwise. How could she keep her from doing mischief? Perhaps by appealing to her better nature and picturing herself as a helpless victim? Moira Amberly had no difficulty in persuading herself that was what she was.

"Just listen to me a moment, my dear. I had no choice but to cooperate with the general's evil designs. He was blackmailing me with some indiscreet letters I had written to a Frenchman I thought cared for me sincerely. I know it was wrong of me to deceive my husband, but he is absent so much, and the comte was so charming, so devoted. I have been very foolish, but I have paid dearly for a few weeks' madness. It would kill me to be deprived of my husband's good opinion and my children. How could I subject them to such disgrace?" she pleaded, facile tears rising into her pale-blue eyes.

"I am not interested in your indiscretions, Mrs. Amberly, and I certainly do not intend to make use of this intelligence to bring you to justice. Your own conscience must be your punishment. What I claim for my silence is some information, which I am sure you will give me," Sarah said, ruthlessly. There was no doubt she had made her judgment of the vain shallow woman who had risked her family's welfare, not for a great love, but for an inconsequential dalliance.

"I am at your mercy, Sarah," Moira begged, her begging manner hiding her vicious temper at being taken to task by this gauche girl.

"It is obvious that the general has played his traitor's game for many years, and harmed not only his country, to which he owed his loyalty, but also many innocent people. I suspect he had some hand in my father's disgrace and I am determined to discover it and bring it home to him, but I need evidence. If you help me, I need not reveal your own despicable actions." Sarah's voice was steely. Here at last was the evidence she had searched for, the confirmation of what she had always known in her heart, and the opportunity to clear her father's reputation from the shame that had dogged it for twenty years.

"But Sarah, I know little. I was forced to spy on Colonel Valentine aboard ship but, as you heard, I found nothing of any moment." Moira excused herself, hoping to brush through this difficult scene.

"There are your plans to entice my Uncle Ronald to reveal state secrets, although I think General Apsley-

Gower has made a grave misjudgment there. My uncle is not so easily gulled by an attractive woman." Sarah would not be put off. "I will not expose you to his scorn, and even more, to his punishment, if you tell me about the general's diary. What did he mean by that?"

"All I know is that he has kept a record of his machinations for these many years, but where he has secreted it I do not know. Some safe hiding place, you can be sure. He has rooms off Piccadilly, but surely he would not keep incriminating evidence there," Moira offered shrewdly.

"Where else could he keep it, but close to hand? How unwise of him to confide to paper his treachery, but how fortunate for me. He no doubt has your letters in the same cache," Sarah said thoughtfully.

"I will do anything to get those letters. Tell me what I can do?" Moira insisted, all attempt to deny complicity gone. Her willingness to turn on her former colleague was yet another example of her self-serving, consciousless attitude toward the world. But Sarah could not waste time caviling at Moira's attitude.

"Here is what I want you to do. And if you do not betray me, you might get your incriminating letters returned. Remember you have a great deal at stake, your husband's respect, your children, your position in society. If you cooperate with me, you might yet rub through this affair without too much damage." Sarah cared little for Moira's safety, but she was not above using a bit of blackmail herself if it would accomplish her aim, to clear her father of all wrongdoing.

Moira, furious at the position in which she found herself, had no choice but to accede to Sarah's plan. As an accomplice she was not to be trusted, but Sarah knew she held Moira's fate in her hands and she intended to use her knowledge. Briefly she told Moira what part she must play and the two parted, suspicion and anger on both sides, but Sarah was secure in the knowledge that Moira must accede to her demands or lose all that she cherished.

Chapter Thirty-seven

Sarah returned to the ballroom in a fever of impatience to put her plan into action, but for the moment she realized she must mask her impetuosity, her eagerness to discover the proof that would absolve her father. In the excitement of learning she was in an ace of achieving the purpose that had brought her to England, she pushed the disturbing encounter with Lucien from her mind. Her long absence from the ballroom had not gone unnoticed by that angry gentleman, who approached her as soon as she made her entrance.

"Where have you been, Sarah? Was it your ill-mannered intention to cut our supper dance, which is now underway?"

"I should think you would be covered with shame at your lecherous actions, Colonel. Practically engaged to one girl and pressing your unwanted favours on another." Sarah, her temper always quick to flare, would not be put in the wrong.

"We are going to get this whole imbroglio sorted out once and for all," Lucien grasped her wrist and dragged her behind him, impervious to the shocked stares of the onlookers.

At another time Sarah would have giggled at the faces of the guests, but her ire, raised by Lucien's high-handed treatment, banished all amusement from her mind. How dare he take her to task after his own performance? However, before she could voice her irritation at being forcibly removed from the ball-room, she was bundled into the morning room, where, with the door slammed ruthlessly behind them, she was forced to face her furious abductor.

"Now, why did you run from the terrace before I could answer Angela's nasty insinuations? I have had enough of that young woman's interference and I have told her so. I love you and I want to marry you, and Angela means nothing to me." Lucien, famed for his polished address, had lost all control under the tempest of his emotions. His proposal may have lacked style but his sincerity could not be doubted when he caught Sarah in his arms with no attempt to deal gently and kissed her ruthlessly.

Sarah emerged from the embrace blushing rosily and completely bemused by his bald words, speechless before his embrace.

"Oh, Lucien, do you mean it? I thought you were promised to Angela," she exclaimed artlessly.

"Of course I mean it. I love you and want you for my wife. I know you might feel reluctance to give your heart to a hated Englishman, but I am sure I can persuade you we are not all the desperate characters you have been led to believe. You cannot think I would prefer that shallow trifling Angela to you, darling." Lucien continued to embrace her, the warmth in his normally cold grey eyes surprising Sarah.

"I thought you were just flirting with me. I haven't much practise in trusting Englishmen you know, and you *are* quite a desperate character," Sarah teased, convinced now of Lucien's true feelings, and not above tormenting him a bit in return for all the unhappiness the thought of his preference for Angela had caused her.

"Desperate to claim you for my wife, you little spitfire," Lucien said huskily.

"But Angela told me you were promised, and she was only waiting for the season to end to announce it. Your families would both hail such a match, I was given to understand," Sarah spoke chidingly.

Lucien, aware that he was not entirely blameless, hurried to explain. "It's true my father wanted me to marry, and a match with Angela would not have been unwelcome. Our families are close friends and neighbors in the country. At one time I might have considered marrying her, not that my affections were deeply engaged. But then I was knocked off my feet by an enchanting termagant of a colonial and lost my heart."

Sarah glowed under his ardent gaze and threw her arms around his neck, all impetuous passion, now that she was sure she need no longer hide her own warm reactions to his lovemaking.

"We colonials are a violent people, thrusting all before us to conquer our enemies," she concluded whimsically, recalling their meeting and tempestuous courtship.

"And I am not letting you off so easily. Whatever

my fault in the affair of Angela, you are not blameless, enticing poor Robert Parry, and then trying your lures on De Lisle. But I think he will be too occupied with his charming comtesse to spend much time fawning over you in the future. You had me in a pother over that gentleman, I can tell you. We almost came to cuffs over you, you know. And it turns out he is not the villain I thought. I admit I misjudged the fellow. He has done some good work for Dundas, wresting some very important Frenchmen from Napoleon's clutches. He may be a brave, clever fellow, but he gave me some bad moments. Still, I am forever in his debt for rescuing you from that den." Lucien tried to look severe, but Sarah, now secure in his affections, did not seem impressed.

"The marquis has been a good friend to me and I hope his comtesse will make him happy. I believe he just used me to gain a foothold in the society that at one time he rejected. I was never seriously interested in him, but I admit I encouraged him just to get your back up. I was successful, wasn't I?" she asked saucily.

"You were, you minx. But remember, Sarah, I am not your enemy. I have conquered you, it's true, but you, in turn have defeated me. I will do my best to make you happy, my dearest, but you must trust me now," Lucien answered gently.

"Oh, Lucien, I want nothing more than to be your wife, but there are so many problems," Sarah sighed, remembering Moira Amberly and the general.

She knew that she should tell Lucien what she had discovered, but, if she did, he would take over the investigation and thwart her plan to expose the general as the culprit who had betrayed her father. She did not want the secret, the heavy burden of her discovery to lie between them, but she felt she must uncover the proof of her father's innocence. Lucien and his superiors would be more concerned with his current treachery and would want to trace the general's co-conspirators and his contacts with the French and to expose his present chicaneries. That long-ago betrayal would not interest them half as much. If the general denied that earlier involvement, she had no recourse. She must get her hands on that diary, the only proof that would convict him and clear her father of any dishonour. She frowned in the contemplation of failure.

Lucien, mistaking her hesitation for doubts about their future together, swept her ruthlessly back into his arms, kissing her fiercely, his lips warm and demanding on her cheeks, hair, and throat, causing shudders of ecstasy through her whole body, drowning her in emotion, causing her to forget all but her love for this former enemy, the man who had stolen her heart.

"There is no problem we cannot solve, once we are wed, my darling. Say it will be soon," Lucien pleaded, his usual aloofness buried beneath a storm of passion that drove all doubts from Sarah's mind and heart.

Before she could voice her objections, she was lost again in the turmoil of his arms, neither of them aware that the door had opened and an intruder watched their idyll.

"Come, come, my dears. This is all very well, but you must recover yourselves and return to the ballroom. I take it I can congratulate you, Lucien." Lady

Ravensham's gentle voice shattered their absorption and they broke reluctantly apart.

"Yes, Lady Ravensham, Sarah has consented to marry me, and very soon, I hope." Lucien held Sarah's hand tightly and watched the delightful colour rise in her cheeks.

"Oh, Grandmother, what have I done? Am I in disgrace with you, behaving in such a fashion?" Sarah asked in some confusion.

"Not at all, my dear. I am delighted that Lucien has won you. You are so well suited and now you will not leave me, unless you intend to return to America to be married," she questioned, her worries about Sarah's allegiance returning.

"Oh dear, I hadn't thought. There is Grandfather," she replied, offering the obvious objection, unwilling to bring up her other problem. "What will we do, Lucien?" she asked gazing in consternation at her lover.

"It will sort itself out. Your grandfather must be assured that this marriage is for your happiness, and I can settle his doubts on that score, Sarah," Lucien replied with a return to his former arrogance, which caused Sarah to wrinkle her nose at him, ready to protest. But he cut short her arguments. "All I can think of now is that you have at last promised to be my wife. I will brook no interference now. And I have Lady Ravensham to thank for her good offices. She encouraged me when I thought my suit was hopeless," he confided, rewarding that lady with a beguiling smile.

"No impediments can prevent your marriage, if you truly love each other. I will see to that," she stated firmly, thinking of Angela and Joshua Allen and sweeping all difficulties before her. Sarah had no notion that her grandmother could act so forcefully. "And we will take this occasion to announce your engagement, a perfect climax to this evening," Lady Ravensham glowed with happiness at the idea, overriding Sarah's faint demurs.

Lucien agreed, eager to set the seal on his happiness. An official engagement would remove any hesitation on Sarah's part and he would sweep her along, countering all her objections to an early wedding. He had no intention of waiting until she returned to America.

Sarah, overcome with happiness after her recent slough of despair, gave in to Lucien and her grandmother and accompanied them to the ballroom in a daze of rapture. She was content for the moment to forget the treachery of the general and Mrs. Amberly, Angela's spite, and her grandfather's possible objections. With Lucien by her side she could conquer the world, she felt just then.

Chapter Thirty-eight

Lady Ravensham's announcement created all the stir she expected. Among the first to tender his best wishes was De Lisle, who raised a wry eyebrow at Sarah's obvious embarrassment at being the cynosure of the company.

"I am not sure I envy Valentine, Sarah. You are a wayward, stubborn minx, not at all amenable to control, but I imagine the marriage, stormy as it may be, will bring you both happiness," he said, enjoying her rosy blushes. "I would hesitate to take you on myself."

"Fortunately you will not have that opportunity, De Lisle," Lucien answered wryly.

"So I see. Well, I wish you both the best if you are determined to enter the parson's trap. Perhaps, I will follow your example one of these days," he admitted ruefully.

"I pity your wife, my lord. You will make a difficult husband," Sarah riposted, recovering her spirits.

"Not at all. They say rakes make the most devoted of husbands. Now Valentine here has always been the most respectable of fellows. Perhaps he will not make such a tame benedict," De Lisle quipped.

"I am not worried, Theron," Sarah answered, looking askance at her fiancé.

"You are a baggage, Sarah, but marriage will blunt that independence," Lucien said teasingly, knowing he could arouse her with such a provocative statement. De Lisle agreed, and they parted in good charity with one another.

Angela's reception of the news was not quite so pleasant. She extended her congratulations in a tempered tone, unwilling to show her obvious chagrin, but unable to hail the match with enthusiasm. However put out she was by Lucien's preference for her cousin, she had enough conceit to mask her irritation and behave with a certain circumspection, although she could not resist a snide remark.

"Well, Sarah, you certainly stole a march on us all. I never believed Lucien would place marriage above his army career. However did you manage to capture him?" she said.

Lucien, not forgetting Angela's efforts to put a rub in his way and entertaining no charitable thoughts toward the haughty beauty, answered for Sarah. "I did the capturing, Angela, and a merry chase she led me. Sarah will make an exceptional officer's wife. She is not that enchanted with society life," he stated firmly, not loath to let Angela know he thought her frivolous and selfish.

"Well, Lucien, I hope neither of you will regret your choice. My best wishes." she had the last word, eager to sow doubt and dissension, in her own disappointment. Since neither of the engaged pair cared much for her opinion, the interlude passed off with a surface politeness.

Robert Parry's response to their engagement was a rueful mixture of regret and pleasure at his friend's good fortune. He admitted with his pleasant lopsided grin that he might have chanced his own hand if it had not been quite apparent how the land lay.

"You are a lucky dog, Lucien, but you deserve the best. And Sarah, if you need a godfather for your first offspring, I am applying now for the post," he said, unable to resist teasing the pair and delighted by Sarah's rosy blush.

"We will keep you in mind, Robert," Lucien replied suavely, not one whit discomforted by his friend's joshing.

General Apsley-Gower offered his felicitations with his usual benign smile. Sarah had the utmost difficulty in facing him with composure. She hoped that he laid her diffidence to the occasion, a newly engaged girl in the first flush of her happiness. She was astounded at the mask he assumed, the avuncular, benevolent friend of the family tendering his wishes for her future. How could she have been so deceived? When she remembered the fate he had planned for her, it was all she could do to swallow her ire and pretend to accept his platitudes. Although Lucien looked at her strangely, aware of the aura of aloofness, so unlike her usual response to this old friend of her father's, she hoped he would not question her in the press of guests closing around them. She felt guilty about hiding her secret from him, and it cast a slight shadow over the proceedings. After the general had removed himself she was able to behave more enthusiastically.

The ball, with its romantic climax, had proved a great success, and Lady Ravensham, on bidding Sarah good night, expressed her delight in the outcome, signifying her joy at the betrothal again and again. Whatever unease Sarah felt at deceiving Lucien was temporarily forgotten in the passion of their lingering farewell, and she retired to dream of a blissful future. She was determined to face the dilemma of the general's treachery in the morning. For the rest of this amazing evening she would put all thoughts of revenge from her mind, and she dropped into an uneasy sleep.

The morning brought more sober counsel. She feared that if she told Lucien what she had discovered he would take over the investigation, but she also understood her arrogant lover. He would object strongly to her meddling in affairs of state. After all, the general's betrayal had now become not just her own concern, but the concern of the British government. Every day he endangered the lives of officers and men bravely serving their country. What right had she to delay the long-overdue retribution he deserved? And then, too, she doubted if Lucien would accept her version of Moira Amberly and the general's revealing conversation. Moira was perfectly capable of denying the whole interview, and Sarah wondered if Lucien might think she had exaggerated and blown up the whole affair. Despite her sincere love for him, Sarah had felt from the beginning of their relationship that he looked upon her efforts to vindicate her father with some impatience. Now, in the first exhilaration of their engagement, he might soothe her with promises and reassurances, but would he follow up on her information and secure the evidence that would exonerate her father? Wouldn't he rather do all in his power to catch the general out in his current conspiracies? No, the only solution was for Sarah herself to find the evidence and confront him with it. Just how she was to accomplish this daunting task she had not decided, but her resolution was firm. If Lucien expected a docile wife, content to let him make all decisions in their marriage, he would be surprised. Love had not completely swamped Sarah's independent spirit, and she doubted if it ever would. In that De Lisle was quite correct. She smiled ruefully. Lucien was indeed taking on a handful.

Her plan to unmask the general did not occupy her mind to the detriment of other questions. Her elation over Lucien's declaration dimmed whenever she thought of her grandfather's reaction, and she could not deny the lingering remnants of her old repugnance toward her country's former enemies. Lucien had carried her along with the force of his passion, but was this enough to form the basis of a fruitful life together? Eventually this swamping of her senses must settle down into domestic tranquillity, based on companionship, a community of interests, and a comfortable cooperation. Away from Lucien's dominant personality, the drugging passion of his kisses, Sarah's instinctive distrust of the English surfaced, threatening her newfound happiness.

Fortunately Lucien called on the afternoon following the ball to take her for a ride in Hyde Park, and his appearance temporarily drove away all the bewilderment that had ruined her night's rest. He seemed to sense her uncertainty and hurried to lay her fears to rest.

"You do not appear to have had a peaceful night. Too much excitement at the ball or doubts at having cast your fate with such a desperate Englishman after all?" he teased, but beneath the banter she sensed an anxiety.

"If you mean I am looking hagged, say so," Sarah reprimanded him sharply. Although her creamy complexion lacked its usual translucent glow and her dark eyes seemed shadowed, Sarah, in truth, showed little evidence of her disturbed night. Dressed in a lime-green silk redingote, frogged over an ivory walking dress, her curls restrained by a dashing Hussar cap, she was a sight to please the most discriminating eye.

"I meant nothing of the sort. You look enchanting, but a trifle worried. You do not regret giving your life into my hands, do you, my fierce little colonial?" Lucien asked, taking her in his arms for a brief kiss to silence all her objections.

She emerged glowing but still argumentative, "I will, Lucien, if you continue to call me a colonial. I love you, I know that, but there are so many problems. My grandfather, for one," Sarah confided, unwilling to risk Lucien's probing into her disquiet and hoping he would be distracted by the one obvious problem.

"Yes, we must talk about that, but there is no difficulty that cannot be solved now that I am convinced you are mine," his usual enigmatic hard glance softened as he looked into her eyes. "Come, let us have a peaceful tool about the park, and we will discuss our plans."

Sarah's pulse pounded beneath his warm gaze and for the moment decided to banish all troubling thoughts in the enjoyment of the projected outing. The bright, clear sky and the emerald greenery of the park matched her spirits. No matter what lay ahead she had the confidence that Lucien's love inspired. He was right. They would overcome any obstacle by the force of their affection. For the first time in her life Sarah felt secure within a man's love and protection. Her various Philadelphia beaux had never inspired more than the most lukewarm feelings of friendship. Only to her grandfather had she revealed the depth of her need for love and tenderness. Now Lucien would benefit from all that untapped emotion. She wondered at her willingness to surrender so wholeheartedly to this man, who in some ways was still a stranger to her.

"I feel I have a tiger by the tail with you, Lucien. Perhaps I was overhasty," she challenged him gaily.

"Too late, my girl. Your fate is cast. I will never give you up," Lucien's voice was steely despite the loving smile he gave her.

"Not a compassionate conquerer, I see," she joked, only partially reassured. Lucien was not a man to allow her to toy with him, and she was no Angela content with a tepid affection. She knew his eventual anger at her deception would be formidable.

"I do feel for your concern about your grandfather, my dear, but you need not despair. You will see him before too long. I will most probably be sent to America again shortly. I know I should ask him for your hand but I cannot brook such a wait. I am all impatience to claim you as my wife. The voyage would make a fine honeymoon, don't you agree? We must urge your grandmother to plan the wedding without delay. I see no reason to wait, do you?" he pressed her.

"Oh, Lucien, do you mean we will return to America together? How pleased Grandfather will be. But such haste. Any well-brought-up English miss would never allow herself to be bustled into marriage in this hurly-burly way. An engagement of at least six months is *de rigeur*, I understand," Sarah pointed out coyly.

"Nonsense. I don't intend to cool my heels any longer now that I have your promise. And I will not go off to America without you, my termagant, so begin collecting your trousseau," Lucien said with finality.

Their ride was now interrupted as the occupants of various carriages hailed them, tendering congratulations on their betrothal and reminiscing about the splendours of the ball. Sarah was conscious of the barely concealed envy of many of the fashionable ladies they encountered, most of whom would have eagerly welcomed Lucien as a suitor or a lover. She was not above preening herself a bit at the eligibility of her fiancé, then reproved herself for such pettiness. Basking in the approval of the ton, Lucien's warm protection, and the knowledge that she would be returning as his wife to her grandfather, she almost banished the remembrance of that interview with Moira Amberly until she saw the object of her disquiet approaching them. This time the elegant matron was escorted by a young guardsman, another of her *cicisbeos*, Sarah warranted.

"Ah, how delightful to see you and the colonel enjoying the first day of your betrothal," Mrs. Amberly cooed archly, after introducing the unexceptional young man, who reddened under Lucien's sardonic gaze.

Really she was too composed. Sarah, while answering her greetings perfunctorily, could not help but remember her last sight of the cool beauty dissolved in tears and confessing her guilt. What a facile actress she was. Not one trace of shame or concern marred her smooth features, and the look she turned on Sarah was guileless. But Sarah, determined to pursue her advantage, would not allow Moira to get off without a warning.

"I do hope you will come to call shortly, Mrs. Amberly. We have a certain matter to discuss," Sarah spoke more sharply than she meant to, despite her fear of arousing Lucien's suspicions.

"Of course, my dear. At any rate I intended to pay a courtesy visit to your grandmother, to thank her for last evening's delightful entertainment," Moira did not return Sarah's piercing look, and a certain nervousness was now apparent in her actions. Obviously she was regretting her confidences and Sarah suspected she would not hurry to make the promised call. They parted with mutual false assurances of good will. Lucien was not deceived by the exchange of courtesies.

"You seem strangely eager to see that rather time-serving matron again, Sarah. I thought you did not find her to your taste," Lucien queried.

"I don't particularly number her among my friends, but Grandmother insists I behave with propriety toward her, since she was kind enough to serve as my chaperone," Sarah hastened to reassure him, feeling guilty, for she quite endorsed his judgment of Mrs. Amberly.

"Mm, I don't remember your being in such charity on the voyage. But perhaps you felt in her you had a rival," he suggested with maddening aplomb.

"Such conceit! You think every woman alive is susceptible to your charms. I don't know that I want a husband who is so suggestible."

He laughed and countered with a flattering display of her own attractions and the long list of rejected beaux she must have repulsed before he had conquered her. Their conversation then turned on the voyage and Lucien's agreeable admission that the kiss that had troubled Sarah so much aboard ship had sealed his fate. Their outing ended on a much more light-hearted note than it had begun, and with Lucien's promise to escort her to the Lansdowne rout that evening. For the moment she put aside all torments and questions and basked in the warmth of his love.

Chapter Thirty-nine

Lucien's father, the Earl of Lenminster, on learning of his youngest son's engagement, posted up to London, opened the family mansion on Brook Street, and welcomed Sarah into the family with every appearance of delight. Sarah found him much like Lucien, a rather fierce old man with his son's dark flashing eyes, a shock of white hair, and the carriage of a conqueror.

"Well, miss, this is quite a surprise. I had no idea Lucien was thinking of tying the parson's knot. He seemed wedded to the army. You look a civilized sort for a colonial. I hope you can persuade him to resign his commission and return to Hereford. His brother Alistair could use some help managing the family acres, as I am getting quite past it," he glowered at her, as if expecting her to crumble beneath his sharp eyes.

"Not at all, sir. I am quite looking forward to following the drum," she answered demurely, but looking him straight in the eye. She had not liked his

312

reference to her as a colonial, but she decided she would take issue with him on that score at another time. A bit nervous at this first exposure to her future father-in-law, she still would not quail beneath his demanding manner. She suspected much of it was a pose, to hide his real delight that Lucien had at last decided to enter matrimony. Lucien, eyeing them both with a quizzical air, stood ready to protect Sarah if his father became too irascible, but he had every confidence in her ability to handle the situation.

"Humph," the earl growled. "No namby-pamby chit, I see. Just as well. But Lucien," he said, turning to his watchful son, "are you sure you know what you're doing? Miss Ravensham seems a bit independent. Can you handle that?"

"I think so, sir," Lucien grinned, pleased that Sarah could stand up to his father, whose gruff manner belied his real pleasure in the match, he was certain.

"Well, I cannot be unhappy at a match between our families, good Hereford stock, both of you. And I hope you have no foolish ideas about childbearing. I want an heir, and before I go to my reward. Alistair and that milk-and-water madam he's hitched up with cannot seem to produce one," he said outrageously, with a frankness that should have shocked Sarah, but which she found rather endearing. In some ways the earl reminded her of her grandfather.

"I hope Lucien and I will have a full quiver of children, sir, but it's early days to be speaking of that. I do thank you for your welcome," she said pertly and was rewarded with a chuckle and a nod of approval.

"You'll do my girl. See to it that Lucien brings you down to Lenminster soon. I'm not too fond of London. It kicks up my gout, you know," he answered.

"I am most anxious to go to Hereford and see my father's home," Sarah said, determined to bring up his name, anxious for the earl's reaction to that old scandal.

"Yes, yes, my dear. You must not let all that past tragedy cloud your happiness. I am sure Lucien has reassured you on that point. Your father was a brave officer, not capable of what he was accused of. Never believed a bit of it," he said gruffly, embarrassed by the reference but eager to lay any fears to rest that her father's imputed disloyalty might have influenced him against her.

"Thank you, sir. I appreciate your belief in him. He was not guilty, I know," Sarah stated stubbornly, her chin tilted. If the earl had joined her father's detractors, she would have taken him to task on the spot. Fortunately that would not be necessary. The interview ended with mutual satisfaction on all sides, and Sarah sighed with relief when Lucien escorted her back to Park Street after agreeing to the earl's giving a small family dinner to show his approval of the engagement.

"Well, Sarah, you handled the governor with your usual address. I knew he could not resist you. Not that it would have mattered a whit if he had taken you in dislike. Nothing will prevent our wedding at a very early date. I have written to your grandfather, as I suspect you have, and we can decide upon a day right now," Lucien insisted as they drove toward the Ravensham house.

"I think your father is an old dear. I am surprised he wants you out of the army. Are you at odds over your career?" Sarah asked.

"Well, he wants me on the estate, but that would never do. I think Alistair would resent it. After all, he is the eldest, the heir, and we have never gotten along too well. I can't stand his wife, a flibbertigibbet type who wants to spend all her time in London. You will meet her and Alistair at dinner tomorrow. I thought father was enough to swallow this afternoon. Will you resent following the drum, Sarah, when you could be queening it with the ton or playing lady bountiful on the family acres?" he asked, quite sure of her answer.

"Don't be ridiculous, Lucien. I will only resent your army career if it takes you away from me. And I would not want our countries to come to blows. I am still a loyal American, you know," she answered, peeping at him with some disquiet. The only bar to their happiness was their different loyalties. But Lucien was prepared for that.

"If that lamentable situation should ever arise, I hope our love will bridge any differences. I would never enlist against your countrymen, Sarah, for I know what pain that would bring you. I can only hope you trust me enough to believe that," he said seriously, intent on impressing her with his sincerity, for he realized that doubts on that score troubled her.

She melted under his warm gaze, content to leave

315

the future in his capable hands, although she would not want him to know how eager she was to place every decision in his hands. She still had a mind of her own, her own ideas about their life together, but those nebulous worries must not be allowed to intrude on this halycon time. If only she could resolve this problem of the general's treachery, she felt no cloud could darken their happiness together.

Chapter Forty

Lady Ravensham's delight in Sarah's engagement had effectively banished most of the legacy of past family tragedies. The shadow had gone from her eyes and her sprightly manner belied her years. At last she could look forward, not backward at a life that had encompassed more than its share of unhappiness. If she spared a thought for Angela's chagrin at the news, she could only feel that young woman might have learned a valuable lesson. She took great pleasure in the coming nuptials, which touched Sarah, and placed no obstacle in the way of an early marriage. On the contrary she acceded to Lucien's demand for an early date with alacrity, completely caught up in plans for an impressive ceremony. The ton would not be able to gossip about the match with Lady Ravensham's approval and that of the earl evident on all suits. She realized that the newlywed pair would be off to America soon after the wedding, but she knew this would only be a temporary absence, and, although Sarah would be following Lucien to a variety of army posts, eventually she would return to England.

Sarah felt she was caught in a whirlwind, between Lucien's impetuous desire for an early wedding and her grandmother's elaborate plans. She found it hard to concentrate on more mundane matters, gazing often at the glowing sapphire on her hand in surprise, daydreaming about the future. She had written to her grandfather about the news, for his approval was necessary, a mere formality, she thought, once he was certain that Sarah's happiness was assured.

She was strangely reluctant to cast a damper over this halcyon period in her life by dealing with Moira Amberly's disclosures. But time was passing and she must find proof of her father's innocence and bring the general to account for his past and present treachery. She had met the general on several occasions since the ball, and it had required all her poise to face him calmly, to mask the dislike and fear he inspired in her. Naturally honest and straightforward, she wondered if her acting abilities had proven up to the charade of demure innocence. It was obvious that the general was still in the pay of his French masters and who knew what chicanery he was up to. He must be stopped. First, however, she must perfect her plan to secure the evidence that would irrefutably prove his treachery.

Lucien had departed reluctantly on a mission to Plymouth and she knew that his absence created an opportunity she must not lose. Her first task was to secure Moira Amberly's cooperation, either willingly or by threats. Sarah had no hesitation about employing the latter method if that was what was needed, for Moira had made no effort to contact Sarah, feeling perhaps that if she ignored her former charge, Sarah would forget that damning conversation in the excitement of her betrothal. In that, as in much else, she was mistaken, Sarah vowed.

While she was hesitating about giving an excuse to her grandmother that would explain her visit to Mrs. Amberly one grey May morning, Angela arrived with her mother to pay a call. Restraining her impatience and her lack of enthusiasm for their visitors, Sarah welcomed their guests with her grandmother over the chocolate cups. Obviously Angela had a purpose for the call and had dragooned her mother into accompanying her, for neither had been much evident since the formal announcement of Sarah's engagement in *The Gazette*. Sarah rather enjoyed Angela's dilemma, a mean-spirited reaction she admitted, but entirely human, and she wished she could have heard the interview between her cousin and Lucien, about which he had been very reticent. Sarah suspected that Angela wanted to secure her position with her grandmother, and in all events that turned out to be the purpose of the call. She was all sweetness and light, admiring Sarah's ring and asking for details about the ceremony. Sarah realized she expected to be asked to be a bridesmaid, but Sarah's charity did not extend that far.

"Have you set the date, yet, Sarah?" Angela asked.

"Yes, we have chosen the last Saturday in June. Lucien must sail before the end of the month for America, and naturally I am all impatience to present my husband to my grandfather, who has met him, but not as my affianced, of course," Sarah replied with composure.

"You certainly lost no time in securing Lucien,"

Angela snapped, her facade of charity slipping slightly.

"On the contrary, Sarah led him a merry chase," Sarah's grandmother intervened. "I knew his intentions from the first day he brought her to me, but I had to contain my impatience to see how Sarah's own sentiments lay." She did not know the full extent of Angela's deviousness, but she was certain Sarah's cousin had done her best to thwart the lovers.

"Lucien is a cool one. We had no idea how he felt. Rumour had it his interests lay in quite another direction although Lucien was ever one to keep his own counsel. We heard his attentions were fixed on an opera dancer," Angela claimed airily.

"Really, Angela, that is no way to go on. What will your grandmother think. Well-behaved girls do not discuss such matters, very unbecoming." The younger Lady Ravensham reproved her daughter to everyone's surprise. She did not usually criticize Angela and seemed completely under her daughter's thumb.

"Nonsense, Mother," Angela responded sharply. "It's just among the family. I was merely warning Sarah that Lucien is not above casting an amorous eye elsewhere. One of the reasons I never took him seriously myself, the other being a disinclination to follow the drum. To be the wife of a serving officer is not at all to my taste." Angela settled the sleeves of her blue muslin with an irritable twitch.

"I don't recall that you were given the choice, Angela," the elder Lady Ravensham said tartly. "Jealousy is an uncomfortable emotion and one you would be wise to abandon."

Angela's blue eyes widened, surprised that her

usually gentle grandmother should strike out at her. "I meant nothing, Grandmother. I am all delight in Sarah's happiness." Having planted her poisonous darts, she was content to retire from the arena, but Sarah would not let her withdraw unscathed.

"Perhaps I misunderstood your interest in Lucien, Angela. I thought you had indicated you would receive an offer from him with compliance," Sarah spoke bluntly, tired of all these innuendoes. Angela reddened angrily and was about to retort unwisely. Before she could reply, her mother hurried to soothe the troubled waters.

"It is quite evident that Lucien's old friendship with Angela was a tepid emotion that vanished beneath the force of his feeling for Sarah, and we can but be happy that he will now form a lasting connection with us through her," Lady Ravensham's firm tones held a warning. Really she had allowed her daughter free rein for too long. It was time the girl was married, and secured a husband to put up with her haughty airs. Perhaps Sir Peter Gresham would come up to scratch. His title was inferior but he had a large rent roll and an amiable disposition, both necessities where Angela was concerned. Lady Ravensham was heartily tired of her daughter's ways. It was overtime that she asserted herself as to the conduct she expected.

Angela, routed by all three of her companions, had no choice but to retire in the best order she could. Family felicity must be preserved, and both her grandmother and her mother had surprisingly welcomed this match and had let her know they would put up with no interference from her. She would have to admit that Sarah would be an integral part of the family and her only recourse was to accept one of her importuning beaux as soon as possible. It would never do to let the ton know her nose was out of joint by this betrothal.

"I do wish you happy, Sarah, and perhaps I will not be far behind you. I have almost made up my mind to accept a very eligible offer, which will allow me to lead the life in London I prefer," Angela announced in determined tones. Her colonial cousin would hear no more of her chagrin and must be assured that Angela had never really intended to honour Lucien with her hand.

Sarah was not deceived but willing to forgive Angela her deception, secure in the knowledge of Lucien's love. The ladies parted in better charity with one another, and Sarah turned her mind to the coming interview with Moira Amberly. She was determined to expose the matter of the general's treachery once and for all so that she could enjoy her happiness with no cloud to mar its perfection.

Chapter Forty-one

"Grandmother, if you won't be too disappointed I would like to cry off the theatre party this evening. With Lucien away I can catch my breath for the nonce. It has been a hectic if happy time, but I do feel a headache coming on and would like a quiet night for once," Sarah pleaded, hoping her grandmother would not insist that she, too, remain at home. It had been difficult to have a moment to herself lately.

"Well, I believe the Lenminsters will be unhappy at your absence, but I quite understand your need for a respite. I will make your excuses. Are you sure you do not want me to keep you company?" Lady Ravensham asked, a bit worried by Sarah's pale face and shadowed eyes.

Feeling the veriest criminal for deceiving her grandmother so, Sarah insisted, urging her grandmother to join the planned entertainment. How difficult this was all being. It had proved more awkward than she had realized to plan this deception—with the added complication of forcing Moira Amberly to lend her talents to the effort—but she might never have another opportunity to discover the evidence, and every day's delay made it more important. Lucien would be returning from the west tomorrow and she could never escape his vigilant eye. Her plans were set and she could not abandon them now.

"No, Grandmother. You go and enjoy yourself. I know how much you like being with the earl," she teased, distracting Lady Ravensham by alluding to that doughty gentleman's penchant for the dowager's company. Sarah wondered if the two, even at their advanced ages, might not comfort each other in their loneliness. The earl treated her grandmother with great tenderness and affection, more than that demanded by old friendship and neighborliness.

With final assurances that a night's rest would restore her spirits, Sarah saw her grandmother off to the evening's festivity and then repaired to her bedroom to cope with her abigail's ministrations. Polly, genuinely fond of her charge, and aware that Sarah was not feeling up to snuff, had a host of nostrums available to press on her mistress, but Sarah succeeded in thwarting her more strenuous efforts. She agreed to eat a light supper and to retire with a cloth wet with eau de cologne on her aching brow, but she begged Polly to leave her alone, as all she required was rest. Reluctantly, the abigail promised she would be undisturbed until morning. As soon as she left, Sarah rose and darted to her wardrobe, shrugging off her dressing gown and hurrying into a dark frock and serviceable shawl for her trip through the streets of London. She had to wait for the June evening to darken to cloak her escapade, but the wait was nerve-wracking.

Peeking out her door, she felt the house had quieted down for the evening and the servants had gathered in their hall. Going to the dining room, she slipped out the terrace windows, leaving them unlatched, and hoping she would return before Peverel locked up for the night and her grandmother came back. Wrapping her shawl about her, Sarah entered the shrouded streets and cast her eyes about for a hackney cab. This was the most dangerous part of her adventure, for she knew what peril she might encounter, an unescorted female on London's streets. Unfortunately, the general's rooms were too distant for her to walk to them.

Hailing a vacant hackney on Grosvenor Street, she directed the coachman to the general's rooms, staring haughtily at his leering look. No doubt he thought she was undertaking a lover's tryst, but she cared little for that now. Her heart beating rapidly, she dismissed the hackney at the bottom of Clarges Street and slipped into the general's rooms with the key Moira Amberly had obtained for her by means Sarah had not ascertained, nor did they interest her.

This evening had been selected because it was the general's man's evening off, and the arrangements had included Moira Amberly's promise to keep the general occupied so that Sarah would be undisturbed. Mrs. Amberly had been shocked and frightened by Sarah's daring plan to effect entrance into the empty rooms, but she had not been able to suggest any other method of rescuing her damning letters. She cared little for Sarah's own mission, her whole intent being to secure her own release from the general's toils. Sarah placed little reliance on her willing cooperation, but Mrs. Amberly's fear of her clandestine amour being revealed to her husband and the consequent disgrace and banishment had persuaded her to play her role.

Once inside the rooms, Sarah gazed about in some surprise. The general was more of a sybarite than she had realized. All the appointments were of the last stare, heavy ruby velvet and damask, gleaming silver trophies, cutlery and crystal of the most luxurious. No doubt afforded by his French paymasters. The large sitting room was paneled on two sides and lined with glass-fronted bookcases. On another wall was a large secretary, unlocked, which after a cursory search, she decided could not hold any papers of importance. All she found there were a few invitations, some tailors' bills, accounts from the livery where he stabled his horses, and a laconic engagement book, whose entries were innocuous. She groaned as she looked at the books. Possibly the diary was hidden in one of them, but there were scores, and she did not have the time to scan every one. Surely there must be a safe or hidey hole where the general kept his diary, easily accessible, for he must write in it often.

Sounds from the street were muffled by the heavy velvet curtains drawn across the tall windows, and the room was in darkness, but Sarah feared to light a taper for it might be glimpsed from the outside. At first she started at every sound, her heart in her throat, but she reproved herself for such nervousness. She had made up her mind to find the proof of her father's innocence and she must not be deterred by want of courage now.

After an hour's careful scrutiny of the bedroom with its massive mahogany accoutrements, Sarah was no nearer to accomplishing her task. She had turned over all the fittings in the chest, raised the mattress, and burrowed in the wardrobe to no avail, desperation driving her on. The diary had to be somewhere, but the hiding place remained a mystery. Returning to the sitting room, she glanced sorrowfully at the fireplace. Could there be a hidden cache revealed only to its owner, a secret that he guarded carefully? She ran her fingers around the molding of the Adam mantel. Nothing. She must persist, for having come this far she would not be defeated in her quest.

Perhaps the diary was hidden behind the rows of leather-bound volumes. She removed several, but, as she was running her hand along the back of the bookcase, she heard steps along the outside corridor coming to rest at the door. Could the manservant be returning? What could she do? Hurriedly she looked about the room for a bolt hole and darted quickly behind the heavy curtains screening the windows as the door opened. What had gone wrong? Surely that was the general's heavy tread she heard, and then she was certain of it as she heard his angry mutter and the strike of the tinder. He had lighted the tall brass candelabra on the mantel and was rummaging about the fireplace. Eager anticipation banished her temporary fear of discovery and she peeked from the curtain to see the general standing before an open wing of the bookcase, a red volume and a packet in his hands, obviously taken from the yawning chasm within the bookcase.

"Stupid female. To think she could cozen me. She was up to something, I know. Probably hired some ruffian to search the place while she distracted me.

I'm too downy a bird to be caught by such tactics, and she will pay for her effrontery in trying to gull me," he muttered to himself. The general's normally kind expression had darkened into a fierce and cruel mien. As Sarah watched, he opened the pages of the diary and he sneered. Anger replaced fear and Sarah opened her reticule, taking from it a pistol, which she had providentially brought along. She would not brook defeat now and stepped from her hiding place.

"I believe I will take that, general," she spoke firmly. "I am sure it contains proof of my father's innocence." Sarah leveled the pistol at her father's former comrade in arms, the cool feel of the metal in her hand giving her a sense of security.

"Ah, Sarah. I suspected Moira was up to something, and, it seems, I was right—to cozen me into a fruitless interview to give you the opportunity to rifle my rooms. And you are quite right. I was the culprit who sent your father to his disgrace and death. I feel no compunction over it. He had a good run, always the fair-haired boy, and winning your mother into the bargain. I was determined that he should pay. I was tired of playing second fiddle to that honourable young gentleman," the general boasted, obviously reveling in the disclosure of his actions.

"I think you are despicable to have deceived everyone. Have you no loyalty or honour?" Sarah's passionate distaste and horror seemed only to amuse the general.

"Loyalty and honour are expensive luxuries I cannot afford, my dear. My forebears were not as provident as yours, and I have only my wits to rely upon," he drawled.

"You are a traitor, and I intend to prove it. Give me that diary and Mrs. Amberly's letters," she spoke with more assurance than she felt, realizing the vulnerability of her position but unwilling to let the black-hearted general know of her hesitations.

"You won't really use that toy, you know. I can't believe a gently bred girl would shoot a man in cold blood," the general faced her down, irritation and amusement warring as he confronted her ruthless young judgment, but unworried at his predicament.

"I will shoot you without a qualm—you, the man who caused my parents such unhappiness," Sarah crossed over toward him, the gun clutched firmly in her hand. "Give me that diary."

"I think not, my girl. I haven't played this game all these years to be challenged by some colonial chit who is no better than she should be." The general frowned, realizing at last the fierceness of his accuser. "Now give me that gun, and get out of here. We will say nothing of this assignation. No one would believe you anyway. I have covered my tracks well, played the very pattern of a discreet and courageous officer. Who will pay attention to the ramblings of a silly young woman, deranged by thoughts of vengeance, and the daughter of a traitor?" the general goaded, attempting to throw Sarah off her guard. He had noticed that the hand holding the pistol shook slightly. She was not as cool as she appeared.

"I will offer the authorities irrefutable proof. You were foolish to confide your treachery to the written page, General," she responded, resolution in every line of her face.

"Perhaps, but I wanted to keep a record. Foolish

vanity, no doubt. Still, that's of no account. You will never have it," he lunged forward, and involuntarily, Sarah pulled the trigger, and the bullet pierced his shoulder. He fell back, the diary dropping from his hand.

"You little devil, you will pay for this," he muttered, grasping the wound, as he fell to the floor.

Neither combatant was aware of the man bursting into the room. Lucien surveyed the scene. Sarah with the pistol still smoking in her hand, paralyzed by what she had done, the general at her feet.

"Oh, Lucien, thank God. I have never been so frightened. He is the traitor—the man who betrayed my father and sold secrets to the French. It's all there in the diary," Sarah ran to his arms, babbling hysterically, eager for the security they offered. Appalled at what she had done, she had no other thought but to lay her burdens on Lucien's shoulders.

"What have you done, Sarah? Why are you here? But explanations can wait. I cannot leave the general to bleed to death." Lucien put her gently from him and turned to succor the man on the floor, who had passed into unconsciousness.

"He deserves no charity, but I suppose we must help him," Sarah said, as Lucien bent over the wounded man, trying to staunch with a padded kerchief the flow of blood darkening his evening coat. "What shall I do?"

"I must get you out of here. You cannot be found in his rooms," Lucien spoke sternly, and Sarah wondered if he believed her. He seemed so angry, but he must realize she had only done what she had to do.

"We must get a physician, and I must get you back

to your grandmother's. I don't want you involved in this." Lucien looked at his hands, holding the blood-soaked pad. "Can you hold this here, while I fetch my groom in the street?" he asked her, looking at her pale face, afraid that she might swoon. "I will send him for aid."

Sarah shook off her queasiness and answered stoutly, "Of course. I am not afraid of a little blood." She knelt beside him.

"You will make a fine soldier's wife, Sarah, if I survive to meet you at the altar. God knows, you give me pause. But hold here a moment. Questions and recriminations can come later," Lucien smiled grimly at her. "You are a veritable tiger, my darling. No wonder you colonials put us to the rout. I will mete our proper punishment later. Right now we must clear up this mess." With a warning stare, which promised that he would be satisfied with nothing less than a full accounting of what had brought her to such a pass, he hurried from the room.

Chapter Forty-two

After all the events of the evening, Sarah slept dreamlessly, to her surprise. She had been escorted home by Lucien's groom, and had managed to sneak through the terrace windows and upstairs to her bedroom before her grandmother's return. Lucien had been left to deal with the situation she had caused. Sarah, less concerned with the wounded man's plight than the explanations she must offer Lucien, had not been so distraught that she had neglected to turn over Moira Amberly's letters and the diary to Lucien after having assured herself that the general's confession was on record. Not that she cared a whit about Moira Amberly's fate, but she had promised that lady her assistance, and she was not one to break her bargain.

When Polly, her abigail, entered her bedroom the morning after the decisive confrontation, she found her mistress sitting up cheerfully, all traces of the supposed headache banished, and musing over the prospect of the general's defeat at her hands.

"Are you quite recovered, miss?" Polly asked as she drew the draperies and settled Sarah's tray of tea and toast across her lap.

"Oh, yes, Polly. I am feeling much more the thing this morning. Is my grandmother still asleep?" Sarah asked, eager to relay the news to Lady Ravensham.

"I believe so, Miss Sarah. She was very late last night, Evans tells me, but suffered no harm from her outing. It seems set for another fair day," Polly answered as she bustled about the room putting it to rights.

Sarah had bundled her telltale gown, with its bloody streaks, into the back of the closet, and remembered guiltily that she must dispose of it before Polly's shrewd eyes could find it. Lucien wanted to protect her and she must do all she could to hide her previous evening's activities from even kindly eyes. Finally Polly retired, leaving Sarah to compose a story that would reassure her grandmother without revealing the danger to which Sarah had been exposed.

Sarah recalled the telling paragraphs in the diary. It was all there, the account of Apsley-Gower's efforts to involve her father in treachery, the envy and malice that had inspired the deed. From the very first he had hated Major Ravensham, who had always proved to be his superior in school and the army and who had won the place on Howe's staff that Apsley-Gower had coveted for himself. The culmination of that jealousy, which had been masked so cleverly, had been Richard Ravensham's winning of Elizabeth Allen. Apsley-Gower had wanted her as much for her patrimony, Joshua Allen's tidy fortune, as for her own gentle beauty. Still Sarah acquitted him of entirely base motives. He had evidently been genuinely in love with her mother.

Philadelphia, during Howe's occupation, had been a hotbed of intrigue and gossip, colonial Tories relaying information to the occupying forces and colonial rebels, in turn, supplying General Washington with British maneuvers and designs. Apsley-Gower, not attached to the general staff but privy, through his friendship with the unsuspecting Richard Ravensham, to much of what went on at that exalted level, had learned of the planned retreat and of Burgoyne and Clinton's troop movements, and had written a damning account in a letter to Washington's aide, Tench Tilgman, signed with Richard's name.

He had managed to send this letter, or a fair copy, to George Germain, at the War Office in London, pleading implicit secrecy as the cost of revelation, excusing his devious actions on the grounds of his longtime friendship with the Ravenshams, a poor return for the favours and hospitality they had tendered him. His treachery had also secured his own promotion, so long desired. Somewhere in the dusty War Office files that letter must still be shelved, long forgotten if any one beside Germain, now many years dead, had ever mentioned it. Germain himself, a vindictive and ambitious man, had evidently taken Apsley-Gower's unsubstantiated word, but he could not be faulted for that, the letter itself seemed irrefutable.

And Sarah's poor father had gone to his death never suspecting his dear friend. For that and her mother's sorrow, Sarah could never forgive him. She hoped he would recover from his wound and face trial for his misdeeds. Then, too, there was his intrigue with the French revolutionaries, which had continued for several years. The general had lived well beyond his means and needed their bribes to pay for his rich life style. All in all, the kindly devoted intimate of the Ravenshams had proved to be the falsest kind of friend, to his boyhood comrade, his army associates, his country, as well as the family who had offered him nothing but benevolence.

Moira Amberly's letters, Sarah barely glanced at, but their purple prose and passionate avowals of love condemned that lady on every page. No wonder she risked so much to get them back, and even now she was not out of the woods. Sarah was sure that the general would drag her down with him as she doubted he had any charity in his heart.

Her own relief at vindicating her father was clouded somewhat by the thought of facing Lucien, who had been appalled at her behaviour. Sarah giggled a bit. Angela would never have behaved so recklessly. He might well regret tying his future to such a rash, heedless hoyden. If he was angry, had taken her in distaste, well, she would just have to accept that he had second thoughts about her becoming a conformable wife. She would never be a pattern card of respectability, but she did love him, despite his arrogance, his British reserve, and all the other qualities she believed she had firmly rejected in a possible husband.

He had every right to be angry that she had not trusted him with the information about the general and asked for his help. Her overwhelming pride had forced her to solve the mystery of her father's supposed guilt herself and, if all went awry with her personal happiness, at least she had solved that problem. She could not regret her actions, although she shuddered to think how nearly she had come to grief.

In better charity Sarah arose and dressed, her mood lightening as she looked on the glowing May morning from her window. English weather was among the many surprises that had greeted her in this land she had expected to hate. Now she must carry the good news to her grandmother.

As usual, Lady Ravensham was resting on a nest of pillows in her huge canopied bed. She greeted her granddaughter with a smile, appreciating the lovely sight she made in her sprigged yellow muslin morning gown.

"Your headache has vanished, I see, my dear. You do look especially happy this morning, anticipating your wedding, I vow," Lady Ravensham twinkled as she returned Sarah's kiss.

"Yes, that too, but, Grandmother, you cannot have heard. We have discovered proof of Father's innocence." Sarah perched on the bed and told her grandmother an edited account of the previous evening's dramatic events.

Lady Ravensham's reception of the news was worth all the anguish Sarah had suffered, although she was shocked and appalled at learning of the general's guilt and the danger to which Sarah had been exposed. Her granddaughter rather glossed over Moira Amberly's role in the nefarious affair, but Lady Ravensham was not deceived.

"Oh, Sarah, it is so hard to realize that Julian should have proved such a false friend, a traitor, a man of jealousy and malice. And you might have been killed, or in some way injured if Lucien had not arrived so providentially," Lady Ravensham paled at the thought.

"Well, he did, although I am not sure how he happened to burst into the general's room at just the right time. I still have not had all those questions answered, and he was too cross with me last night to tell me how he learned of my attempt to discover the general's treachery. I fear I will have a rather sticky interview with him," Sarah confided, somewhat abashed at the prospect.

"I think you will be able to talk him around," Lady Ravensham reassured her with a smile. "Although normally Lucien is not a man to be cozened."

"I will have to throw myself on his mercy and plead extenuating circumstances," Sarah said ruefully. "Do you think he will forgive me?"

"It was wrong of you not to confide in him when you learned of Julian's machinations, my dear. I am sure he is hurt to think you thought so little of him, and you would have relied on his protection and care. I shudder to think what might have been the outcome of your heedless action," Lady Ravensham reproved gently.

"I know, Grandmother, but I felt it was my responsibility, and I was not sure he would believe me or act promptly. What could he do without proof? The general was his superior officer, one he was accustomed to trust. It was unthinkable that he could have been a traitor. And, I must admit, I wanted to offer him a *fait accompli*. What do you think will happen now? Will Father be given a clean bill now that the truth is out?" Sarah was fiercely determined that the past injustice should be righted.

"There will be quite a scandal. Ronald will be overset, because I think he always believed firmly in his brother's guilt. It's so long ago, perhaps it will be best to let it all be forgotten. Of course, Julian's implication with the French will have to be dealt with. What a dilemma!" Lady Ravensham frowned, thinking of all the ramifications of Sarah's revelations.

"Never, I will not let Father's memory be smirched a day longer. If Lucien does not agree, I know Grandfather will see to it," Sarah asserted stoutly, banishing the fear that her interference in affairs of state might have jeopardized her love.

"Now don't be hasty, Sarah. Lucien sincerely cares for you and realizes how deeply you felt about the allegations against Richard. It will all sort itself out and, my dear, pay no attention to the criticisms of an old lady. I wish I had your courage and loyalty." Lady Ravensham sighed, remembering her own timidity in dealing with her husband.

"Don't fret, grandmother. All will be well. We must rejoice in Father's innocence, and the discovery of the general's duplicity. I am sure Mr. Pitt, for one, will be relieved that I have unmasked the traitor in his midst," Sarah soothed.

"Yes, our personal affairs are not half so important as that, discovering Julian's traitorous behaviour. How could he have turned against the country he had vowed to serve? It is hard to understand. He was so close to us all. I thought he loved and admired Richard, but all the time he was animated by envy and malice." Lady Ravensham's shock and sorrow at her old friend's conduct depressed her and Sarah hastened to relieve her grandmother's anxiety.

"Well, it has all turned out well, and how could you suspect him? He played his part of the grieving, sympathetic friend so well. He deserves all that his greed and jealousy has brought him." Sarah was unforgiving. Although she knew that her grandmother's sheltered life had not prepared her for such treachery, she herself could only rejoice that she had uncovered the truth, freed the family from the burden of her father's disgrace.

"Yes, and then there is that Amberly woman. I never liked her. And I am sure there is more to her involvement than you are telling me," Lady Ravensham queried, but Sarah was not to be drawn. She felt little sympathy for Moira, but she had promised to protect her as best she could.

Leaving her grandmother to mull over her news under the disapproving Evans's ministrations, Sarah contemplated the coming interview with Lucien. She feared it would not be so easy.

Chapter Forty-three

Her apprehensions concerning the explanations she must offer Lucien were quite justified. Later that morning he arrived for the promised interview, and Sarah's nerves suffered from the postponement. He was at his most formidable and sardonic when he finally met her in the morning room. He made no attempt to embrace her but quelled her with a stare.

"Well, young woman, you have a lot of explaining to do. You have created quite a situation and do not think discovering a traitor excuses your actions. Why did you not confide your suspicions to me, Sarah? Do you still not trust me?" he asked grimly.

Sarah reddened, aware that Lucien was justified in his harshness. In her anxiety to prove her father's innocence she had rushed rashly into action, not understanding that her interference would be regarded as a breach of faith by the man to whom she had promised love and obedience.

"I regret that I did not tell you, Lucien, but I was

afraid you would dismiss my suspicions of the general. I wanted to face you with irrefutable proof," she offered.

"It did not occur to you that I was in a better position to unmask the general, I see. You still have little faith in the British, a bad augury for our life together," he continued in that haughty voice that had once infuriated her.

Sarah, angry and guilty, was too proud to throw herself on his mercy. She rushed heedlessly into speech. "If you had wanted a prissy amenable wife, you should never have chosen me. I am perfectly capable of making my own decisions. Perhaps you should have settled on Angela after all. She would never have embroiled herself in such an affair, I am sure. Too worried about the proprieties. If that's what you expect from me, it would be better we abandoned all thoughts of a life together," Sarah could have bitten her tongue as her temper mastered her. What was she doing quarreling with Lucien, whom she loved with all her heart?

Mastering his own emotion with difficulty, Lucien grasped her in his arms. "You little fool, don't you understand I was frightened out of my mind when I burst into the general's room? I couldn't bear to lose you now," and he kissed her fiercely, abandoning all restraint.

Sarah emerged from the embrace flustered but reassured. He could never have kissed her that way if he did not really care for her.

"I am sorry, Lucien. You may beat me if you wish, and I promise not to threaten any more spies or shoot them," she said roguishly, trying to lighten the atmo-

341

sphere.

"I probably should beat you, but you are such a captivating little baggage, I will kiss you instead, a much more enjoyable punishment, I vow," and he suited his action to the words. Sarah, gasping with the force of his passion which she now realized hid his real concern and anxiety, hastened to calm matters.

"It's just as well I know how to handle a pistol. Who knows? That experience may prove useful in our, no doubt, tempestuous life together. Now tell me what has been done about the general, and Mrs. Amberly?" She tugged him toward the settee and sat down with his arm about her, her head on his shoulder, and snuggled up to him with an engaging smile.

"What a hornet's nest you have raised, my dear, but I am forced to forgive you. Really, Sarah, your bravery is only exceeded by your rashness, but, since you have solved a vexing problem for the War Office, I will be magnanimous this time." He smiled ruefully, realizing that Sarah would not be tamed, and that she would probably embroil them both in situations of intrigue and danger in the future. He would not want her different. He loved her as much for her loyalty and courage as for her whimsical charm and radiant beauty.

"Now, tell all, Lucien. I am consumed with curiosity," Sarah pleaded.

"Well, General Apsley-Gower is hovering near death, and I only hope he does not recover, for that would put the state to the scandal and trouble of a trial and an execution. It seems he has been dealing with the French for many months, relaying all kinds of information from the very top level. Both Pitt and your Uncle Ronald were amazed and embarrassed by the revelations in that diary. How egotistical of him to keep such damning evidence, but I suppose he felt, in his twisted way, some pride in his traitorous actions. In his conceit he believed he had fooled us all, and he had. He never counted on a chit of a girl exposing him." Lucien smiled at her, taking the sting from his criticism.

"It was just good luck that I heard his conversation with Mrs. Amberly on the night of the ball. I wouldn't have been in the library at all if I hadn't been fleeing from what I considered your ungentlemanly advances," she joked.

"I was just about to propose to you when that busybody Angela appeared on the scene, and you dashed off in a pet," he reproved.

"Well, I had reason to suppose you preferred her. And you might have been better off," she teased.

"No doubt, but unfortunately I had become enslaved by a colonial coquette. Now don't get up in the boughs, my darling termagant. We still have some explanations to be made. I returned Mrs. Amberly's letters to her, and she made a full confession of her implications in the general's intrigues, but she will come out of the affair not too badly. She has agreed to be banished to the country on pain of disclosing all to her husband. She should not get off so easily but, after all, she did not succeed in her efforts to deliver Hamilton's message to the general or to entice your Uncle Ronald into indiscretions. He would be shocked to think that she entertained such an idea, and unbelieving, I think."

"He's too prosy to contemplate casting out lures to encroaching ladies, I fear. Poor Aunt Margaret. She's too much under his thumb," Sarah reflected.

"Lucky Uncle Ronald. I quite envy his ability to keep a wife in subjection," Lucien answered whimsically. Sarah decided it would be wiser to ignore such provocation, although she passed him a speaking look.

Lucien then explained that her father would be cleared of all imputations and given a posthumous honorable discharge. An announcement would be made in the War Office journal, but for state reasons it had been decided not to go into details about the general's treasonable activities. He would pay the price, and certain contacts would be rounded up, thus frustrating the French spy ring. In his madness, Apsley-Gower had fully written down the damning evidence in the diary.

On her questioning about Lucien's opportune arrival at the general's rooms, he explained that he had returned early from Plymouth and was riding to Park Street in the hopes of seeing her when he noticed the general rushing from the door of Moira Amberly's dwelling on Mount Street. Uneasy, for some reason, at the general's untypical action, he had followed him to his lodgings, wanting to confront him for an explanation.

Sarah sighed gratefully, relieved that her father was cleared of all wrongdoing, that she could set her grandfather's mind at rest and could now contemplate her future with Lucien, undeterred by any cloud over her family's honour. The rest of their conversation was concerned purely with private affairs, and very little of that, as the time was taken up in a more romantic fashion.

Sarah looked around the dining room reassured by Joshua Allen's unchanging and ruddy face at the head of the board. For a moment it seemed that time had retreated and she and her beloved grandfather were dining alone on one of those numerous occasions in her girlhood, before Lucien had erupted into her life to change it beyond imagination. She looked at her husband of two months where he sat on Joshua Allen's left hand, toying with his wine glass and laughing at some jest the elder man had made. The dying sun of the late August day bathed the comfortable and familiar room in a warm glow, highlighting the portrait of her mother, which smiled down upon them from the mantel above the fireplace.

So much had happened since she had last sat here, heedless of what fate held in store for her. Then she had been a careless innocent girl, unaware of her English relations, the general's treachery, and most of all, unconscious of the role that maddening English colonel would play in her life. She smiled reminiscently, recalling their wedding, and the honeymoon that followed the formal ceremony in St. Margaret's her grandmother had arranged so skillfully. She had moved through the ceremony in a haze of happiness and later was only vaguely aware of the guests gathering in the Park Street drawing room to offer their congratulations. She was conscious only of Lucien's resplendent and suddenly unfamiliar figure in his regimentals at her side. She recalled William Pitt, the normally austere prime minister relaxing as he murmured thanks and good wishes to them, Angela, preening herself while she tendered casual congratulations and reminded them of her own engagement so recently announced, her grandmother's pride and joy, Aunt Margaret's wistful gaze, and Alan's exuberant hope for future meetings.

She had come to acceptable terms with her English family and rejoiced in the loving close relationship with her grandmother, but Lucien so overshadowed her horizon little else mattered, even the happy outcome of her confrontation with the general. The two-week honeymoon in Devon, under the balmy skies by the shining sea, had surprised her only with the passion that Lucien's possession of her had evoked. Then there had been the long voyage from Plymouth, so different from the outward journey, where her nights were heightened by a reaffirmation of that passion. Whatever the future held for Lucien and herself, as they followed the vagaries of his army career, she was completely secure in the knowledge of that all-encompassing love, the wonder of that union she had hardly believed possible.

Her musings were interrupted by a roguish query from her grandfather to her husband.

"It seems you have completely tamed his wayward miss, Lucien. I wish you would share your secret," Joshua Allen urged whimsically.

"Alas, I believe the shoe is on the other foot. Your granddaughter has routed me on every suit. I will have my hands full," Lucien riposted, his warm glance on his wife.

"Let that be a lesson to you, Colonel. We colonials

are a stubborn lot, unwilling to be mastered by you redcoats," Sarah said, sparkling, quite willing to be teased.

"This redcoat has signed an unconditional surrender, which will last forever, although no doubt skirmishes will still be fought," Lucien returned.

"Naturally," Sarah agreed. "We are a determined breed, determined on the 'pursuit of happiness' if you remember."

"I agree with that, my darling, and with you I will be content to live always beneath the flag of truce." Lucien's satisfaction at having the last word did not dismay Sarah. She had her own methods for keeping this particular redcoat in subjection.

GOTHICS A LA MOOR—FROM ZEBRA

ISLAND OF LOST RUBIES
by Patricia Werner   (2603, $3.95)

Heartbroken by her father's death and the loss of her great love, Eileen returns to her island home to claim her inheritance. But eerie things begin happening the minute she steps off the boat, and it isn't long before Eileen realizes that there's no escape from *THE ISLAND OF LOST RUBIES.*

DARK CRIES OF GRAY OAKS
by Lee Karr   (2736, $3.95)

When orphaned Brianna Anderson was offered a job as companion to the mentally ill seventeen-year-old girl, Cassie, she was grateful for the non-troublesome employment. Soon she began to wonder why the girl's family insisted that Cassie be given hydro-electrical therapy and increased doses of laudanum. What was the shocking secret that Cassie held in her dark tormented mind? And was she herself in danger?

CRYSTAL SHADOWS
by Michele Y. Thomas   (2819, $3.95)

When Teresa Hawthorne accepted a post as tutor to the wealthy Curtis family, she didn't believe the scandal surrounding them would be any concern of hers. However, it soon began to seem as if someone was trying to ruin the Curtises and Theresa was becoming the unwitting target of a deadly conspiracy . . .

CASTLE OF CRUSHED SHAMROCKS
by Lee Karr   (2843, $3.95)

Penniless and alone, eighteen-year-old Aileen O'Conner traveled to the coast of Ireland to be recognized as daughter and heir to Lord Edwin Lynhurst. Upon her arrival, she was horrified to find her long lost father had been murdered. And slowly, the extent of the danger dawned upon her: her father's killer was still at large. And her name was next on the list.

BRIDE OF HATFIELD CASTLE
by Beverly G. Warren   (2517, $3.95)

Left a widow on her wedding night and the sole inheritor of Hatfield's fortune, Eden Lane was convinced that someone wanted her out of the castle, preferably dead. Her failing health, the whispering voices of death, and the phantoms who roamed the keep were driving her mad. And although she came to the castle as a bride, she needed to discover who was trying to kill her, or leave as a corpse!

Available wherever paperbacks are sold, or order direct from the Publisher. Send cover price plus 50¢ per copy for mailing and handling to Zebra Books, Dept. 3248, 475 Park Avenue South, New York, N.Y. 10016. Residents of New York, New Jersey and Pennsylvania must include sales tax. DO NOT SEND CASH.

THE BEST IN HISTORICAL ROMANCES

TIME-KEPT PROMISES   (2422, $3.95)
by Constance O'Day Flannery

Sean O'Mara froze when he saw his wife Christina standing before him. She had vanished and the news had been written about in all of the papers—he had even been charged with her murder! But now he had living proof of his innocence, and Sean was not about to let her get away. No matter that the woman was claiming to be someone named Kristine; she still caused his blood to boil.

PASSION'S PRISONER   (2573, $3.95)
by Casey Stewart

When Cassandra Lansing put on men's clothing and entered the Rawlings saloon she didn't expect to lose anything—in fact she was sure that she would win back her prized horse Rapscallion that her grandfather lost in a card game. She almost got a smug satisfaction at the thought of fooling the gamblers into believing that she was a man. But once she caught a glimpse of the virile Josh Rawlings, Cassandra wanted to be the woman in his embrace!

ANGEL HEART   (2426, $3.95)
by Victoria Thompson

Ever since Angelica's father died, Harlan Snyder had been angling to get his hands on her ranch, the Diamond R. And now, just when she had an important government contract to fulfill, she couldn't find a single cowhand to hire—all because of Snyder's threats. It was only a matter of time before the legendary gunfighter Kid Collins turned up on her doorstep, badly wounded. Angelica assessed his firmly muscled physique and stared into his startling blue eyes. Beneath all that blood and dirt he was the handsomest man she had ever seen, and the one person who could help beat Snyder at his own game.

Available wherever paperbacks are sold, or order direct from the Publisher. Send cover price plus 50¢ per copy for mailing and handling to Zebra Books, Dept. 3248, 475 Park Avenue South, New York, N.Y. 10016. Residents of New York, New Jersey and Pennsylvania must include sales tax. DO NOT SEND CASH.

FIERY ROMANCE

CALIFORNIA CARESS   (2771, $3.75)
by Rebecca Sinclair
Hope Bennett was determined to save her brother's life. And if that meant paying notorious gunslinger Drake Frazier to take his place in a fight, she'd barter her last gold nugget. But Hope soon discovered she'd have to give the handsome rattlesnake more than riches if she wanted his help. His improper demands infuriated her; even as she luxuriated in the tantalizing heat of his embrace, she refused to yield to her desires.

ARIZONA CAPTIVE   (2718, $3.75)
by Laree Bryant
Logan Powers had always taken his role as a lady-killer very seriously and no woman was going to change that. Not even the breathtakingly beautiful Callie Nolan with her luxuriant black hair and startling blue eyes. Logan might have considered a lusty romp with her but it was apparent she was a lady, through and through. Hard as he tried, Logan couldn't resist wanting to take her warm slender body in his arms and hold her close to his heart forever.

DECEPTION'S EMBRACE   (2720, $3.75)
by Jeanne Hansen
Terrified heiress Katrina Montgomery fled Memphis with what little she could carry and headed west, hiding in a freight car. By the time she reached Kansas City, she was feeling almost safe . . . until the handsomest man she'd ever seen entered the car and swept her into his embrace. She didn't know who he was or why he refused to let her go, but when she gazed into his eyes, she somehow knew she could trust him with her life . . . and her heart.

Available wherever paperbacks are sold, or order direct from the Publisher. Send cover price plus 50¢ per copy for mailing and handling to Zebra Books, Dept. 3248, 475 Park Avenue South, New York, N.Y. 10016. Residents of New York, New Jersey and Pennsylvania must include sales tax. DO NOT SEND CASH.

PASSIONATE NIGHTS FROM ZEBRA BOOKS

ANGEL'S CARESS (2675, $4.50)
by Deanna James
Ellie Crain was a young, inexperienced and beautiful Southern belle. Cash Gillard was the battle-weary Yankee corporal who turned her into a woman filled with hungry passion. He planned to love and leave her; she vowed to keep him forever with her *Angel's Caress*.

COMMANCHE BRIDE (2549, $3.95)
by Emma Merritt
Beautiful Dr. Zoe Randolph headed to Mexico to halt a cholera epidemic. She never dreamed her caravan would be attacked by a band of savages. Later, she refused to believe that she could love and desire her captor, the handsome half-breed Matt Chandler. Captor and slave find unending love and tender passion in the rugged Commanche hills.

CAPTIVE ANGEL (2524, $4.50)
by Deanna James
When handsome Hunter Gillard left the routine existence of his South Carolina plantation for endless adventures on the high seas, beautiful and indulged Caroline Gillard learned to manage her home and business affairs in her husband's sudden absence. Caroline resolved not to crumble and vowed to make Hunter beg to be taken back. He was determined to make her once again his unquestioning and forgiving wife.

SWEET, WILD LOVE (2834, $3.95)
by Emma Merritt
Chicago lawyer Eleanor Hunt was determined to earn the respect of the Kansas cowboys who openly leered at her as she was working to try a cattle-rustling case. The worse offender was Bradley Smith—even though he worked for Eleanor's father! She was determined not to mistake passion for love; he was determined to break through her icy exterior and possess the passion woman who lurked beneath her.

Available wherever paperbacks are sold, or order direct from the Publisher. Send cover price plus 50¢ per copy for mailing and handling to Zebra Books, Dept. 3248, 475 Park Avenue South, New York, N.Y. 10016. Residents of New York, New Jersey and Pennsylvania must include sales tax. DO NOT SEND CASH.

REGENCIES BY JANICE BENNETT

TANGLED WEB   (2281, $3.95)

Miss Celia Marcombe's dark eyes flashed with righteous indignation. She was not a commodity to be traded or bartered to a man
as insufferably arrogant as Trevor Ryde, despite what her high-
handed grandfather decreed! If Lord Ryde thought she would let
herself be married for any reason other than true love, he was
sadly mistaken. He'd never get his hands on her fortune—let
alone her person—no matter how disturbingly handsome he
was . . .

MIDNIGHT MASQUE   (2512, $3.95)

It was nothing unusual for Lady Ashton to transport government
documents to her father from the Home Office. But on this particular afternoon a gust of wind scattered the papers, and suddenly an important page was lost. A document desperately
wanted by more than one determined gentleman—one of whom
would murder to get his way . . .

AN INTRIGUING DESIRE   (2579, $3.95)

The British secret agent, Charles Marcombe, had done his bit
against that blasted Bonaparte. Now it was time to nurse his
wounds and come to terms with the fact that that part of his life
was over. He certainly did not need the likes of Mademoiselle
Therese de Bourgerre darkening his door, warning of dire emer-
gencies and dread consequences, forcing him to remember things
best forgotten. She was a delightful minx, to be sure, but it would
take more than a pair of pleading emerald eyes and a woebegone
smile to drag him back into the fray!

*Available wherever paperbacks are sold, or order direct from the
Publisher. Send cover price plus 50¢ per copy for mailing and
handling to Zebra Books, Dept. 3248, 475 Park Avenue South,
New York, N.Y. 10016. Residents of New York, New Jersey and
Pennsylvania must include sales tax. DO NOT SEND CASH.*